DARK WATERS

DARK WATERS

Mary Minton

Thorndike Press
Thorndike, Maine USA

This Large Print edition is published by Thorndike Press, USA.

Published in 1998 in the U.S. by arrangement with Chivers Press Ltd.

U.S. Softcover ISBN 0-7862-1274-8 (General Series Edition)

The text of this Large Print edition is unabridged.
Other aspects of the book may vary from the original edition.

Set in 16 pt. New Times Roman.

Printed in Great Britain on acid-free paper.

Library of Congress Catalog Card Number: 97-91169

ISBN: 0-7862-1274-8 (lg print : sc)

CHAPTER ONE

The household had hardly settled down after the dismissal of Elvie, the parlourmaid, when the arrival of a letter the following morning caused another upset. Kendra Hollis had just come out of the dining room, where she had gone to draw the curtains against the sunlight, her mistress's orders, when Mr Bagley came storming out of the morning room, waving a letter aloft. His veins stood out like cords and his protruding eyes seemed to bulge more than ever.

He put a finger inside his cravat to ease it away from his throat then shouted at Kendra who was about to turn away.

'You there, wait!' He shook the letter. 'When my scoundrel of a nephew calls today you are not to allow him in. Do you hear? Not under any circumstances. Do you hear girl?'

'Yes, I understand.'

'Then why don't you reply? Standing there like a lump of wood.'

Kendra, who until six months ago had been used to giving orders to servants, still found it difficult to show any deference to this ill-tempered man, or to his disagreeable wife. She looked at him with a direct gaze.

'Apart from the fact that I have never met your nephew, Mr Bagley, it is not my place to admit visitors. I was employed as companion to your wife.'

He glared at her. 'Well, you're going to have to act as parlourmaid as well, aren't you? And may I remind you, Miss, that you have no need to give yourself airs and graces. Your father was no more than a common thief.'

Kendra clenched her hands but managed to keep her anger under control.

'My father was a gambling man, but not a thief. He would have paid all his bills had he not been killed.'

'He would never have paid his bills and well you know it.'

There was a sneer on Mr Bagley's heavily jowled face. He wagged a podgy finger under her nose.

'So just you remember and try not to play the lady with me. You're no better stock than that chit of a parlourmaid.' He left her and went thumping up the stairs to his wife, no doubt to air his grievances to her.

Kendra felt like shouting up the stairs that the 'chit of a parlourmaid', as he called poor Elvie, would not have been in trouble had he not raped her in the first place, and then paid regular visits to her attic room afterwards. He had apparently told her if she mentioned anything to her parents about this he would deny it and tell them he had found her naked in a barn with a stable boy.

And this tale he must have told her father

2

when he had arrived the day before and angrily demanded to know who had got his daughter into trouble. The father apologised, bowed himself out then thumped Elvie all the way down the road.

Elvie was partly to blame for what had happened. She was an attractive girl who liked fun. She teased all the boys she knew and had played up to Mr Bagley. She loved trinkets and Kendra suspected that the ones she had were given to her by Mr Bagley.

What worried Kendra was the thought that he would need someone else to satisfy his lust. Even during the past two months he had, on pretext of reaching over her, let his arm touch her breasts. He pressed himself against her when meeting in doorways. Last night she had knocked his hand away when touching her body had been a deliberate action.

She had been annoyed when she saw his secretive smile. Her wages were three weeks overdue and when she mentioned it last night he said, 'All in good time, all in good time. The longer I have it the longer it will be saved for you.'

With a sigh Kendra turned into the dining room when Mary, the little skivvy, came sidling in and began to clear the breakfast dishes onto a tray.

'The master's in a fine old temper this morning,' she said, 'and he i'nt the only one either.' Mary rubbed the back of her hand under her nose and wiped it on her pinny. 'Mrs Webster's been on to me ever since she came this morning, to do this and do that and hurry up about it. I've only got one pair of 'ands,'aven't I?'

Mary looked at Kendra with scared eyes. 'Mrs Webster says I'll 'ave to watch out or the master'll 'ave me, like he did poor Elvie. My father 'ud kill me if I went home with a bellyful.'

Kendra felt a swift compassion for the little skivvy. Any man would need to be in a desperate state to take this half-starved looking girl to his bed. She was thin to the point of being emaciated. Her eyes were crossed and she had a perpetual cold. She stood, twisting hands that were red and sore from constant scrubbing of floors and washing clothes.

'Mary—' Kendra spoke gently, 'if Mr Bagley makes any advances towards you, you must tell your father.'

'Oh, I couldn't, Miss. Me father is a violent man. 'E'd kill the master then go to the gallows and me mother wouldn't 'ave no money for food and we'd all starve.'

Mary suddenly gave a lop-sided smile. 'You'd be safe enough from the master, Miss, you being a lady and all that.'

A lady? Oh, yes, there had been wealth in the family. She had been well brought up, taught all the social graces, educated, but was now a pauper. And as much dependent on other people for her keep as poor Elvie and Mary.

Mary suddenly picked up the tray and stood listening. 'Is that 'im? Is that the master coming now?' She went scuttling into the passage, the crockery rattling on the tray.

When Kendra heard the heavy footsteps she waited, thinking that Mr Bagley would be going out as he usually did at this time in the morning. He did not even look into the dining room but, to her surprise, went into the morning room, which was only used for prayers.

He had left the door open and from where Kendra was standing she saw him go to the family Bible, which stood on a pedestal in front of the window. He unlocked the Bible then, taking a quill he dipped it into the ink and scoring across a page muttered, 'There and there and that puts an end to him! Never will he set foot in this house again.'

When he slammed the Bible shut Kendra turned away and began fiddling with the curtains in the dining room.

The next morning he called, 'You there, I'm going out and I'll be out for the rest of the day. Your mistress wants you and don't keep her waiting. She's in a bad mood and remember what I told you about my nephew. If you dare let him set foot in this house you'll regret it.'

He paused and when he spoke again his voice was raised.

5

'I'm speaking to you, girl. Why don't you answer me when I'm talking. Did you hear what I said?'

Kendra turned slowly and faced him. 'Yes, Mr Bagley, I heard.'

'Then answer me when I speak to you. Go on up to your mistress. I don't pay you for doing nothing.'

Kendra drew herself up. 'May I remind you, sir, that I have not yet been paid my wages for the six months I've worked here.'

'You'll get it when I think fit and not before.'

'I would like it now, Mr Bagley. I am entitled to it.'

His veins bulged again. 'Don't you start giving me orders or you'll never see them. And stop looking at me in that arrogant way. I don't know how you have the nerve to give yourself airs after the way your father behaved. How old are you, nineteen? You should have been wed by now, but I'll warrant that no one offered for you.'

'They did, but I was not ready for marriage.'

'Think yourself lucky that you have a good home here, you're well fed and, I'll say it again, I'll pay you when I think fit. Now go to your mistress.'

He stormed out and Kendra gripped the edge of the table to stop herself from picking up a vase and hurling it after him. Tears suddenly filled her eyes. What had happened to her? Six months ago such violence would never have occurred to her. But then there had never been anything to get angry about. If only her father had not died.

She relived the time her father had been carried home on a stretcher after a fall in the hunting field. She could see again the still form and hear one of the men say, 'He was not in his cups, Miss. It was simply that the master misjudged the height of the hedge.'

It was true her father had lived life to the full, taken chances, gambled away a fortune, but he was so loveable, so loving. He would be horrified if he knew the position she was now in.

Kendra ran her fingers over the contours of her face. Mr Bagley had once called her a plain bitch. This was because Mrs Bagley had insisted that she wear her hair drawn tightly back and caught up in a bun. It did make her look plain. But her husband was wrong when he said she had had no offers of marriage. There had been many offers but there was no man up to now that she had wanted to marry.

She had told her father that she would wait until she found a man she could love, as he and her mother had done. Her father had never stopped talking about the great love there had been between them. Kendra was twelve when her mother died. Her father was grief stricken and she suspected it was then her father had started gambling. It became an obsession with him. Yet in spite of it Kendra had never felt neglected. Her father's sister had moved in with them.

Ten minutes after bringing him home he had regained consciousness but his voice was no more than a whisper. 'Kendra, my darling girl, forgive me. Your Aunt Margaret will take care of you. But stand up for yourself. Be strong and never . . .' a faint smile touched his lips, 'never marry a gambler.' They were his last words.

His sister had looked after her but she had hated the scrimping and scraping there had been and had wanted to marry a man she had met but the man did not want Kendra. He wanted there to be just the two of them. Kendra had told her that she would manage and her aunt and her husband went to live in Australia. And it was not until then that Kendra realised how much her father's debts were.

Eventually the solicitor got her the job with the Bagleys.

He had not known them, someone had recommended them to him. Kendra had never complained of the unsuitability of the job. He was old and ailing and thought he had done her a good turn. Anyway, she had no choice, she was destitute.

Kendra was suddenly aware of Mrs Bagley's sharp, penetrating voice. Although she was on the floor above she could always make herself heard.

'Kendra, where are you, girl? I need you,

come at once.'

Usually the summons was accompanied by the thumping of her walking stick on the floor, but there were times when the stick slipped and she would not make the effort to reach for it.

For once Kendra ignored her mistress. Let her wait. Mrs Bagley was always supposedly suffering from one complaint or another but she could fill herself with sweetmeats and eat every scrap of her food. She must have known what was going on between her husband and Elvie, but she made no effort to stop it. It was time this lazy and whining wife took on her marital duties.

Perhaps Mr Bagley was content to let his wife remain like a bladder of lard when someone as pretty as Elvie was willing to minister to his needs. Kendra was determined on one thing at that moment, Mr Bagley would not interfere with her life in that way.

She was about to make her way upstairs when she began to wonder whose name had been struck out of the Bible. The door of the morning room was ajar. Kendra hesitated a moment then going over to the room she pushed the door wider and stood a moment, staring at the big Bible.

She found something rather awesome in the way a shaft of sunlight, streaming in through a chink in the curtains, put a warm glow on the big Book. The silver filigree clasp had been left undone.

Kendra's heart began to beat a little faster. Dare she take a look inside? A Bible was sacred. She reached out a hand and touched the leather. It was warm and smelled musty. She glanced over her shoulder. Then finding that the Book had been unlocked she took a deep breath and opened it.

And there on the vellum page inside she saw where a name had been crossed through, again and again. Appleday Devereux? What an odd name. What had the nephew done to put Mr Bagley in such a fury? The fact that he had made Kendra think she might like him. She hoped he would call. It would at least help to break the monotony of her days.

Mrs Bagley's voice had reached screaming pitch. Kendra closed the Bible carefully, went out and made her way upstairs. And was greeted by her mottled-faced mistress.

'Where have you been, girl, how dare you ignore me when I call, I could have been dying, but a fat lot you care. Who do you think you are to treat me in this way? You're nothing, a nobody, we gave you a home when no one else wanted you, we—'

'What is it you need, Mrs Bagley?' Kendra forced herself to speak calmly.

The wobbling chins stilled, washed-out blue eyes regarded her belligerently. 'You've made me forget what I needed. You can get me some fresh water to drink. You never think to fill up the carafe, I have to ask for everything. And while I think about it, you stop making eyes at my husband. Oh, yes, I've seen the way you look at him, I know your type, well let me tell you he wouldn't cast a second glance in your direction, he likes a woman with flesh on her bones, like me.'

Kendra felt suddenly sorry for the gross figure propped up in the bed with a mound of pillows. There was a strange, starved look in her eyes, a woman no longer attractive in any way and knowing she could rouse no feelings in her marriage partner. Mrs Bagley reached for her box of sweetmeats, her comfort, and popped one into her mouth.

'Mrs Bagley—' Kendra spoke gently, 'if I helped you downstairs you could perhaps sit in the porch, it's lovely and sunny.'

The loose lips took on a pout. 'You know perfectly well I can't get downstairs.'

'I think you could, if I helped you.'

Mrs Bagley was belligerent again. 'Why do you taunt me, you enjoy it, don't you? You know I can't walk properly. You don't care about the pain I suffer, nobody cares.' The self-pitying tears started and Kendra knew she was going to have a bad morning, trying to get her mistress into some semblance of normality.

Mrs Bagley got on about the nephew who might possibly call and reminded Kendra he was not to be allowed inside the house.

'That Pel was no good since the day he was born, a bad egg.'

11

'Pel?' Kendra queried.

'Short for Appleday, a stupid name, his mother was stupid for wanting him called that. She doted on him, so did his father, and his grandfather—at least the old man did until he found out what he was, then he cut him right out of his life.'

'Why? What had Mr—Appleday done?'

'What hadn't he done? He absconded with money, with treasures, a gambler, that's what he is, gamble on anything. Went off to America, he should have stayed there, nobody wants him back here, and he certainly is not going to get into this house. Now remember that girl. He is *not* to set foot inside the front door. But my husband said he's already told you that. Don't be taken in by him, he has charm, has Pel. Oh, yes, he'd charm the birds out of the trees, but he would never get round me because I know what he is, so be warned, girl.'

It was nearly one o'clock before Kendra got Mrs Bagley settled, and then to sleep. She had gobbled up the box of sweetmeats, devoured a cold collation at midday which Mrs Webster had prepared. Mrs Webster came in from the village to cook breakfast and a meal at four o'clock, Mr Bagley being too mean to pay for a full time cook.

When Kendra came downstairs she was met by Mary who was greatly agitated. Her mother had had a fall and her father had come to take

12

her home to look after the children.

Mary screwed up her apron. 'What am I to do, Miss? What will the master say? I'll lose me job. I might be able to get back tomorrow if I can get a neighbour to look after the little 'uns, but I'll not be back today. Oh dear, what'll I do, there's the dishes and the kitchen floor to wash, Mr Bagley told me it *had* to be washed today and will come to inspect it.'

'You go, Mary, I'll see to everything.'

Mary's eyes went wide. '*You* Miss, I bet you ain't never washed a floor in your life, or even washed up a cup.'

Kendra thought wryly, if only Mary knew the struggle she and her aunt had had. She said, 'Then now is the time to start. I think I hear your father calling you.'

Mary started towards the kitchen then paused, to explain where Kendra would find the scrubbing brushes, the pail, the floor soap and a coarse piece of sacking to tie over her dress. With that she went scuttling away to the kitchen from where her father had been shouting for her.

As Mary went into the kitchen she wailed, 'Oh dear, I don't know what the master will say when he knows I've gone.'

A coarse reply came, 'Any trouble from 'im and I'll bash his face in.'

Kendra winced then she went and lifted the kettle from the hob. She would wash the dishes first. The sooner she got them done and the

13

floor washed the better it would be. She wanted these jobs out of the way before she had to deal with the 'wicked' Pel Devereux.

With the dishes washed and put away she made preparations for washing the floor, and was fastening the piece of sacking on when she caught sight of herself in the cracked mirror.

Heavens above, she did look plain. It was her wretched hairstyle that made her look plain. Her hair curled but it was stretched so tight the curls were not noticeable. She began to pull out the pins, then shaking it free she took a piece of cord and tied it back, leaving tendrils at the side. Much better.

She gave a sudden grin, knowing deep down that she did not want this Pel Devereux to think she was a skivvy. And felt glad she could still feel this way after months of slaving at the Bagleys. There was still some life in her. Even if she did know that Mr Bagley had described his nephew as a wastrel and a thief as well as a gambler.

Look at how Mr Bagley had maligned her father. He had accused him of being a thief, but this was not true. He would have paid all his debts to friends in time had he not been killed so tragically.

His friends all admitted it and many of them refused to take what money he had. With a sigh Kendra brought an old cushion and dropped it onto the floor. Then, getting down on her knees she dipped the scrubbing brush into the

14

pail, rubbed the coarse soap onto the bristles and began to scrub. Wielding the big brush made her arm ache and she sweated. She had not been used to washing floors of this size. The only floor that needed washing at home was the kitchen floor and it was about a quarter of the size of this one and also it was tiled. This floor was rough stone.

After a while she got up and opened the kitchen door wider, then stood, drawing in breaths of the sweet summer air. Beyond the back garden was a patchwork of fields. How lovely, how peaceful, how beautiful the birdsong. She had been brought up in the country and would miss it when she went to London, but it would have to be London when she left. She had been only once and that was when she was a child, but had been impressed with its business. Surely there would be a woman somewhere who needed a companion and would treat her as a human being, not as a slave. With a small sigh Kendra got down on her knees again and resumed her task.

She was wringing out the floorcloth when a shadow fell across the stone floor. She glanced up, expecting to see a tradesman, and instead saw an elegantly dressed man regarding her in a speculative way. Then he smiled suddenly and swept off his hat, and at his smile Kendra's heart began a slow pounding. The word rogue sprang to her mind.

'The name is Devereux,' the stranger said.

'Appleday Devereux, but my friends, *and* my enemies, call me Pel.' He paused then added, 'Although I am expected I fear I will not be welcome.'

Kendra got up from her knees. He was not at all like the image she had conjured up of Pel Devereux. She had imagined him to be shabbily dressed, a little unkempt, but this tall, broad-shouldered man was immaculate. He was also attractive with his very dark eyes and thick black hair.

'Well?' he queried. 'Am I right?'

Kendra wiped her hands on the piece of sacking then drew a finger across her upper lip, which was beaded with perspiration.

'Yes, Mr Devereux, you are right. I have orders not to admit you.'

He looked her up and down. 'You speak well, not the usual type of menial.'

'I am trying to earn my living, Mr Devereux, which is something, I take it, you have never done.'

A look of amusement came into his eyes. 'And sauce with it. Who are you?' He stepped inside. 'Sorry, I must ignore orders. I happen to be famished. I have not had a proper meal since last night. I came round to the back hoping to find a kindly cook who would find me a crust. Instead I find a *crusty* female who regards me with disdain. Now, where is the pantry? Ah yes, I see it, door opened wide to beg me to enter and partake of the delicacies.'

16

He brushed past Kendra and for seconds she was so bemused she stood watching him. Then she hurried after him. 'Mr Devereux, you must not touch any food. If you do either I or young Mary will be accused of stealing.'

He came out with a loaf of bread in one hand and a cheese dish in the other. He brushed past her once more and put the food on the table. 'You have no cause to worry, I shall take the entire blame, both for coming in against orders and for helping myself to these. A knife?' He crossed to the dresser and began pulling open drawers. 'This will do. Is there any ale or cider available?'

'None, and I do wish you would go, Mr Devereux. Your aunt and uncle will never believe I couldn't have prevented you coming in.'

'My aunt and uncle? Is that who they claim to be?' Pel Devereux gave a derisive laugh. 'The female of the species was my grandfather's housekeeper and the male specimen his butler!' He began to slice into the bread with vicious cuts. 'They cheated me out of my inheritance, stole it, they're thieves. I want it, and what is more I mean to get it.'

He eyed Kendra once more in a speculative way. 'You puzzle me, your voice, your bearing. Who are you, what is your name?'

'It doesn't matter who I am, Mr Devereux. I work here and I want you to leave, otherwise I could lose my job. Like you, I happen to be destitute.'

'What makes you think *I* am destitute?'

'You would not be stealing from this pantry if you had money to buy food.'

'I should just like to explain something to you. When I arrived back in England and learned what had happened I came post-haste, never stopping for meals. You will not lose your job, I shall admit to the Bagleys that I helped myself, and I think they will have no cause for complaint, seeing they stole my inheritance.'

'You obviously have no proof they stole anything from you, or you would have gone to the law. So how do you expect Mr Bagley to hand over your—property—presuming he has it, of course. He's a mean man, a very mean man, I have not been paid my six months' wages. They are now three weeks overdue, I'm at my wits' end to know how I can get my ten pounds.'

Pel Devereux dismissed this as a paltry sum. What he was after was worth thousands. 'It was my mother's jewellery, she willed it to me. Before I went to America I left it with my grandfather for safe keeping. My mother had requested that certain of the pieces be given to my bride on her wedding day. I respected her wishes and my grandfather knew I did. He would never have given the casket to anyone else. We had a great affection for one another but he told me that although, when he died, he would leave me a sum of money, the rest of his

18

estate would go to a distant cousin, a married man and a responsible person. I understood this and accepted it.'

'Then why did you not get the casket when he died?'

'Because I knew nothing of my grandfather's death until six months later, I was in various parts of America and the letter from the solicitor had been following me around. As soon as I received it I booked passage for England. And then learned that my mother's jewellery was missing.'

'Why should you think the Bagleys have it?'

'Mrs Bagley was seen handling it one evening. Although she denied this I know they have it, and I'm not leaving here until I get it.'

'Knowing Mr Bagley, I fear you will be leaving empty-handed.'

'I shall prove you wrong.' Although the words were quietly spoken Kendra was aware then of a ruthless undertone.

The next moment he was smiling at her and she remembered Mrs Bagley saying, 'Oh, Pel Devereux has charm, he'd charm the birds from the trees...'

'You still haven't told me who you are, your name, where your home is. I would like to know, *please*.'

Kendra found it impossible to resist Pel Devereux's coaxing smile. 'My name is Kendra. I have no home, not now, but my father was Dermot Hollis.'

19

'Dermot Hollis—?' Devereux got to his feet. 'The gambler? A genial man with one green eye, one blue?'

'Yes, that was my father.'

'Well!' Devereux threw up his hands, and gave a shout of laughter. 'I can hardly believe it. And you are his daughter.' He sobered suddenly. 'You used the word, *was*, when you spoke of him.'

'He died over six months ago.'

'Oh, God, I'm sorry. I had no idea. He was a wonderful man, one of the most popular men I knew. How did he die, what happened, why did you have to find work in a house like this?'

'Because my father was a gambler, Mr Devereux. Don't misunderstand me. I loved him, loved him dearly, but the house and everything in it had to be sold to pay his creditors.'

A wry smile touched Devereux's lips briefly. 'So you have no kindly leanings towards men who gamble.'

'I have no kindly leanings towards you.'

'So you would not be prepared to search the house for my mother's jewellery? If you found it I would make it worth your while. With extra money in your pocket you could achieve independence, pick and choose a suitable position in London.'

Kendra unfastened the piece of sacking from her waist and began to fold it. 'Mr Devereux, you must take me for a fool. I'm not sure I even

20

believe your story about your mother's jewellery. Even if I did I am not going to risk transportation to Australia for helping to *steal* a casket of jewellery, for that is how the magistrates would consider it.'

'I'm not asking you to take it, I wouldn't do that, I'm only asking that you search the house.'

'No! Quite definitely not.' Anger put colour in Kendra's cheeks. 'I've suffered enough discomfort, enough insults, without leaving myself open to other abuses. Have you ever read about the suffering of people transported to Australia, women especially, they are treated worse than animals, the pawns of men's lusts, their brutality.'

'Oh dear, what a hornet's nest I've stirred up.'

Kendra felt she could have struck him for the amusement in his voice. 'I want no involvement in your feud with Mr Bagley.'

Devereux crossed one leg over the other and eyed her this time in a rather lazy fashion. 'Do you know, Kendra, there's something about you I rather like. I admire your fighting spirit. It's not often one finds this in a person in—' he paused, 'let us say in such a situation as you occupy.'

'In other words, a menial. I want my six months wages, Mr Devereux. You were inclined to dismiss ten pounds as a paltry sum, but to me it means a way of escape from this household, it would get me to London.'

'I think you should realise that an unaccompanied woman in London is also liable to abuse and the unwanted attentions of men.'

'I should imagine that with my looks any man would steer a course away from me.'

'Only some men, Ma'am, only some.'

Kendra was trying to work out the implications of this remark when he added, 'I've decided to come back later to see Bagley, and I think I prefer that he knows nothing of my call.'

'How do you suggest I account for the *stolen* bread and cheese? Mr Bagley misses nothing.'

'Deny any knowledge of it.'

'I refuse to lie for you, Mr Devereux.'

'Such piety is commendable. Tell him of my visit if you wish.' He picked up his hat and swept her a bow. 'I bid you good-day, Ma'am.'

Kendra, seething, crossed the kitchen and closed the door after him. Piety indeed! He made her sound like a psalm-singing spinster. But then telling the truth would come amiss to a man who would be willing to steal. She cleared away the bread and cheese dish, wiped up the crumbs, then finished washing the floor.

It was half-past two when she finished and she decided to go up to her attic room and have a wash down. Mr Bagley would not be back until four o'clock and Mrs Bagley always had a sleep in the afternoon.

She felt hot and sticky and the attic was far

from cool. The only window in the room was a small one in the roof. Kendra removed her dress and shift. Once she paused to run her hands over her body. Then she stood thinking about Pel Devereux, all that tale about his mother's jewellery. If it was worth thousands of pounds his grandfather would not have let it out of his sight.

But the grandfather had died . . . and the Bagleys? Something about Mr Bagley began teasing at Kendra's mind. It had something to do with stealthy movements. Whatever it was it eluded her.

Suddenly she tensed as she thought she heard a creaking stair. There was no lock on the door, no chair to tip up under the knob. She had found a small piece of wood which she wedged under the door every night.

Then she was staring. There was no wedge under the door. She had forgotten it while daydreaming. There was the creaking sound again. But Mr Bagley never came home in the afternoon. Not unless . . . Perhaps he had come to be there when Pel Devereux arrived.

She quickly pulled on her shift and looked for something to defend herself. Picking up the water jug she rushed to get the wedge under the door.

Before she reached it Mr Bagley walked in. She backed away and with her heart thudding madly she said:

'Get out of here. This is my room.'

23

'No, Miss clever sides. It's my house, my room and you better be nice to me or you'll find yourself without a place to sleep. Neither have you any money nor will you get any until I say so.' He leered at her and started to advance slowly.

'Stop right there.' She held up the jug. 'I'll have no compunction in throwing this at your head. And, it isn't the first time I've done it.'

Kendra was surprised at how strong her voice sounded. He stopped. 'And if you do, what do you think will happen? The magistrates would not take kindly to a girl bashing her master. You would end up in Newgate, with the criminals and the whores.'

'And if you take a step further you'll end up with a cracked skull. One man I threw something at ended up in a madhouse.'

He put a foot out to take a step and she threw the jug. It missed him by inches but it was enough to make him shout at her, 'You bitch. I'll get you for this.'

Kendra picked up the bowl of water. 'Get out, get out!'

He went to the door then turned. 'By God, I'll have you for this.' He went out, slamming the door.

Kendra put the bowl on the floor and dropped to her knees. She was shaking now. How could she have told a lie so easily. Cracking a man's skull indeed. But it had done the trick.

24

She would have to get out of here, before he had a chance to carry out his threat. He had been wrong to say she had no money. She had five pounds her father had given her once, in case of emergency. Many times she had been tempted to spend it, but had kept it just in case. The money would not get her very far but it would get her out of this house.

Thank goodness Mr Bagley had not mentioned Pel Devereux. He had obviously taken it for granted that he had not called.

It was then that Kendra remembered the stealthy movements of Mr Bagley one time. It had been on a night not long after she had come to the house when, having a raging thirst after a heavily salted meal, she had gone downstairs to get a drink. On reaching the window of the first floor landing her attention was caught by the figure of a man going down the garden path. There was something so furtive about his behaviour, glancing around him and over his shoulder that she was on the point of running to tell Mr Bagley when the moon came from behind a cloud and she saw it *was* Mr Bagley. Curious to know what he could be doing at that hour she watched. He went into the garden shed, came out with a box under his arm and a spade in his hand. He then climbed the stile leading into the next field.

Kendra was more puzzled than ever. The place where he was digging was the grave of a pet dog—at least according to the headstone it was, but according to young Mary it was a werewolf.

Now she was turning over in her mind the possibility that jewellery could have been in the box . . . Pel Devereux's inheritance. After all, if a man was going to bury a dog he would not be likely to bury it in the grave of another dog. But, if he wanted to hide something, what better place than one which the villagers avoided like the plague.

'Are you upstairs, girl?' Kendra jumped. Mr Bagley.

'I want you down here and don't give me any excuses.'

'I'm coming now,' she called. She wrote a quick note to Pel Devereux, asking him to meet her at ten o'clock at the old oast house. She had information to impart. Then she pushed the note in the pocket of her dress and ran down the stairs.

As she reached the bottom stair there was a knock on the front door. She heard Mr Bagley call that he would answer it, but she raced along the passage into the hall. And had the door open and the note pushed into Pel Devereux's hand before Mr Bagley came into the hall. He was out of breath and pushed her aside.

'Go to your mistress. Now.'

Mrs Bagley could be heard yelling for Kendra. Kendra hurried away, thankful that Pel Devereux had not shown a sign that he had received a note.

Thank God. She made her way back to go upstairs.

CHAPTER TWO

Kendra could hear the two men arguing downstairs and, although Mr Bagley was shouting, she found it impossible to hear what was being said because of Mrs Bagley making her tongue go.

She was the most badly treated woman in 'he world, no one cared about her, and she informed Kendra that one day she would kill herself and then her husband would be worried.

Kendra made no reply and of course that was a mistake. Kendra was the coldest companion she had ever known. She didn't care what happened to her either. Useless to tell Mrs Bagley that she was her own worst enemy. Kendra just let her go on and on and in the end Mrs Bagley was in tears.

Tears that stopped suddenly when her husband came into the bedroom.

'So what did Pel Devereux have to say?' she demanded.

Her husband's face was blood red. 'Nothing new. I hate his guts.' He turned to Kendra. 'And you can get out of here. Tell Mrs Webster

27

I want my tea at four o'clock.'

Mrs Bagley added, 'And tell her that my husband and I want to have it in my room. I'm sick of eating alone.'

Mr Bagley opened his mouth and closed it again. Kendra left.

In the kitchen Mrs Webster, who had just come in, said, 'So what's going on? I just heard the tail end of what seemed to have been a big argument between a young man and the master. Who is the young chap? A good-looking fellow.'

'His nephew. Mr and Mrs Bagley want to have tea together in the bedroom.'

'Oh, they do, do they. Well you can carry the tray upstairs, I'm not taking it up. My legs are playing me up today. I'll have to try and find another job.'

Kendra felt thankful that she would be leaving the house that night, then began to worry in case Pel Devereux did not show up. No . . . curiosity would bring him.

Ten minutes later a young boy came to tell them that Mary would not be coming back.

'Good,' Kendra said. 'I'll let Mrs Bagley know.'

This caused a row between husband and wife. According to Mr Bagley his wife was harsh with the girl. She said she never had anything to do with her.

Kendra left them and went downstairs.

It was the longest night Kendra had ever

known. She went over and over all that Pel Devereux had said. If only she could believe that he was the wronged person. The trouble was he behaved so arrogantly.

She prayed that Mr Bagley would be in bed by half-past nine. Sometimes he went at that time and at others he would be later. There had been occasions when she was aware of him prowling around. Then, of course he would be coming to be with Elvie.

To Kendra's relief Mrs Bagley said, at nine o'clock, that she wanted to be settled in bed for the night, and insisted that Mr Bagley came too. They had had a trying day. He was sitting in an armchair, brows drawn together, brooding.

He was not very willing to go to bed, but gave in when his wife started to make a fuss.

'All right, all right, I'll go,' he said, giving a big sigh.

Kendra sighed too and only hoped he would go to sleep soon. She packed her small valise then waited. The waiting seemed endless too and half fearfully she kept watching the door, thinking that Mr Bagley might wake and come up to her room.

At last she got up, crept down the narrow stairs then went to the bottom of the main staircase and stood listening. The snoring of husband and wife was unmistakable, Mrs Bagley with her whistling snores and her husband with his deep stentorian ones,

29

alternating with a number of gurgles.

Satisfied that there was no pretence of sleep she hurried back to her room and, at ten minutes to ten, she put on a thin cloak and laid a note on her bed saying she found it impossible to go on working in a household where wages were withheld. She then snuffed out the candle and tiptoed across the room in stockinged feet, her valise in one hand, her shoes in the other.

At the bottom of the main staircase she stood listening once more. Although the snores of husband and wife had not changed, Kendra held her breath until she was outside. Then she ran round the main path until she reached the back of the house, where she stopped to put on her shoes. Afterwards she ran along the narrow lane that led to the oast house.

Would Pel Devereux be there? She slowed to a walk to regain her breath. What if he didn't come? If he didn't she would sort out that problem then.

Her footsteps slowed as she neared the stone-built ruin. Nothing stirred. Then suddenly there was a beat of wings and a bat flew past her face, causing her to cry out in fright.

'Miss Hollis—?' Kendra's hand flew to her mouth as the tall figure of Pel Devereux emerged from the ruin.

'Oh, what a fright you gave me. I wondered whether you would come.'

30

'How could I stay away with a message so intriguing. I only hope my lengthened stay will be worth my while. What information have you to impart?'

'I think I know where your mother's jewels are hidden.'

Devereux did not show a quick interest as Kendra had expected. 'Oh, yes, and where might that be?'

'I shall tell you but on one condition, that you let me travel with you to London.' His gaze went to the valise by her side.

'Miss Hollis, if you think you can fool me into giving a promise to let you accompany me, with a tempting tale that you know where my mother's jewellery is hidden—'

'If it is not where I think then you are under no obligation. I shall walk to the Coaching Inn on my own.'

'Tell me one thing, why are you so anxious to leave the Bagleys? I know I promised you a reward should you find the jewellery—but you *were* anxious to get your wages.'

'I decided to sacrifice them. Mr Bagley, having sacked the parlourmaid, after getting her with child, turned his attentions to me.'

'The devil he did!' Devereux's eyes were blazing. 'He should be horsewhipped. If only I had known—'

'His attempt to molest me did not succeed, but as I have no lock on my bedroom door and no way of keeping him out—'

31

'You were wise to leave when you did, but I must say that I do not wish to be responsible for you when you get to London.'

'I shall be as pleased to be rid of you, Mr Devereux, as you will be of me. Shall we go?'

She picked up her valise but he took it from her, and asked where this 'secret place' was situated. When she told him, in a grave, he stopped and eyed her with distaste. 'Is this some kind of jest?'

'It is no jest, the grave is supposed to be that of a pet dog buried many years ago. The villagers believe a werewolf is buried there. The grave is in the field at the back of the garden shed. We can get a spade from the shed.'

'What makes you think the jewellery could be buried in such a macabre place?'

Kendra explained about the night she had seen Mr Bagley go with spade and box to the grave, the deductions she had drawn from his actions, and Devereux raised his eyebrows. 'How clever of you.' He gave her a quick glance. 'I take it you are not superstitious?'

'Let me say I do not believe in werewolves.'

'What will you do if a howling starts up when I begin digging?' he teased.

Kendra clutched at her throat. 'Oh, stop it, this is no time for jesting. I think I shall leave you to do the excavating, seeing you are likely to enjoy your task.'

'Oh, no, I want you with me. If a howling starts I will need you to support me when I flee.' Devereux was laughing softly.

'And I want to be on the lookout for Mr Bagley. If he happens to wake and find out I'm gone he might get very suspicious.'

Pel Devereux did not trouble to reply, nor had the thought occurred to him that he might have opposition.

He said, 'I shall go and get the spade,' and there was a grimness in his voice.

There was a quarter moon, making the night light enough to see what they were doing.

Although the Bagleys slept at the front of the house there was the chance that if Mr Bagley got up he might see what was happening from the landing window, from where Kendra had seen him digging that night. She kept looking about her.

Pel Devereux was soon back with the shovel. 'I'll get started. The sooner we are out of this spot the better.'

Recent rain had made the soil easier to turn, but with each spade thrust Kendra, who kept glancing at him, noticed that he was becoming more and more tense.

He looked up once. 'If these jewels are not here—'

'Oh, get on with it,' she snapped.

Then, metal struck metal and he gave a long drawn out sigh. 'Oh, thank God.'

'It may not be your jewellery.'

'I know it is.' He began digging with a fury. At last he said, 'Ah'. Then he bent and lifted the box.

He brought a key from his pocket and opened it, and even in the semi-darkness Kendra could see the jewellery sparkling. He handed the box to her. 'Hold that for a minute. We'll get away from here as quickly as possible.'

He brought out a leather bag, emptied the jewellery into it and putting the box into the hole began to fill it in. He then spread some matted grass over it and straightened. 'That's it, I don't think it will arouse suspicion. Come along.'

He picked up the bag. 'You be walking ahead. I must replace the spade. Don't want Mr Bagley to get ideas.'

For a brief moment Kendra wondered if he was planning to leave her now he had the jewellery but a brief smile, a consoling pat on the shoulder and a 'Well done', dispelled her suspicions.

She had reached the roadway when he caught her up. He asked her if she could ride and when she told him yes he said, 'Then I shall hire horses at the inn where I had supper. I've already prepared them that I might need them, and vaguely hinted at an elopement. People enjoy a little intrigue and with a bribe to keep our direction a secret—'

'Is all that necessary? We should be well away before Mr Bagley could find the note I left.'

'Not if he made up his mind to go to your room.'

Kendra gave a shiver. It was certainly a possibility. They walked quickly and she was breathless by the time they had reached the small inn. Devereux left her to go to the stables and returned with a boy leading two geldings. Devereux reminded the boy of his promise and handed over some money.

Minutes later Kendra found herself cantering side by side with Devereux over a field, the wind billowing out her cloak. She had expected they would make for the Coaching Inn some six miles distant to pick up the early morning stage, but Devereux took a different direction. 'To put anyone likely to follow off the scent,' he explained.

They had travelled quite a distance when he suddenly reined his horse and sat listening, his head cocked. Then he dismounted and stood listening again.

'What is it?' Kendra asked.

'A rider—no two—quick, get into the shelter of the trees.'

Thick forest land bordered the road and it took only seconds for them to seek sanctuary behind thick-trunked trees. Kendra's horse, spooked by the waving branches, began to whinny. Devereux urged her to go further on where there was open land. She stumbled over exposed roots, her heart thudding madly. Who were the riders? She led her horse to the clearing ahead, then *she* stood listening. In the stillness of the night there was a menace in the thudding hooves drawing nearer. Harness jingled, a horse snorted. A man's voice called something but she was unable to hear what was being said. When the hoof beats faded into the distance Devereux appeared, leading his horse.

'Bagley and another man,' he said. 'We'll cut across this field and through that copse yonder. We must change direction yet again.'

'Who was the man with him?' Kendra asked fearfully. 'What was it he said?'

'That, according to the stable lad, they were on the right road. The wretched boy had informed, and I paid him well.'

Kendra moistened dry lips. 'You were right about Mr Bagley coming to my room. I thought him to be sound asleep. Who *was* the man with him?'

Devereux shrugged. 'A groom perhaps?'

'Or the law. He threatened if I complained about him for withholding my wages he would say I was lazy, that I neglected his wife and stole money from him. Oh, God if I am to be pursued—'

'You won't be,' he said grimly. 'I shall see to that. Come along, let's go.'

At that moment all Kendra cared about was getting as far away from the wretched Mr Bagley as possible but after they had ridden for a while the strain of all that had happened began to tell. She begged to rest a while.

Devereux looked about him. 'I could do with a rest myself. I had no sleep at all last night. There's a barn over there, not the most luxurious of accommodation, but under the circumstances—'. He rode ahead and Kendra followed, wondering if he meant them to share the barn. It was then suspicion began to go through her mind. Had he contrived this? How did she know that one of the horsemen had been Bagley? She had only Devereux's word for it. How did she know he had a right to the jewellery? It might have been willed to Mr Bagley, he might have buried it to prevent Devereux getting his hands on it.

Devereux, who had investigated the barn said, 'There's enough straw for bedding. We shall have to dispense with proprieties under these circumstances.' He went to tether the horses, leaving Kendra staring after him, her heart thumping.

Dispense with proprieties? Surely he did not intend them to share a bed? If he did she would certainly have something to say about it!

When he came back he was carrying the horse blankets. 'Soon have you nice and cosy.' He sounded most cheerful. In the barn he divided the bundle of straw, put half on one side of the barn and the other opposite. Then he dropped a blanket on each portion.

It seemed all right but Kendra was uneasy. 'Mr Devereux—'

'The choice is yours, Madame. Right or

left—?'

'Mr Devereux—I'm not at all happy about sharing this barn.'

'Well, *I* intend to take advantage of having a roof over my head, the nights get extremely cold. If you prefer to sleep outside I shall carry your "palliasse" out for you.'

'Mr Devereux! *You* may be used to sleeping with women in barns but I—'

'Miss Hollis—if you think I have evil intentions towards you let me put your mind at rest. I am not in the mood for making love and if I were you would be perfectly safe, you are simply not my type of woman. Does that satisfy you?'

Ouch! He certainly knew how to touch the raw spots. 'I think you have made the situation quite clear,' she said coldly.

'Then I suggest you be sensible and try and get some sleep.' As Devereux spoke he laid down on the straw, shuffled it about a bit then drew the blanket over him. 'Good-night.'

Kendra laid down but it was not to sleep. She was furious for having given the impression she might be desirable to him. Not his type indeed! He certainly knew how to put a woman in her place. No doubt he still thought of her as a menial. If he had been less cruel she would not have taken the share he offered for the recovery of the jewellery. Now she would not leave him until she got it.

The ground felt rock-hard under the thin

38

layer of straw. If he had been a gentleman he would have let her have all the straw. Draughts seemed to be coming from everywhere. If only she could have got bedded into deep straw. Devereux, breathing deeply, evenly, seemed to be asleep. Hateful man.

She felt rigid with cold. How could she fall asleep in this state? Exhaustion finally took over. But in her dreams she was cold, lost and naked running across the floor of a valley seeking a cave, the shelter of bushes, to get out of the appalling wind which swept down. 'I'm cold, I'm cold,' she kept wailing. 'Somebody please warm me. Cold—cold—cold—'

Then suddenly strong arms went around her and she was being held close to someone, the warmth of the person's body seeping into her own. Oh, what heaven. The wind had died down and the sun was beating down and she had never known greater comfort and happiness . . .

Kendra roused and lay for a moment in a euphoria of peace. Then she became aware of a weight on her thighs, and rousing herself went rigid as she realised what it was. Devereux was beside her, his leg across her, one hand cupping her breast.

She tried to draw away and he stirred. Soft lips touched her cheek. 'Eleanor, darling,' he murmured.

Kendra pushed his leg away. 'Mr Devereux!'

'What—what is it?' He spoke sleepily,

turning away from her. Then as she struggled to get up he awoke. 'Miss Hollis—' He sounded bewildered.

'How dare you,' she said. 'How dare you sneak up on me, come to my bed.' Kendra was trembling with anger.

He sat up, ran his fingers through his thick dark hair and looked at her. 'Yes, of course, you were cold—you asked me to warm you. I think you were dreaming, but you were shivering, your teeth were chattering—' Devereux raised his shoulders in a helpless gesture. 'What was I to do? Let you catch your death of cold—?'

'You could have given me your share of the straw, your blanket, *if* you were so anxious to help me.'

Devereux spread his hands. 'A typical woman! Take all! *I* could freeze. You don't deserve any consideration. You don't know how lucky you were that I didn't attempt anything. After all, you did invite me to your bed.'

'In a dream. How do I know that nothing did happen?'

He gave a dry laugh. 'Oh, you would have known if I had made love to you, Miss Hollis. You most certainly would. None of my women friends have any complaints about that. They beg for more. I don't know if you can get a man to make love to you but you certainly need it. I'm sorry I can't oblige. My women friends

40

have to be special. Warm, loving.' He got up. 'I shall give you my blanket and my straw if you feel so strongly about it.'

Kendra was furious with herself for being so stupid. Of course she would have known if Devereux had done anything more than hold her. Now she had to suffer insults. She got up.

'I don't want your straw or your blanket. I was dreaming that I was warm,' she lied. 'I shall go to sleep again.'

'May I have your permission to stay in the same barn, Ma'am?'

'Oh, go to sleep.'

She dropped down on the straw again and pulled the blanket over her.

Kendra heard him chuckling. Although she realised she *would* have known had Devereux tried to do more than hold her, she still felt a sense of shock at having been held in a man's arms—in bed. There was something so wanton about it. A tremor went through her body. A pleasurable tremor. She found herself wondering what it would be like to be lying naked with a man, his flesh touching hers. She turned over, and over again, rustling the straw. Lord above, where were her thoughts leading her?

In spite of her determination to put such lascivious thoughts from her mind they persisted until it dawned on her it was not exactly flattering to have a man lie beside you and *not* attempt anything, especially as that man was now lightly snoring. So much for romance! Kendra slept then.

* * *

When she aroused the next time the barn door was open, sunlight streamed in, and Pel Devereux was outside talking to the horses. She got up, stretched her cramped limbs, brushed the straw from her clothes and went out. He greeted her as though the incident through the night had never happened.

'A beautiful morning. Do you feel better for your rest?'

She blinked in the bright light. 'Yes, yes I do.'

'Are you ready for some breakfast? I took the precaution of having some food packed at the Inn.'

'How resourceful of you.'

'Ah, but I happen to be a very resourceful fellow. Bread and cheese?' He undid a package. 'I have some water too.' He indicated a pocket flask. 'Collected it from the river.'

Kendra could not help but admire his virility, his exuberance, he was really a most attractive man. Very strong, she would imagine. She felt again the pleasurable tremor as she imagined his arms around her, his lips on hers. She took a piece of the bread and a portion of cheese.

She looked up and met Devereux's gaze. 'You had a rough time yesterday one way and another,' he said. His voice was surprisingly gentle. 'And I was hard on you last night, suggesting you were not my type of woman. I said it to get you to accept the situation, it was the only way I could think of to convince you that you would be safe with me.' A roguish twinkle came into his eyes. 'Although I must admit I found it difficult to behave myself when I came to your bed.'

'Mr Devereux, you must not use that phrase! Anyone hearing it would certainly put the wrong interpretation on it. You would not let your—wife hear such a thing.'

'That would be no problem, I have no wife.'

'Then who is Eleanor?'

He turned his head sharply. 'What do you know of her?'

'It was a name you mentioned last night in your sleep.'

'Oh, did I?' He gathered up the last of the crumbs of cheese. 'When we've finished the meal we must make a move.'

'Can we stop at the river, I should like to freshen up.'

'You can bathe in it if you wish, I know of an excellent spot where you can have complete freedom.'

'I doubt whether I shall be bathing,' she said, 'but I will appreciate a wash.'

'I think I shall have a swim.'

How tempting it sounded. Kendra's thoughts went winging away once more on things she ought not to be thinking about,

43

swimming with Devereux in the river—naked. She could see the droplets of water glistening on his dark hair, his body—a strong body, broad-shouldered, narrow-hipped, firm thighs. Hot colour rushed to her cheeks. What madness was this, and all because of a dream. She must get her thoughts into some form of sensibility. She got to her feet.

The sun glinted on the water like so many dancing silver coins. The privacy for ablutions Devereux had mentioned was a U-shaped inlet, surrounded by thick-trunked trees, interspersed with bushes.

Devereux waved a hand. 'There you are, Ma'am, the perfect place for anyone wanting to bathe. You could undress, swim and be totally unobserved.'

Kendra looked around her. It did seem perfect, but there could be people near. She looked at Devereux. 'And where would you be, sir?'

He laughed. 'Might I not be permitted one small peep?'

'Indeed not. In any case I shall not be undressing.'

'How foolish. You are missing such an opportunity for swimming. But then perhaps you are unable to swim?'

Kendra assured him she was an excellent swimmer. She had learnt with her cousins during holidays.

'Well then—' Devereux swept her an

exaggerated bow, 'I shall leave you to your frolics. If you need your back washing, just call me.' He left, laughing.

Kendra had brought her valise with her and she took out a piece of soap and a flannel. Her intention had been to simply wash her hands and face, but as she stood on the grass the water looked so inviting she longed to immerse her whole body in it. What passed for a bath at the Bagleys constituted standing in a large bowl of warm water and washing down. Kendra looked about her. Dare she undress?

She walked to the water's edge and saw to her delight it was sandy at this particular spot and shelved gently. She could keep on her shift, but then that would not be the same; it would become water-logged and she would be unable to soap herself easily. Anyway, she had no towel so she would need her shift to dry herself. With this thought the decision was made. Kendra drew clean underwear from her valise, looked cautiously around her, then hastily undressed, and with her last garment shed she splashed quickly into the water. The iciness of it made her gasp, but it was certainly refreshing.

What freedom! She soaped her body, rinsed, splashing the water over her, soaped again and kept bobbing up and down, with the excitement of childhood when taken to the seaside.

In her joyousness she began to sing, 'Sweet Lass of Richmond Hill' and realised it was months ago since she had sang. Friends of her father had always been urging her to play the piano and give them a song. She had a good voice, many people had told her so. Now in the still, bright morning the notes soared clear and sweet. She was in the middle of the chorus when a voice called, 'Is that you singing, Miss Hollis?'

Devereux's voice came from far enough away to make her feel safe.

'Yes, yes it is—was,' she corrected herself.

'Sing some more, you have an excellent voice.'

The interruption had made Kendra self-conscious. It was different singing at home. She called, 'Some other time.'

'Don't hurry, plenty of time.'

She felt reluctant to leave the water, yet knew she had to come out sometime. What was more, Devereux could come for her without any warning. He might even have been out of the water and dressed when he called. Even so, she could not resist splashing water over her back and doing a little more bobbing up and down before making her way back.

She glanced around her then picked up her shift. She pulled it over her head and began rubbing it against her body. When she was dry she could put on a clean shift and dry her legs and feet.

Her body tingled. She began to hum to herself. Then suddenly she tensed, thinking she

46

heard the snapping of a twig. She glanced quickly over her shoulder. Not a bush or leaf stirred. She reached for her clean shift then was tense again.

She had a horrible feeling that someone was watching her. She quickly pulled the clean shift over her. Was that a bush moving? Everywhere was still. No, it had moved again. A face appeared, then a man stood up. Kendra screamed.

He came out of the bushes, a tramp, dirty and from where she was she could smell him.

'Pretty lady,' he said, and came forward, smiling.

Kendra screamed again and kept on screaming. Devereux came running then stopped as he saw the man.

'Clear off,' he said.

'I just want to touch the pretty lady.'

Kendra pulled on her dress, while Devereux came up to the man. 'And I told you to clear off. I don't want to hurt you, but I will if you don't leave at once.'

Kendra began pushing the things back into her bag. The man had turned away, but kept glancing back, a broad grin on his face. 'I'm going pretty lady. I wouldn't have hurt you.'

Devereux followed him until he was out of sight, then returned. 'I think he was harmless but one can't be sure with these vagrants. They use all kinds of ruses. Are you all right?'

'Yes, thank goodness you were at hand.' Her

legs felt weak. 'I'll just sit down for a moment.'

'You are having a very mixed time, aren't you?' He spoke gently and she was glad he did have feelings. 'I'll wait for you, in case there are any more vagabonds hanging around. Although I couldn't see anyone else, I think I would have been aware of them.'

Kendra had difficulty in fastening the buttons on the bodice of her dress. When it was done she said, 'I think I'm ready to leave, Mr Devereux. It was the sudden shock of seeing the man that upset me.' She got up and felt steady again. 'Such a shame, the water was so lovely.'

'I know, I enjoyed my swimming. Now, have you got everything? The horses are just beyond the bushes. But I think we can walk beside them for a while, get your sea legs, as the saying is. We don't want you falling off your horse.'

'I'm sure that wouldn't happen. I feel a bit of a fool now for screaming.'

'Not at all, you were sensible.'

They walked beside the horses for a short distance and Devereux said, 'I think when we get to London I shall take you to some friends of mine. You can stay there for a time. The Garfields are lovely people and most hospitable, you'll like them.'

Kendra protested. 'No, I couldn't possibly impose on your friends. It wouldn't be fair to them.'

'They'll be pleased to welcome any friend of

mine. Anyway, I'm taking you and no more protests.'

Kendra, who had not been looking forward to finding accommodation in London, or a suitable post, gave in. After all, a few days would give her a chance to find something she really wanted.

The rest of the journey passed without further incident but Kendra was bone tired by the time they arrived in London. They had left the horses at a coaching inn on the outskirts and travelled by hired carriage the rest of the way.

Kendra, who was used to visiting the homes of her father's gambling friends and finding them denuded of pieces that would help to pay gambling debts, expected Devereux's friends' home to be the same. And was surprised on arriving at an imposing residence in Grosvenor Square to find an air of stability and graciousness. It was there in the beautiful Aubusson carpets, the exquisite porcelain, the silver, the paintings and luxurious furnishings.

Mr Garfield, an elderly man who greeted her with a gentle courtesy, told her that any friend of Pel's was more than welcome and apologised that his wife was out and would not be back until late. Then he added, 'But Mrs Coates, our housekeeper, will see to all your wants, Miss Hollis.'

The middle-aged Mrs Coates put Kendra at ease right away. She took her up to her room, said dinner was at seven, but if Kendra would prefer it she could have a tray sent up to her room. For which Kendra was grateful, as she was tired after travelling.

'If there is anything you need, anything at all, Miss Hollis, just ring. You may hear voices in the room below but I doubt whether the men will disturb you. A card game will be in progress later.'

Kendra smiled and said once her head was on the pillow she doubted whether an earthquake would rouse her. She refused the offer of a maid to help her unpack, knowing her wardrobe would not stand up to inspection, but accepted the offer of warm water being sent up for her to wash. Mrs Coates then withdrew.

Kendra stood looking about her. There was fine furniture here too, luxury, the graciousness she had known in her early childhood at home. To Kendra there was something about the life of a gambler. When her father had got them into dire straits he was always looking around frantically for something to sell. Her own mother's jewellery had gone that way. Although it had been pawned at first there had not been money at the time when it was due to be reclaimed.

Her father expressed his grief for allowing this to happen, and Kendra now wondered if Pel Devereux's mother's jewellery would go the same way. Mr Garfield must be a gambling man, but he was either cautious, or had amazing luck.

Kendra had opened her valise to get out her nightdress when there was a knock on the door and Devereux called, 'Are you respectable, Miss Hollis? May I come in?'

'Quite respectable.'

He peered round the door. 'Ah, there you are.' He came in, smiling broadly. 'How do you like it?' He waved a hand indicating the furnishings. 'Much better than sleeping in a barn.'

'Mr Garfield is most kind, but I feel an interloper. I understand a card game will be in progress this evening.'

'That should not affect *you*. I enjoy a game here, the stakes are high. I feel lucky.'

'You could end up losing all the jewellery,' Kendra said quietly.

'What a Job's comforter you are, to be sure.' A sudden coldness had come into Devereux's voice. 'Please give me credit for more sense, Miss Hollis. I happen to be a professional gambler, not some small town amateur waiting to be fleeced.'

'Even the best of professionals can be on a losing streak, confidence will not turn a bad hand into a good one.'

'A professional never loses on bad hands, Miss Hollis, only on good ones, you should know that.'

'Yes, I do, but—'

51

'You are afraid you might not get the reward I promised you. If you wait one moment I shall settle my debt.'

He came back with the leather bag and tipped the contents out onto the bed. The display in daylight made Kendra gasp. Pendants of rubies, of emeralds, diamonds, brooches and earrings set with precious stones, gold bracelets, necklets, silver as well as gold.

'Oh, how exquisite,' Kendra breathed.

Devereux selected certain pieces and set them aside. 'These are to be given to my bride on our wedding day, at my mother's request. I shall honour it.' He waved a hand over the rest. 'But from these you are free to choose what you will.'

'But that would be an impossible task, Mr Devereux. I might choose something much too expensive. They all look too expensive. I expect a modest reward, not a piece of jewellery. I would not know where to sell it. What I need is money in my hand.'

'And you shall have it in a few days' time, as I told you.'

'I've suddenly decided I should like to leave in the morning. I can find some accommodation. I feel out of place in these surroundings. I have only one decent dress—Mrs Garfield will wonder when she meets me who—'

'Leonora is a marvellous person, very warm, most kind. She will arrange for a dressmaker to make you clothes.'

'But I will not be here long enough to need expensive clothes. Even if I do stay it will be for no more than two or three days.'

'No, I want you to stay longer. I feel you brought me good luck when you discovered the hiding place of the jewels. I need you, you must stay.'

Kendra gave a small sigh. She knew all about the superstitions of gamblers. Her father would never put his left boot on before his right. If he saw a black cat and thought it likely to cross his path he would turn away from it. Black cats might be lucky to some people, he would say, but not to him. He had numerous superstitions.

'I shall stay until tomorrow,' Kendra said firmly, 'then I shall leave, with or without my reward.'

Devereux took her hands in his and said softly, 'I want you to stay and not solely for the reason of bringing me luck. I find myself drawn to you.' Kendra was about to say that flattery would not make her change her mind when he added, 'Don't ask me why, I only know there is something about you that attracts me.'

He rubbed his thumb gently over the back of her hand, sending delicious little shivers up and down her spine. 'I do need you, Kendra, please stay.'

She said hesitantly, 'Well—', and knew he had won.

'Good, I shall see you at dinner.'

She explained about having a meal sent up and he shrugged. 'If that is what you wish. I shall see you in the morning. And, Kendra, thanks for agreeing to stay.'

There was something so sincere about him that she tried hard to push aside the thought of Mrs Bagley's words that 'Pel Devereux could charm the birds out of the trees.'

CHAPTER THREE

Kendra had a sound and dreamless sleep that night and was awakened the next morning by a maid bringing morning tea and hot water for her to wash. She said, 'Mr Devereux sends his compliments, Ma'am, and asks if you would care to breakfast with him in about half an hour.'

'Thank Mr Devereux and tell him yes, I shall be pleased to have breakfast with him.'

Kendra felt light-hearted. She had salvaged one simple morning gown when she left home and this she brought out, a sprigged muslin in pale blue.

'Oh, that's pretty, Ma'am,' said the little maid. 'My name is Jenny, would you like me to do your hair for you when you're ready, I do the mistress's hair for her.'

'Yes, I would, Jenny, thank you very much.'

The girl was adept. She brushed Kendra's

hair until it shone, curled strands round her fingers and looped up the curls, framing her face. Kendra felt gratified at the result when she went down to the morning room and saw Devereux's surprise at the change in her. He took her by the shoulders and held her away from him. 'Well, good-morning, and who is this beautiful young lady?'

She smiled wryly. 'I can see you had a good game last night.'

'Yes, indeed. I hope I did not disturb you when I went up to bed at five o'clock.' His face was alight, his eyes alive. 'I could do no wrong and I owe it all to your influence.'

'Mr Devereux—'

'I won a very large pot on a couple of pairs! Come and have some breakfast and I shall tell you about it.' He went over to the sideboard and raised domed covers on silver dishes. 'Bacon—devilled kidneys—?'

He talked in between eating, describing the play of the other guests, the cards they had held, the hands he had held. There was an American, Lloyd Francis, a crazy gambler, a reckless player, gone through three fortunes and looked like going through a fourth, an amiable fellow, most likeable. Devereux stabbed a piece of kidney with his fork. Had he told Kendra that Leonora would be delighted to help her choose materials for dresses, she would summon two seamstresses.

'Mr Devereux—'

There was no stopping him. After she had dispensed with the dressmakers he would take her for a drive, they would go to Madame Tussauds, would she like that, was there anywhere else she would rather see, she had only to say?

Kendra gave a small sigh, thinking how familiar she was with all the feverishness after a good win. What would Pel Devereux be like when he lost, in the depths of despair, morose, or would he be like her father, down one minute and bouncing back the next, there was always another evening, another game.

'Do you have a goal, Mr Devereux? My father dreamed of owning a string of valuable racehorses, he imagined himself leading in a Derby winner. He looked just as you do now when you talked about your winning streak. He was in a world I could never *quite* wholly share.'

'Why not?'

'Because I could never understand such an obsession with gambling.'

'Everyone must have some dream,' Devereux said softly. 'What is yours, Miss Hollis.'

'Oh, the simple things, a home and children.'

'And a husband, of course,' he teased.

'Naturally.'

'And what is your image of this dream man in your life?'

'Quite definitely not a gambler.'

'Why not?' This came from Mr Garfield who

had come in unnoticed. 'Gambling men quite often make very good husbands, Miss Hollis.'

'And here is a living proof,' Devereux declared. 'My friend here has a wonderful marriage.'

'Ah yes, because I have such an understanding wife.' Mr Garfield helped himself from a dish on the sideboard and came and sat down. 'But do not get the idea we have not experienced poverty. There have been times when I have not known where our next meal was coming from.'

'Then you must have learned a lesson from it, Mr Garfield. This beautiful house, your treasures—'

He bowed his head in acknowledgement. 'You are right, Miss Hollis. When my children were crying for food I knew I must never get into such a position again.' He looked across at Devereux and added with a gentle smile, 'So let that be a lesson to you, Pel, my boy.'

Devereux grinned. 'I promise I will not have a wife and children begging me for food, because I shall not marry until I own an empire.'

Mr Garfield's eyebrows went up. 'And you think that empires are not lost in gambling?'

'All right, I shall set a sum aside for my family and tell my wife if I lose everything else I possess she is not to hand over to me that sum, not even if I go down on my bended knees to her.'

'Then I hope you are lucky enough to find a woman who is strong enough and loves you enough to resist you,' Mr Garfield said quietly.

It was on this note that Leonora Garfield came in. 'Who is talking about love at this time in the morning?' she asked laughing. She turned to Kendra. 'Miss Hollis, how nice to meet you, so sorry I was out yesterday when you arrived. Shall I come and sit beside you, then we can talk women talk, the men will be sure to be discussing their card game.'

She was a tall, angular woman, who wore her simple morning gown with elegance, and she had such a vibrant personality, it was some time before Kendra realised she was quite plain-featured.

A maid came in with a silver toast rack and set it down before Leonora.

'I think it will be to your liking, Ma'am.'

'Thank you, Jenny.' She gave the maid a smile, then took one of the triangular portions of toast, snapped off a piece and confided to Kendra she liked it thin enough and crisp enough to crack when she broke it, adding with an impish grin, 'We are all children at heart.' Devereux started to laugh and she said, 'Yes, and men too. You get on with your business, Pel Devereux, Kendra and I are going to talk about clothes.'

She buttered the toast. 'Pel tells me you are wanting some new gowns. I shall order some too. I shall send word to have materials

58

brought to the house, and ask my seamstresses to call. We shall have a lovely time.'

Kendra said quickly, 'Mrs Garfield, I must explain that I have no money. I came to London to try and find a job as a lady's companion. Mr Devereux was kind enough to allow me to travel with him. I would be very interested in seeing what you order from your dressmaker, but I am unable to afford a dress myself. I felt this has to be explained, as Mr Devereux was talking about dresses for me.'

Leonora smiled. 'Mr Devereux is inclined to get enthusiastic when he's on a winning streak. You must come and see what I choose.'

When later Kendra saw the stream of people arriving with bolts of material she wondered how many gowns Leonora intended to order. There were silks and satins in jewel colours and delicate shades, fine French silk velvets and heavier velvets with the bloom of peaches on them. Patterned and striped muslins were a spring garden of greens and pinks and lavender and golds and yellows.

They went to a very large sewing room with a lovely polished oak floor, where materials were draped over stands, over chair and sofa backs. Devereux, to Kendra's surprise came with them, and sat back in a gilt chair, one elegantly clad leg over the other.

He said, in a casual voice, 'I shall leave when Kendra has made her choice. First I would like to see that soft black chiffon draped against her.'

Kendra immediately protested. She was not in need of any dresses and certainly not black, she had just come out of mourning.

'This black chiffon is shot with silk and has a sheen on it. You have a creamy skin, it will suit you. I want you to have it.'

Kendra tried to protest again but Mrs Garfield, catching her eye, whispered, 'Accept it. I can talk to my dressmaker later.'

Devereux waved to a man hovering near. 'Bring me some sketches.'

Kendra was too taken aback to protest further. Devereux was ordering for her as if he possessed her. Well, she would make it quite clear to him that she was not his mistress and never would be. He was even ordering what he wanted, never even giving her a chance to order what she would like. But the next moment she was thinking how wonderful it would be to own beautiful dresses.

So Kendra decided to accept this one but, if she had to have another, it would certainly be a gown that she wanted, not what he fancied. Why shouldn't she? Her father always bought her something when he won, so why shouldn't Pel Devereux with his arrogant ways. Not that she could imagine any time when she might wear them.

However, she had no say in the matter, Devereux took over. He asked to see the delicate green silk. And could the apricot

60

velvet be draped for his inspection? He appealed to Leonora.

'Do you think these suitable for Kendra?'

Kendra stared at him, then fumed that he had asked someone else for an opinion. Leonora, to be fair, replied gently, 'Does Kendra approve?'

This made no difference. Devereux made the decisions, not even glancing at her for a reply. How dare he treat her as a nobody? She had her own pride.

She was about to ask Devereux if she could have a private word with him when he said, as he waved away a piece of red silk, 'No, no, my ward would certainly not suit that shade of red.'

His ward? Well! At least he had given her a more honourable position in the eyes of all the people there. But the clothes, the quantity—it was not only morning and day gowns and evening ones but cloaks, pelisses, spencers—when on earth did he think she would get a chance of wearing them all? And what about the cost?

At last he unfolded his long legs and got up. 'Well that is all for now. I shall be waiting in the drawing room, Kendra, to go for our drive. Try not to keep me waiting too long.'

Leonora raised her eyebrows. 'Typical man, he can spend hours making a choice for you, but you must run the moment he wants to leave. Just let Miss Smith take your measurements, Kendra, then you can go.'

When Kendra went down to the drawing room Devereux was standing at the window, his back to her. For a moment she felt a pang, he looked such an imposing figure with his broad shoulders, narrow waist and long legs. She hardened her heart.

'Mr Devereux, I must have a word with you. These clothes you ordered, what use will they be to me when I take up a position of lady's maid or companion—?'

He turned swiftly. 'You are not taking up any position. You agreed to stay with me.'

'But only for a couple of days, at the most.'

'That was not what you agreed.' He regarded her coldly. 'You cannot go back on your word.'

Kendra spread her hands in a helpless gesture. 'I'm not going back on my word, you must have misunderstood me. And it would be impossible for me to stay on here indefinitely, you must realise that.'

'Edward and Leonora would not mind how long you stayed.'

'But my position is in relation to you—I know you spoke of me as your ward a while ago, but—'

'Because you are such a stickler for the proprieties. I want to take you to various places, introduce you to people I know, I want you to have enjoyment.' He smiled suddenly. 'Don't you like the idea of being my ward? I quite like the role of guardian.'

Kendra could see the pattern. Pel Devereux,

62

like so many gamblers was generous when in funds, they spent lavishly, never thinking of another day, or if they did it would be one where they could make another 'killing'.

She looked down at her muslin gown. 'I shall have to postpone my drive with you. I would look a rather impoverished ward of such a distinguished man.'

'That can easily be rectified, I shall have a word with Leonora. Come upstairs with me.'

* * *

Some time later Kendra came downstairs dressed in an outfit belonging to Leonora, a pale cinnamon gown piped with white, an oval hat with shallow crown in white with a feather in cinnamon curling round the brim, and carrying a parasol with a deeper brown fringe. She looked and felt regal.

Devereux was smiling happily as he helped her into the open carriage, lent to them by Mr Garfield.

'You will set everyone gossiping,' he said, 'they will be agog to know who you are.'

'And you will enjoy every moment of it.'

'Of course.'

Kendra certainly had plenty to interest her. She was intrigued by the number of people in passing carriages who acknowledged Devereux. Some of the women peeked back, no doubt full of curiosity to know who she could be.

She enjoyed the activity when they were caught up in a stream of traffic, it was all so new to her, the noise as the drivers of wagons and drays shouted to one another as they fought for supremacy of the road. A man pushing a barrow edged it into a place one would have thought impossible to put a small chair. Once a barrow, laden with vegetables, overturned, causing chaos. And at one time a carriage drew so close to theirs the wheels all but interlocked. Kendra gasped but Devereux sat through it all calmly, raising his hat to occupants of carriages, explaining the position of the people, the Duke of this, the Earl of that, Lord and Lady so and so. The greetings exchanged were all most friendly. 'Devereux my boy, good to see you back. Will you be at Almacks—at the club—and the cock fighting?' And the ladies' glances coy or affectionate, as they issued invitations for him to visit them soon.

'You own to quite a popularity,' Kendra said.

'I do have my enemies,' he admitted, but in a tone that gave the impression his enemies would number no more than two or three among a vast number of acquaintances and friends.

At Kendra's request he took her to Madame Tussauds. She had read about it and was very interested in the still figures, how real they were. She wanted to inspect everything, the clothes of famous people, of Kings and Queens and knights of old.

Devereux was impatient. Why should people want to see these figures? Living people were so much more interesting and he had so much to show her.

At last she agreed to leave, but afterwards mentioned she had been disappointed not to have seen the Chamber of Horrors. When she told Devereux this he eyed her with distaste.

She said in a low voice, 'It's all right, I don't really want to see the Chamber of Horrors.'

'Good. I have so many beautiful things to show you.'

After taking her to a concert in the Crystal Palace he took her to the Regent's Circus and she was thrilled. She had never seen so many animals, who could do such amazing things. Lastly they went to the Dancing Waters and when they returned to the Garfields she thought it was the most exciting day she had ever spent and was breathless telling Leonora about it.

'The Waters were so magnificent,' she enthused. 'Water cascaded from a series of basins, there were the water temples, the Grand waterfalls, the dancing fountains. Then we—'

'Speaking of dancing,' Devereux interrupted, 'I have a present for you. The Magic Sailor.'

It was a toy, which he placed on the floor, then taking out a cheap tin whistle he began to play and this toy sailor began to dance, and appeared to be following the rhythm of the music. Kendra and Leonora were helpless with laughter.

Leonora wiped her eyes. 'Pel, where did you get it?'

'I didn't see you buy it,' Kendra said.

'Ah, but then I never let my right hand know what my left hand is doing.'

Both women demanded to know how the toy worked and Devereux laughed and showed them the button that had to be pressed. 'There you are, it will amuse you and you can think of me when you have him dancing.'

He spoke lightly but Kendra knew it was something she would always treasure, the token of a very happy day.

She and Leonora spent the evening together, talking mainly about clothes, while the men went out to play cards. Leonora seemed quite reconciled to being what she called a 'poker widow'. 'It has its compensations, being married to a gambler,' she said. 'A wife is always needed to commiserate over losses, or to share her husband's excitement over wins. Oh yes, we have had our bad times,' she smiled, 'but life has never been dull with Edward.'

Kendra thought about this when she went to bed that night. Life had never been dull living at home, and it would be different if it was a husband you were waiting up for. She remembered how that afternoon Pel had twined his fingers in hers and the way he had looked at her had given her a feeling of belonging to him.

But perhaps she was fooling herself. It might be something he did with every woman he escorted. And yet—he did regard her as someone special, if only because he thought her to be lucky to him. He needed her. It was good to feel needed. This was what she had missed most since her father had died.

She thought of her dream of the night before, when she and Pel had been naked. It brought a throbbing to her body which made her want to be in Pel's arms, to feel his flesh warm against her. Was this wrong, or was it something that happened to most women when thinking of a man in this way? Evie, the parlourmaid, had spoken of how beautiful feelings could be if you loved a man and how hateful if a man took you only for lust.

She should be pleased that Pel had promised to take her to meet his grandmother the next day. Kendra had been surprised he had a grandmother, as he had never mentioned any family.

*　*　*

The house both inside and out had the air of a mausoleum and the elderly lady with the parchment skin, who greeted them from a day bed, looked to be at least ninety. But her voice when she greeted Devereux was strong.

He was a bad boy, a very bad boy, why had he not been to see her?

'Because, dear Grandmother,' he said, 'I have been visiting America.'

'America, what were you doing there? Is England not good enough for you? But then you always were a restless soul. Who is this with you, why are you not introducing me. Is the lady your fiancée?'

Devereux, with a quick conspiratorial glance at Kendra, said, 'Yes, she is,' and introduced her.

The old lady demanded that Kendra come closer so she could see her better. She picked up a pair of lorgnettes and eyed Kendra from head to toe.

'You are not pretty, thank goodness. Can't stand pretty young ladies with their simpering ways. I thought you rather plain, at first, but now I see you have a beauty of your own. I imagine, too, you will have a lot of common sense.' She paused then added wryly, 'You will have your hands full when you marry this grandson of mine, but he does have some good points. This is something you will have to find out for yourself.'

Devereux laughed. 'I lived with my grandmother for twelve years. It is easy to see from whom I inherited my "plain" speaking.'

The old lady waved a hand, dismissing them.

'Go now, I am very tired, but make sure you come again and soon, and bring your fiancée with you. Wait, just one moment. Why were you named Kendra?'

'Because my mother's maiden name was Kendrick. If I had been a boy that is the name he would have been given, but as I turned out to be a girl—'

'That is all, I like my curiosity satisfied. Good-day to you both.'

When they were outside Kendra said to Devereux, 'You had no right to tell your grandmother I was your fiancée.'

'It pleased her, she has always been advocating my settling down. By tomorrow, by even another hour she will have forgotten you.'

Kendra soon learned what it meant to have a restless man as an escort. He whisked her from place to place, from the Embankment to see the House of Commons, to Buckingham Palace, to several of the parks, to the Cathedral, then Kendra cried, 'No more, I'm exhausted.'

He eyed her in surprise. 'Why? We've driven to all the places.'

'And done a great deal of walking. But missed so much beauty. There was wonderful architecture, both at the Houses of Parliament and the Cathedral, yet I had hardly any time to take it all in before you whipped me off somewhere else.'

A coldness came into his face. 'In future you

had better go with Leonora then you can browse around all day if you wish.'

'Mr Devereux, I have no wish to hurt you, but I think you must realise that we are two totally different people. London is new to me. You have lived here, know it all. This is the first time I've been shown any of it and I am grateful. It's just that I would like to stroll around, not to rush from place to place.'

He gave a sudden grin. 'I'm always in a hurry. Sorry about that. Do please call me Pel. We are good friends, aren't we?'

'Yes, of course,' she answered softly.

'So where do we go now and, I promise to stroll.' He drew her arm through his and Kendra was happy.

Although they walked along Piccadilly and Pel did allow her to look in certain shop windows it was only for a minute and he was off to the next one. Kendra guessed she would just have to accept it.

They had lunch and went to various churches, still not lingering to look around. Nor were there any romantic interludes. But perhaps because of being a gambler's daughter Kendra had hope that something might develop.

Kendra was awake early the next morning. She got out of bed and padded over to the window. Then her pulses leapt as she saw Pel standing under a tree. He was looking up into the branches, his head inclined, as though listening to the bird-song. He was without a jacket and his white shirt was open to the waist. She had been dreaming about him again, and although in a less sensual way than the night before, her body responded to the magnificence of his virile figure. He looked serious at the moment. Had he lost at cards? Remembering her father's need to talk to someone after a disastrous night Kendra dressed quickly and went downstairs.

The dew-soaked grass, sparkling in a sudden shaft of sunlight, soaked through her thin slippers, but she was uncaring. She was almost up to him before he became aware of her.

'Why Kendra, you are up early this morning.'

'So are you.'

'I have not yet been to bed. Our game finished less than half an hour ago.'

'And you lost.'

'No, I made a killing.'

'So why the lack of animation?'

He shrugged. 'Oh, I was just thinking of this and that.' He plucked a leaf from the tree and rubbed it between his fingers.

Kendra waited for a while, and when he made no attempt to qualify the 'this and that' she asked him who had lost in the game, who had suffered the most.

He was silent again for quite a time then he turned his head. 'Oh . . . Lloyd Francis.'

'The American? Poor man, he must be just about destitute.'

71

'Not quite.' Devereux gave a sudden grin. 'I can take him for a sizeable amount yet.' He tapped her on the tip of her nose. 'Don't look so disapproving. If *I* don't, someone else will. And don't feel sorry for him. He takes it all philosophically. Incidentally, he's giving a supper party in his private suite at the Savoy this evening. You too are invited.'

'Why me? I don't know him.'

'I spoke about you, explained you were my ward.'

'Did you indeed. I think Mr Francis must be a most generous person to offer supper after sustaining such heavy losses, and *you* being the winner.'

'He is generous, a most likeable fellow.' Devereux stifled a yawn. 'Oh, please forgive me. I must go and seek my bed. Shall we go back to the house?'

He picked up his jacket from the stump of a tree and proffered an arm.

Kendra found herself looking forward to meeting Lloyd Francis. It would be interesting to talk to a man who had so much money that he could be complacent about giving a party after losing so much. And, what was more, she had been told that one of her evening dresses would be ready.

To her disappointment, however, she learned that it was the black chiffon gown, as Devereux had insisted that this one should be ready first.

She thought she would have no pleasure in wearing black, but when she put it on and saw her reflection in the mirror she was startled at the effect. The low cut neckline was more daring than she had ever worn and the black emphasised the pale column of her throat and the creaminess of her shoulders.

The sheer simplicity had the elegance of Leonora's dress that she had worn the day before, and Kendra found herself looking forward to Pel's reaction.

When he came to escort her downstairs a slow smile spread over his attractive features.

'A transformation,' he exclaimed. 'From an *ingénue* to the toast of the town!'

A little extravagant, perhaps, Kendra thought, but Leonora, exclaimed, 'Oh, Kendra, you really do look lovely. Pel was right, black does become you.'

'Of course I'm right, have I ever been wrong in my choice of women's dress?' declared Pel.

Kendra was surprised at the pang of jealousy that shot through her. How many other women had he been responsible for dressing?

Mr Garfield called to say the carriage was waiting and Devereux picked up Kendra's cloak and put it around her shoulders. The gesture, the way he was smiling at her, sent pleasurable tremors of excitement chasing up and down her spine.

Kendra, having thought of Lloyd Francis as a rather brash man prepared to fling fortunes away, was surprised to find him a quiet, pleasant young man with copper coloured hair and china blue eyes. She liked him on sight, especially when he smiled and his eyes crinkled at the corners.

'How nice to meet you, Miss Hollis. Mr Devereux has talked so much about you, how you are enjoying the sights of London. I think it must be most rewarding to escort a young lady who enters into the enjoyment, appreciates all there is to offer. I envy your guardian. If at any time he is unable to escort you, may I please have that honour?'

Devereux, as though determined to establish his proprietory right, put an arm around Kendra's waist. 'I think I can find time to keep my ward fully occupied, but should there be a time when I have other commitments there is no one I would rather trust her with than you, sir.'

Lloyd Francis acknowledged the compliment with a bow. 'I thank you.'

Kendra enjoyed the men's attention, especially Devereux's, with his air of possession. She knew then she wanted to be possessed by him, and found herself flirting a little with Lloyd Francis to make him jealous. It worked, he made a point of keeping her beside him, and she loved every moment of it.

The meal was served in an ante-room of Lloyd Francis's suite. The food was superb, Kendra enjoyed every course, the elegant surroundings and the attentiveness of all the men. There were to be no cards. The evening was to be devoted to the ladies.

'How fortunate we are, Kendra, how honoured,' Leonora said, her tone and manner good-humoured.

Kendra began to see how the Garfield's marriage was successful. If *she* had been making the remark she could not have resisted saying it with sarcasm; she was learning all the time.

CHAPTER FOUR

Wine was discussed over the meal and the various vineyards from which it came, and although Kendra had no expert knowledge on the subjects she enjoyed listening. Then Leonora, no doubt wanting her to take part in the conversation, suggested she tell Lloyd Francis about the sailor-man toy Devereux had bought her.

Kendra described it and the others laughed with her and Lloyd Francis said to Pel, 'You really are the most fortunate man, Devereux, I cannot bring such excitement to the eyes of the young ladies I escort, not even with the most expensive gifts I offer.'

'Ah, but then Kendra is unique,' Pel said. His gaze held hers. 'Quite unique. So unaffected,

75

so refreshing.'

At that moment Kendra felt willing to die for him. And yet later, listening to Lloyd Francis's quiet voice, she imagined that in spite of him being a gambler, life would be much more peaceful with him. He had that aura. She could see herself strolling with him around Madame Tussauds, discussing each waxwork figure, instead of being rushed around by Pel to pay a visit elsewhere. She felt he would have appreciated the dancing waters, not like Pel who kept saying, 'It is only water, Kendra,' and tapping his foot impatiently while she lingered for a last look.

During the conversation Kendra allowed her wineglass to be replenished and had not been aware of how much she had been drinking until her head began to feel woolly. Twice she giggled at something which was not intended to be funny and at last Leonora got up and said, 'I think we must get this young lady home and to bed.'

Kendra began to protest. Oh, no, she was enjoying herself. It was a wonderful evening. Devereux gripped her under the elbow, 'Come along, no arguing.'

It was his arm around her in the carriage, her head resting against his shoulder. He talked soothingly to her. 'You will be all right in the morning after a good night's sleep. We shall have another day out.' He held her hand and moved his thumb over the back in circles, bringing a tingling sensation to Kendra's limbs.

'I want to see my sailor-man dance,' she said. 'I love him.'

'More than you love me?' Devereux teased her in a whisper.

'Oh, no, *you* more, much more.'

'Then you must show me how much, later.' His voice was coaxing, sensuous, and he started to whisper something else but Leonora cut in, 'Kendra, are you feeling all right? Sit up, my dear, it would be unwise to fall asleep now, we are nearly home.'

'If she sleeps I can carry her upstairs,' Devereux said lightly.

'And you would enjoy that, Pel dear,' Leonora said smiling, 'but Kendra, I feel sure, will be perfectly able to walk up to her room.'

It was Leonora who helped her upstairs and saw her into bed. Kendra had a vague feeling of being thwarted in some way, but found it impossible to think why. With a sigh she settled under the covers. The bed rocked and the ceiling kept moving and she began to wonder if it might fall on top of her. She tried to focus on a piece of furniture in the room. Eventually a raging thirst got her out of bed. She knew there was a carafe of water on a table, but was unable to find it until she knocked it over. Oh dear— she would be waking all the household. She began to giggle. Now what did she do to get a drink of water?

The door suddenly opened and a voice

whispered, 'Kendra, are you all right?'

She waved a hand airily. 'Come in, Mr Devereux. I knocked over a table and the water spilled and my nightdress is soaked and—would you like to see my sailor-man dance?'

'I would not.' He came towards her and put a finger to her lips. 'Shh, you will have everyone awake.' She swayed and leaned towards him and he held her steady. He was wearing only a robe and as she felt the firm strong body, emotions stirred within her.

'Kendra, you must take off this wet nightdress, have you another one? Can I get it for you?'

'It's somewhere—' She looked around her vaguely. 'I think I drank too much wine. Can you make the room stay still?' She giggled. He propelled her towards the bed.

'Now listen, Kendra, I'm going to remove your nightdress then you must get straight into bed.'

'No—' Alarm bells began to ring in her mind. Pel Devereux would see her naked and anything could happen.

He picked up the hem of the nightdress. 'You cannot get into bed in this soaked state.' He tried to raise the gown but Kendra crossed her arms over her breasts, preventing him. With a gesture of impatience he pushed her arms aside and had the nightdress over her head before she could raise a further protest. But as he made to pick her up to put her on the bed she darted away to the other side of it, and crouched down.

'Kendra, for heavens sake stop playing games. Get into bed at once.'

'When you leave.' The mist in the room was beginning to clear.

'I am not leaving until you are safely in bed. In the state you are in you could bring other furniture down on top of you. Now get into bed at once, or I shall make you. You will catch a cold.'

Kendra suddenly wanted Pel to come round to her, wanted him to sweep her up in his arms. As she imagined it, emotions stronger than any she had ever experienced threatened to swamp her. And yet she waited, peeping at him over the top of the coverlet.

'Kendra—' he spoke sternly, 'you are asking for trouble. You were tempting me when you were in the carriage, but because I realised you had had too much to drink I controlled myself. Now I am finding it most difficult to control my emotions. You are a most desirable young lady and if you do not get into bed at once and cover yourself up I shall not be answerable for the consequences.'

Kendra, her body throbbing in a most delicious way, wanted to experience the 'consequences'. Yet, her upbringing told her she was thinking in the most wanton manner. She pulled at the silken coverlet, bit by bit until it was off the bed. Then, after draping it around

79

her she came round to Pel. 'Does that satisfy you, sir?'

She looked up at him with a teasing smile. Pel picked her up, held her close to him for a moment then tossed her on to the bed. Then, after divesting himself of his jacket, he climbed up beside her and leaned over her. 'Temptress,' he said softly. He eased the coverlet away from her shoulders and laid his lips to the pale flesh. His touch brought pleasurable shivers up and down her spine.

'You blame me for tempting you, sir,' she said lightly, 'but you are the tempter, the devil himself. When we were in the carriage you were insinuating all sorts of things about what would happen later.'

Kendra was aware of the mist forming in the room again, and in the mist she seemed to see her father's face. She made to push Pel away, saying in an urgent way, 'But nothing is going to happen, nothing at all.'

'Oh, no?' Pel pulled the coverlet apart and in the soft glow of the night-burning lamp she lay naked to his gaze. Kendra made a desperate attempt to cover herself but was suddenly helpless against the caressing fingers of Pel as they moved lightly over her body, making her draw in quick breaths. His mouth sought hers, at first gently sensuous, then becoming more demanding. The feather-light touch sought secret places making her body one big throb. No words were spoken, only the quick breathing of Pel and her own betrayed the need of both.

Yet in spite of this sweet agony Kendra knew it would be wrong to give in. She moved her head this way and that to escape the imprisoning mouth, she tried to ease her body away from his but was not having much success until her outflung arm caught the fragile table, sending the empty water carafe crashing to the floor for the second time. The weight on her eased.

'Kendra, for God's sake,' came Pel's impassioned whisper. 'Do you want to wake up the whole household?'

She took advantage of her freedom to slide off the high bed. With the silken coverlet held to her she waited, expecting someone to enquire if something was wrong, but there was no sound, only her own ragged breathing. She begged Pel to leave and with a sigh, he too got off the bed.

He touched her cheek gently, 'Never has my ardour been so effectively dampened. Perhaps the interruption was a godsend. But that is no promise that I will not invade your privacy again. I find you one of the most desirable women I have ever known.'

The room was beginning to spin again. Kendra put out a hand and the last thing she remembered was being swept up in Pel's arms.

* * *

81

Kendra awoke to find sunlight streaming into the room. At first she found it impossible to think where she was, then, as remembrance came, warm colour flooded her cheeks. What had happened when she blacked out? Had Pel—? Surely not.

There was a knock on the door. Kendra shot up in bed and called, 'Come in.' It was the maid with hot water. She wished in one way it had been Pel. She had to know what had happened. She felt normal, apart from a slight headache, but then perhaps one did feel normal after being made love to.

Kendra felt she might be able to tell by Pel's face when she went down to breakfast if he had touched her but Pel was not there. Leonora told her that the two men had gone out on business and would not be back until late.

It was midday the next day when the men returned. Both men came into the drawing room, sank into chairs and closed their eyes.

Leonora said, 'Tell me, Edward, do we still have a roof over our heads?' There was a smile in her voice.

Edward opened one eye. 'Oh, yes, indeed, my dear, we are also the proud owners of a couple of thoroughbred racehorses.'

'Good heavens. And you, Pel, how did you fare?'

His eyes remained closed. '*I* am now the proud owner of a Mississippi riverboat and part owner of a showboat. Lloyd Francis owns the other half.'

'I take it he owned both boats until these games of the past two days.'

'He did.' Devereux sat up and shook his head vigorously to rouse himself. 'The half-share in the showboat is about all he now owns, but I must add he is not complaining. I have a great admiration for the fellow. I shall be going to America in a few days' time to take up residence on the riverboat.'

'Oh,' Kendra said, feeling dismay at the thought.

Devereux gripped the arms of the chair and heaved himself out of it. 'It's possible I shall sleep the clock round. I don't wish to be disturbed for any reason.' He went to Leonora's husband who was now snoring lightly and shook him. 'Come along, Edward, bed—'

The two men were at the door when Devereux said over his shoulder, 'By the way, Kendra, I should like you to come to America with me. Think about it, we can talk later.'

Kendra stared at his retreating back. Go to America. Just like that? Who did he think he was, ordering her life? She ran after him. 'Just a moment, Mr Devereux.'

He stopped and eyed her sleepily. 'What is it?'

'Do you really expect me to go to America at your order?'

He gave a deep sigh. 'I said we would talk it

over later. Now, if you will excuse me.' He made to move away.

'No, just one moment. I don't want to go to America.'

'Very well, don't go. I shall be booking a berth after I have had a sleep.'

Mr Garfield, who had come up said in a low voice, 'Think about it carefully, Kendra,' and Leonora told her there was a letter for her.

Then she tugged at her dress. 'Come away.'

Kendra let the men go and grumbled. 'Pel is not being fair, expecting me to go all that way and not bothering to ask me if I wanted to go.'

'It might be a good thing to give it some thought,' Leonora coaxed. 'It really would be a wonderful experience. You would find it very interesting on a riverboat. Just think of all the fascinating people you would meet.'

'And what would my position be? I can tell you now I will not travel as any man's mistress.'

Leonora laughed and said, 'Read your letter.'

It was seldom that Kendra had a letter. She tore the envelope open, read the contents on the page then looked up.

'Believe it or not, it's from Pel's grandmother asking me to spend the day with her tomorrow. She said she would be very pleased to see me.'

'Why not go? You might at least get to know something of Pel's background. He's never talked about it. I didn't know until you told me that he had a grandmother. Has he parents, brothers and sisters?'

Kendra nodded slowly. 'Yes, I think I'll go. I'll have to risk him rushing off to America.'

Leonora smiled gently. 'He would miss his lucky mascot.'

The two of them spent the morning going round the shops. Leonora bought some lovely underclothes, shoes, two coats and Kendra teased her, saying with a laugh, 'You really are a glutton for clothes.'

'I love the feeling of being able to buy them. I never had the chance when we were first married and wondered then if I would ever get a new dress. Do you know,' she added softly, 'I still have that blue dress, carefully wrapped in a piece of sheeting and moth balls. I keep it so that I'll never forget that time.'

'Do you have children, Leonora?'

'We had twins, a boy and a girl. They died the same day they were born. Both Edward and I were grief stricken. I think it was this that turned him into a successful gambler. He became more cautious. But there, we mustn't talk about morbid things. We shall have lunch out then get back home.'

The men were up and having a meal when Leonora and Kendra arrived home. They were greeted cheerfully. 'And what have you been doing?' Mr Garfield asked his wife.

'We've been shopping. At least I have.'

Pel said to Kendra, 'And are you all settled to

go to America?'

'Not really,' she answered lightly. 'I had a letter from your grandmother asking me to spend the day with her.'

'Unusual,' he replied, in equally light vein. 'I wonder why she wants to see you. You are not going, of course.'

'Yes, I am. I'm going to spend the day with her.'

The coldness was there in his face. 'Very well, you spend the day with my grandmother and I shall see if I can get a berth on the ship sailing in the morning.'

Kendra was taken aback with his answer. She had thought they would have another talk, and that he might even suggest they get married. How wrong she could be about this Pel Devereux.

She looked at Leonora, who nodded towards the letter on the table and mouthed, 'Let him go.'

Kendra said to Pel, forcing herself to speak brightly, 'I hope all will go well for you. Thank you for all your kindness. I'm very grateful to you, Mr Devereux, and always will be.'

His expression showed a similar surprise to her own only moments ago. 'It was a pleasure. You will probably be back from seeing my grandmother before I leave.'

When the two men had gone upstairs Leonora grinned mischievously and gave Kendra a hug.

'Pel won't go without you. And, you'll go as a bride. I'm glad you used the soft answer. It never fails.'

'I hope you are right. Now I shall get ready and go and see Mrs Devereux. What shall I wear?'

'Wear the cinnamon outfit. I want you to have it, Kendra. It really becomes you.'

There was opposition from Kendra, she really could not accept it, but twenty minutes later she was stepping into a cab wearing it and feeling excited. What would the day hold?

During the journey Kendra's mind was on America. She would go if Pel suggested marriage. After all, living on a Mississippi riverboat would be much more interesting than being a companion to a lady.

But, she conceded, she would not go with only a promise of marriage when they arrived in New York. She would have to be married here before they left. Would he agree to that? A little of her excitement died.

Who was this girl Eleanor? He was obviously in love with her. He would hardly sacrifice her to marry another woman who was a lucky charm to him. On the other hand, lucky charms had played an important part in her father's life. He once found a four-leafed clover and had an amazing win. Then he also had a gambling coat and would not wear any other, in spite of having it on when he had bad nights and lost a lot of money. And if he saw a loose pin on the ground he would pounce on it and pin it to his lapel for luck. Kendra sighed. Oh, yes, lucky charms were a part of every gambler's life.

Kendra still had some hope left and it could have been this that made Mrs Devereux's house look a little less like a mausoleum than it had done the first time.

An elderly nurse opened the door before Kendra had had a chance to knock, and welcomed her with a smile.

'Mrs Devereux is looking forward to meeting you again, Miss Hollis. This is one of her good days. Will you come this way?'

Ever thoughtful, Leonora had bought a big bunch of delicate pink roses for Kendra to take with her and the old lady was delighted with them.

'How kind of you, Kendra, how fragrant they are. Do sit down. The maid will bring coffee in a few moments.'

The coffee was brought in, and a plate of biscuits, then Mrs Devereux dismissed the nurse, with the sharp assurance, 'I shall be all right, I need to have a private talk with Miss Hollis.'

'Ring the bell if you need me, Ma'am,' the nurse said in a soft voice and withdrew.

'Wretched woman, she wants to know all my business. Now, tell me, how is my grandson? I didn't want to invite him today. I wanted to get to know you.'

Kendra hesitated. 'I think he may be calling on you tomorrow. He was talking yesterday of booking a cabin to go to America.'

'And you, my dear? Are you going with him?'

'I'm not sure.'

'So you would not be getting married before you went?' There was a gleam in the old lady's eyes. 'Would you consider coming here to be my companion? I would very much like you to move in here.'

Kendra guessed now why she had been invited. 'I may be bad-tempered now and again,' Mrs Devereux went on, 'but it's people who annoy me. The nurse I have. She irritates me. There's a chance she might not irritate anyone else. I only know that I don't think I could ever feel bad-tempered with you. And I'm not saying this to flatter. I felt comfortable with you when you were here last and said to a friend who called how pleased I would be if you would come and live with me.'

'I would have to think about it, Mrs Devereux. Pel could decide he wants to marry me and leave London in a few weeks' time. I would not be the perfect wife but you see he . . .' Kendra smiled wryly, 'he's been on a lucky streak since he met me and I think this is the reason he would like me to go to America with him.'

'I see.' Mrs Devereux nodded slowly. 'Lucky omens are important to gamblers.'

'I know, my father was a gambler.'

'Ah, I see the connection now. Are you prepared to wait and see?'

'I feel I will know by the time I get back to the Garfields.'

'What you must be certain of is whether you are truly in love with my grandson. It won't be easy to be married to a man who has another woman in his life. If the lucky charm business stops working . . .?'

Kendra sighed. 'Yes, I know. That is a problem.'

'Well, if you would like to come and live here, you have only to let me know.'

'Thanks, I shall remember.'

'Now, another cup of coffee?'

'Not yet, thanks.' Kendra paused. 'I really don't know very much of Pel's life. Are his parents alive?'

'I am his only relative. My son, Pel's father, and his wife, both died a few years ago. They lived mostly abroad and Pel was their only child. He was looked after by nannies and at a very early age went to boarding school.'

The old lady put a hand to her eyes. When she lowered her hand her eyes were brimming with tears. 'I wrote regularly to Pel and he wrote to me, just notes, really, not saying much, never complaining. He spent some of his vacations at the homes of other boys' families and sometimes he stayed at the homes of some of his tutors. How selfish I was. My husband was my life. When he died I was bereft.'

90

Mrs Devereux drew a handkerchief from her dressing gown pocket and blew her nose. Then she straightened.

'It was not until Pel was sixteen that I invited him to come and stay with me for his vacations. We were two sad people at first, neither having anything to say to one another because of the grief in our lives. Then I began to look forward to his visits and I like to think that he enjoyed them. He was interested in the gardens and helped the gardener to plant shrubs and flowers. He was full of this and would talk to me in the evenings about how he would like to be a gardener.'

'Were his parents alive then?'

'Oh, yes, but never once did they ask him to go and stay with them. When he wrote and said he would like to go abroad and see them they were always going to stay with friends for the summer who had no children of their own, or they were going on safari where no children were allowed. Poor Pel. He gave up writing to them and I think they were glad. I wrote to them, telling them what dreadful parents they were but neither bothered to reply.'

'When did they die?'

'Eight years ago. Within a few months of one another. I don't know if they regretted their neglect of their son but all the money and property was left to Pel. And then, of course, he went mad, spending money like water.' The old lady was silent and looked full of pain.

Kendra laid a hand on hers and said gently, 'Mrs Devereux, if I don't go to America I will come and live with you.'

She looked up. 'Thank you, my dear.'

The nurse came in and said, 'I'm sorry to interrupt but it's time for Mrs Devereux's medicine and she does have a nap at this time. Only for half an hour. Why not have a look at the garden at the back, Miss Hollis. It's quite attractive. I'll get the maid to take you out.'

'Thank you.'

The garden was beautifully set out and ablaze with colour, but Kendra was more interested in Pel's life. He was to be pitied to have parents who never even bothered about him. She had had a father who had loved and cared for her, even if he did waste his money. To be without any love in one's life must be appalling.

She had felt bereft when her father died and badly treated when she had to find some work in order to exist. Now she thought of Mr and Mrs Bagley's dreadful behaviour and wondered if Pel had been speaking the truth about the jewels. He deserved them if it were true, but how could she be sure?

Her father had told small fibs when he was needing money so he could gamble again. Had Mrs Devereux been telling the truth? She was old, and old people did get things mixed up. But it had all seemed so true.

The nurse came out and sat down on the seat

beside Kendra. 'If there's one thing I dread it's getting really old and becoming senile.'

Kendra glanced at her. 'Does Mrs Devereux's mind . . . wander a little?'

'Difficult to tell. She does tell some strange stories but one tends to believe them. Oh, there's Cook calling. Will you be here for lunch, Miss Hollis?'

'Mrs Devereux did invite me for the day, but—'

'Then lunch it is. I'll be back. It's nice to have a young visitor to talk to. Mrs Devereux's visitors are all older.'

It was not long before the nurse was back, saying that Mrs Devereux was awake and wanting to see Kendra.

The nurse's eyebrows were raised. 'Never known her have such a short sleep before at this time. She says you may be going to America and she might not have another chance of talking to you for some time.'

'I don't know yet about going to America,' Kendra said as she got up, 'but I'll come now. I know what loneliness is.'

'And so do I, Miss Hollis.'

Kendra looked at her. So many lonely people in the world and she thought then she would take a chance, if it was possible, and avoid getting to the age of the nurse and still have a lonely existence.

Mrs Devereux talked quite a lot, in a feverish sort of way, as though she might never have another chance. She spoke of old friends and seemed to have quite a lot who came to visit her. Nurse shook her head and seemed sad. Was the old lady living in another world? Had the story about Pel's life been true? Or was it just in her imagination?

Yet when lunch was ready she sat at the table and ate quite heartily. Afterwards she reminisced about her young days and insisted on showing Kendra some small paintings of herself in a ball gown.

She delved into a black leather casket, which seemed to be full of letters, tied with blue ribbon, then brought out a single painting of Pel's parents, done just after their marriage. She handed it to Kendra. 'There they are. As you will see they are both serious looking but take note of the flirtatious look in Estelle's eyes and see the passion in Joseph's eyes. He was so enamoured with her he could never hide it.'

Kendra could not see what Mrs Devereux saw. She said, 'They are both very attractive.'

'Oh, indeed yes. She was so slender, so gracious looking in her gowns and was a tomboy when at play. Joseph was tall and handsome and hated to be away from her.'

The next moment the old lady was asleep.

Nurse whispered, 'Poor dear, she was so jealous of them. And yet she herself was attractive when she was young. I'll just put another blanket over her then leave her to have her sleep. She usually sleeps a long time in the afternoon. Shall we go into the morning room and have a talk?'

Kendra agreed, feeling the nurse was lonely, but when she went on about her life and how awful it had been, never marrying and having children, she felt it was time to leave.

She made the excuse that Mr Devereux was waiting to know her decision about America and she really would have to leave. And felt awful when Nurse said, a sad note in her voice, 'I wish I could go abroad, but it's too late. I wish you well, Miss Hollis, it's been so nice meeting you.'

Kendra promised that if she didn't go abroad she would call again and asked if she would make her apologies to Mrs Devereux.

*   *   *

The men were still sleeping when Kendra returned and Leonora said eagerly, 'Good, you can tell me how you got on with Mrs Devereux.'

Kendra was in the middle of her talk when a maid came in to announce two gentlemen, a Mr Bagley and a Mr Warren.

Kendra jumped up, a fist to her mouth, her heart thumping against her ribs. 'Oh, Leonora, please. Don't let them in. Mr Bagley is an evil man, that is why I ran away. Pel knows what he is like. Mr Bagley will lie, say anything to blacken my character.'

Leonora laid a hand on her arm. 'Don't

worry, I shall deal with him. You stay here, I shall see the gentlemen in the morning room. Your Mr Bagley will not get near you, I promise.'

As Kendra waited she felt she would suffocate from the wild beating of her heart. Fortunately, Leonora was back quite soon, smiling as she came in.

'Well, I have settled that wretched man—for the time being at least.'

'What happened, what did he say?'

'He told me you had stolen some valuable family jewellery and threatened you with gaol. I told him you were our friend and guest, that you were out until late this evening but if he wished to return he could deal with my husband, who is an eminent lawyer.' Leonora smiled wryly. 'There are times, Kendra, when it is necessary to lie.'

'I'm glad you did, what did Mr Bagley say to that?'

'He said he would speak to his own lawyer. Then he shook a fist at me and shouted that he would get you, and that when he did you would pay in full. What a dreadful man he is. He's the type who would pay witnesses to lie for him.'

Through all this Kendra had stood, feeling frozen. Leonora came to her and put an arm about her waist. 'Come and sit down. As soon as Pel is up he must make plans for you to leave.'

At that moment Pel came in. He said he had

heard voices, a man shouting. When he knew it was Bagley he was furious that he had not been downstairs to deal with him.

Kendra looked from one to the other in a frantic way. 'How could he have known I was here, in this house? It's terrifying.'

Leonora said, 'The man with him had numerous notes written in a book. He must have questioned a lot of people.' She turned to Pel. 'The important thing now is for you and Kendra to get berths on the first ship leaving for America. The best of lawyers can be defenceless at times against a man like Mr Bagley. You and Kendra can be married before you leave.'

Pel looked taken aback. 'I thought Kendra could travel as my ward.'

'But I had assumed—Kendra I shall leave you both to talk it over. I must see Cook.'

'Well,' Pel said, when Leonora had gone, 'and what is your decision, Kendra, not that you have much choice. You either travel with me or languish in Newgate for heaven knows how long. And, if you had seen inside Newgate, I think you would not need to consider for a second what your choice would be.'

Kendra, who was beginning to recover from the shock of Mr Bagley's visit, said, 'There's something I have to know. What happened . . . the other night?' She spoke in an urgent whisper.

'Nothing, Kendra, nothing at all. You passed

out. I put you to bed and left. Now you'd better see about doing some packing. I'll go and see about booking passage for both of us.'

'Something else has occurred to me. You told me that the Bagleys were butler and housekeeper to your grandfather. If this is so how did they come to have the family Bible?'

Without having to give thought to the question he replied, 'They once claimed a distant relationship, it was so distant it was considered to be practically non-existent in the family. Bagley and his wife, not having any living relatives, set great store by our Bible, regarding it with awe and reverence.' Devereux smiled wryly. 'Not a side of character one would expect in that type of man, but there, humans are strange creatures. Naturally, with Bagley hating me, and he always has, it would give him a great deal of pleasure to erase my name from the Good Book. They must have taken it when my grandfather died.'

Although the explanation sounded feasible Kendra was not willing to accept it wholly. She stood hesitant for a moment then said, 'I still don't know what to do. I don't want to arrive in America and be left there stranded.'

'What on earth are you talking about?' There was irritation in his voice. 'Are you suggesting I give you your return fare home, as a guarantee that if I desert you you'll be able to come back to London? What audacity!' Pel declared. 'You expect money from me when you are the one hunted by the law.'

Kendra, furious, practically spat her words out. '*You* speak of audacity, when you were the one to steal the jewellery. Yes, I know, I helped you, I was your—accomplice, but don't speak to me of being a criminal. How do I know you were telling the truth about any of it, the jewellery, about the Bagleys being your grandfather's butler and housekeeper? I'm the fool for listening to your tales. And no, I will not be going to America. Get someone else to act as your good luck charm.'

Pel took a step forward. 'Oh, for God's sake, Kendra.' He gave a deep sigh. 'I want you with me. Not only because you bring me good luck, but because I am attracted to you. I mean it.' His tone had softened. 'Kendra—marry me.' Pel was now smiling. 'Think of all the pleasure we could have, all the nights, the many nights when I could initiate you into the art of lovemaking.'

She now hesitated. 'I—don't know if I could marry a gambler.'

'But you will marry one, darling, you want me as much as I want you.'

'What about Eleanor?' Kendra searched his face. 'How could I forget about a woman you dream about, whose name you mention in your sleep? How could *you* forget her?' A man does not speak a woman's name in his sleep then fall out of love with her in minutes. She would always be there in the background. There could

99

come a day when he would want Eleanor, long for her, and I would be cast aside, Kendra thought.

'I wish I could be sure that Eleanor—'

'Kendra, listen to me, if we marry I do not want you continually mentioning Eleanor. I've asked *you* to marry me, now what is your answer?'

'I would have no one to give me away,' Kendra said, and heard a forlorn note in her voice.

'That can easily be arranged.'

An arranged marriage. This is what it would be . . . But if she refused—Kendra had a sudden fear of being alone, friendless in a strange country. She straightened her shoulders.

'I accept your proposal, Mr Devereux.'

*   *   *

Although the Garfields could not have been kinder or more friendly, when it came to making preparations for the wedding, it lacked all the excitement of a more leisurely wedding, the fittings of the wedding gown, the bridesmaids being fitted for theirs, the gossiping days, talking over bottom drawers, the presents, the choosing of the hymns, arranging the reception, sending out invitations. Then there was the wonder of the day itself, the awe and spiritual feeling of arriving at the church, the bridegroom waiting. There were times when Kendra had been so moved by the ceremonies of friends she had wept.

On the morning of her own wedding, which had been arranged to take place three days after she accepted Pel's proposal, she felt nothing but desolation. She longed for her friends and family. When she donned her blue velvet gown trimmed with lace and rosebuds Leonora said, 'You look lovely, my dear, blue becomes you.'

Pel, in silver grey with a satin waistcoat embroidered in blue, gave her an encouraging smile when she arrived at the registry office, and she did manage to smile back.

When the ceremony began Kendra found herself concentrating on a white crotcheted antimacassar on the back of the settee and counting the squares between the motifs. Then Devereux twined his fingers in hers and brought her attention to the words being said. They were spoken with reverence, with gentleness, and she listened intently. But even when the ring was on her finger she did not feel the marriage was quite real. They were showered with rice by Pel's friends but there was no one else to wish them well, no young girl to catch her bouquet—all she had was a small posy, which she felt she must keep.

Then they were in the carriage and driving away, and Devereux said, 'Well, Mrs

Devereux—' and Kendra began to feel a stirring of excitement. She twisted the ring on her finger.

'I'm just beginning to feel married.'

'After tonight you will have no doubts,' he said, putting his lips to her cheek, and she thrilled to his touch. Pel then brought out from his pockets certain pieces of the jewellery that had been set aside to give to his bride on their wedding day. Kendra was astonished, and could only throw her arms about his neck.

CHAPTER FIVE

Devereux managed to get tickets for a ship leaving Southampton for New York the following day, and from then until boarding the ship Kendra felt as though she had been caught up in a whirlwind. Even then it did not end. After all the activity of getting aboard and friends of passengers rushing hither and thither, they found themselves caught up in a party of young people who were seeing off a family who were emigrating. 'Come along,' one man said, 'come and join us,' and hustled them below, where champagne corks were popping and the liquid flowing.

Kendra, remembering the last incident when she had drank too much, went sparingly with the champagne, but it was impossible not to be caught up in the atmosphere. It helped her over the parting with Leonora and her husband and the awful feeling that soon she would be leaving the country of her birth.

When the call came for all visitors to go ashore Kendra and Devereux went up on deck and stood at the rail. The noise and activity seemed to have increased. Passengers lining the rails exchanged greetings and messages with people on the quayside. The ship was part steam, part sail and paddles. Men swarmed up the rigging, the stewards moved among the passengers urging lingering visitors to go ashore, bells clanging mingled with the shrill sound of whistles and the deep-throated blasts from funnels.

The party who had entertained Kendra and Devereux were now ashore and waving and shouting to them. Kendra said she had no idea what they were saying but she thought it nice to have someone to wave them off.

Devereux, perhaps hearing the wistful note in her voice, laid his hand over hers and said softly, 'You will make friends in America.'

'Gambling friends or the wives of gamblers?' The words were out before Kendra could stop herself. Devereux withdrew his hand, his expression changed, and Kendra immediately regretted her words.

'You enjoyed the hospitality of the Garfields. What complaint had you against Edward and Leonora?'

103

'None, none at all. They were wonderful people. I'm sorry, I spoke without thinking.'

'I suggest you think before you speak another time.'

Oh dear, Kendra thought, she was off to a bad start, but the fault was hers. She had been grateful to Leonora and Edward for their many kindnesses and had told them so tearfully before they parted. Pel, who had not been there at the time must be thinking her a most ungrateful wretch. She must watch her tongue in future.

The ship was preparing to sail when a carriage approached at speed. It drew up and a man jumped out. The horses steamed.

Devereux had remarked there was always one last minute passenger when Kendra felt him tense. 'See who it is,' he said.

Kendra recognised the auburn hair of Lloyd Francis. The people on the quayside cheered as he sprinted up the gangplank as it was about to be taken away. He turned and grinned and gave them a wave.

Devereux edged his way past the passengers lining the rails. Kendra followed and was in time to hear him say to the American, 'Well, and what has brought you aboard, sir? Are you hoping to win back your riverboat?'

Lloyd gave him an amiable smile. 'I would be satisfied if I won back your half-share in my showboat.'

'I might find myself with whole ownership.'

'True, that is a risk I must take.' Then, seeing Kendra, he swept off his hat and gave her a bow. 'Miss Hollis, or should I now say Mrs Devereux how good to see you again. I do hope I shall have the pleasure of your company from time to time during the voyage.' He turned to Devereux. 'With your husband's permission of course.'

Devereux, judging by his scowl looked ready to refuse. Kendra forestalled him. 'We shall both be delighted, Mr Francis.'

'If you will excuse us.' A hand was put firmly under Kendra's elbow and Devereux hurried her away, stating that although he was willing to play cards with the American he did not want him intruding into their private lives.

Kendra stopped and faced him. 'Mr Devereux, let me make certain things clear. I am now your wife, but I will not accept you giving me orders as to how I shall run my life. If I want us to spend some time with Mr Francis I do not feel I need to ask your permission. Is that understood?'

'No, it is not understood.' He drew Kendra aside out of the way of people passing continually to and fro. 'You are now my wife, and so you must obey me. I hope you do me the courtesy of accepting my judgement.'

'Only if it is fair,' she retorted.

'I have a reputation for being a just man. Come along, I shall see you to our cabin.' Kendra refrained from making any further

105

comment for the moment.

*　*　*

She was a little disappointed with the ship. There was not the luxury she had expected to find in first class, and the cabin was small. Pel seemed quite happy, and brushed her cheeks with his lips, saying 'I shall come to escort you to dinner.' Kendra stood trembling when he had gone, wishing she could control this emotion he had the power to rouse in her.

She chose to wear a gown in a shade of deep gold that was trimmed at the hem in festoons of fine lace and narrow brown velvet ribbon. She was now able to dress her own hair stylishly, but being unable to button up the back of her dress she sought the help of the women in the neighbouring cabin. They were two step-sisters, who introduced themselves as Miss Baker and Miss White. They were twittery, but eager to help. They praised Kendra's gown, her hair and said they hoped Mrs Devereux would call them at any time—day or night. Kendra smiled, said she would and after thanking them made her escape.

When Devereux came for her he nodded his approval and praised himself for his good taste. Kendra bridled and reminded him that both material and style of the dress were those she had chosen herself. He raised his eyebrows and conceded that she also must have good taste.

106

The dining room was fairly crowded when they arrived but seats were eventually found for them at the long table. Devereux was seated next to an attractive young girl while her companion was an elderly man who was very deaf. The main topic of conversation at first was the weather, the wind was rising, a storm could be brewing, then there was a discussion on the number of days the journey would take, the number varying between twelve and fourteen, although one man said it had taken seventeen days once when the weather was foul all the way.

After a while Kendra began to be aware of the change in the motion of the ship. Her deaf companion said cheerfully, 'Here comes the gale, it will be rough, you mark my words.'

They were on their second course when Kendra experienced a queasiness. She picked at the food, worried in case she should be ill. Although she had been conscious at first of the vibration of the ship caused by the paddle wheel, that vibration was now beating in her head. She concentrated so hard on not being ill she lost the thread of conversation. The face of the woman sitting opposite to her was coming and going. Oh God, she could not be ill here, Pel Devereux would never forgive her. She must go. She got up and immediately Pel was there by her side.

'Come along,' he said, 'I'll take you below. You should have said you felt ill.' He sounded quite concerned.

Before they were out of the dining room Miss Baker was at their side wanting to know if she could help; Devereux accepted it. Miss Baker seemed to know all there was to know about *mal de mer*. Mrs Devereux must lie flat on her back and keep warm, and have nothing to eat and drink for six or seven hours at least, depending on the severity of the attack.

Kendra kept apologising for causing so much trouble, saying she felt ashamed. Devereux told her she had no need to feel that way, as there were many sailors who suffered from seasickness and mentioned Horatio Nelson who had been plagued by it all his life.

This in no way eased Kendra's discomfort but she felt less guilty knowing that such an eminent man had suffered a similar condition.

Devereux left her in the hands of Miss Baker with the promise he would call and see how she was later. Kendra did feel a little better once she was flat on her back, but she was so cold, the linen sheets felt icy. Miss Baker rushed out and came back with two travelling rugs to put over her. Then she too left with the promise she would be back soon to attend to her.

Later the storm blew up. It worsened through the night. The ship pitched, it tossed, it rolled, it shuddered. Kendra felt so ill she wished she were dead, wished she had never heard the name of Pel Devereux and vowed she would not set foot on his riverboat or any other kind of boat as long as she lived.

Before dawn the storm died down, and by breakfast time the next morning Kendra, although not wanting food, felt somewhat better. She did decide, however, to stay in her cabin.

When Devereux called to see how she was he suggested it might be wise if she could keep the jewellery he had given her about her person. Kendra agreed to arrange it. That morning she occupied herself making pockets in underskirts. The work, and the worry of having been given such expensive items, helped her to forget her occasional bouts of queasiness. Miss Baker and Miss White were constant visitors, Devereux came twice more to enquire after her and Lloyd Francis came once.

After the cloying administrations of the two step-sisters Kendra was greatly relieved when, the following morning, she seemed to have found her sea legs. She left on her own to go into breakfast and surprised Pel Devereux who was talking animatedly to a young and attractive girl. He got up and drew out a chair. 'Why, Kendra, how good it is to see you fully recovered. Have you met Miss Trenton?'

Kendra acknowledged the introduction and said she hoped that Miss Trenton had not suffered because of the storm. The girl replied she had kept well, but her parents, with whom she was travelling, had still not recovered from their illness. She got up then, asking if they would excuse her as she wanted to see how her parents were faring.

Devereux, watching her leave, mused, 'A lovely girl, so sweet, so warm-hearted.'

'She seems quite young, fourteen would you say?'

'Miss Trenton is seventeen and a half, a little younger than you, Kendra my dear. Jealous?'

His teasing smile made Kendra furious. 'I can think of no reason why I should be. I am not vying for your favours, Mr Devereux. In fact, during the storm I wished you at the bottom of the sea.'

'Kendra, how could you?' His voice was full of mockery. 'I did not order the storm. I was worried about you.'

She sought for something to take the smile off his face. 'The storm did one thing for me, I know I shall never set foot on your riverboat.'

Dismay replaced the mockery. 'But that is ridiculous. There is no comparison between travelling on an ocean-going ship and a riverboat. The Mississippi is never rough, not like the Atlantic.'

'Well, that is how I feel at the moment.' Kendra looked around her. 'Has Mr Francis been down for breakfast?'

'He has, and if it is of any interest to you he won back my half-share of his showboat.'

'I'm glad. I felt the boat was important to him.'

'Oh, I have plenty of time to win it back from

him.'

'And time to lose the riverboat. Then you would certainly be feeling your luck was in reverse and you would be questioning my value as your lucky charm.'

'One bad night does not mean a run of ill-luck.' Devereux's expression suddenly softened. He laid his hand over hers. 'Don't ever leave me, Kendra, I need you, not only because of the cards—'

They were interrupted by the steward bringing Kendra's breakfast and then Devereux's attention was taken by a man coming into breakfast and recognising him, and Kendra was left wondering what Pel had been going to say.

After breakfast he asked her if she would care to walk on the promenade deck and she said yes, it would be wonderful to get a breath of sea air after having been confined to her cabin.

The steward had said the breeze was fresh. It was more than fresh, the ladies were having difficulty in preventing the skirts of their gowns from billowing. Kendra smiled to herself, not having this problem, the weight of the jewellery in the secret pockets at the hem of the dress she was wearing kept it beautifully in place.

Kendra, curious to know what Devereux had been going to say in the dining saloon reminded him of their unfinished conversation. He had to think about it for a moment then he said, 'I asked you not to leave me, that I needed you and not only because of the cards. Having you with me is like having a second skin.' He spoke gently. 'And if I lost you it would really hurt.'

'Why, Pel,' she said, unconsciously using his Christian name.

'I'm not entirely sure I'm in love with you,' he admitted, to her profound shock, 'but I want you, I want to make love to you.'

'I see,' she said, stunned, and drew away from him. 'I can't help feeling you really are despicable.'

'I don't understand this feeling myself, Kendra. I have been honest with you, perhaps too honest. I could have lied, said I loved you. Perhaps I do—in a way, I don't know. I only know you have something that draws me to you just as it draws other men to you. I get jealous, want your favours.' He took her hand, pulled her arm through his and smiled down at her. 'Give me what small favours you can spare.' Kendra wished his smile did not hold so much charm.

They kept passing people who greeted them and Devereux raised his hat, acknowledging their greetings. Once he said about a man who had just passed, 'He has a house and plantation I envy. I should like to own one similar.'

'Oh, so you are thinking about settling down?'

'I do hope to have sons,' he said with a grin

and Kendra blushed.

After that their conversation was general. They had quite an invigorating walk then Devereux, after settling Kendra in a deck chair with a rug over her, said he must leave her as he had some business to discuss with a colleague. He had only just moved away when he came back and said, 'Kendra, do not encourage Lloyd Francis.'

'Jealous?' she teased.

'Not at all. I despise such a man. He will never have any money, he will lose at cards whatever he gets. Yes, I know he won from me last night, but that was a flash in the pan. He has no skill.' Devereux leaned over, knuckled her chin and went away laughing.

Oh, Pel Devereux—Kendra shook her head in despair. Was it love she felt for him or was this emotion he roused in her a sensual thing, a feeling that would not last once they were separated?

When he came back for her later they walked in silence for a few moments, then Kendra said suddenly, 'Oh, I never told you about going to see your grandmother that day. So many things happened at once. Did you manage to call and see her before we left?'

'Yes, I did, for about a quarter of an hour.'

When he did not continue further Kendra prompted, 'And . . .?'

'And what?'

'What did she say about you going to

America?'

'Not very much.'

'Did she tell you that she had told me about your young life?'

'Yes she did.' He looked grim. 'I was not very pleased.'

'You should have been pleased to have your grandmother give you a home at vacation time. You would have been very lonely without her.'

'I was lonely with her. You probably have no idea what it is like to be without your parents. I loved my mother, adored her and she didn't give a damn about me.' His tone was bitter. 'She was a beautiful woman, who always had a trail of men following her. She enjoyed that.'

'Your father must have been a very patient man to stay with her for so long.'

'He worshipped her and gathered up the crumbs. But that was their lives, they did stay together. My father did have the money of course. He was wealthy until shortly before he died. I don't know whether my mother had all his money from him. Nor, may I say, do I worry about it. Now, if you don't mind, can we close the subject please.'

There were a lot more things that Kendra would have liked to talk about but was sensible enough to stop there.

Then the two step-sisters came up giggling. Earlier, Pel had teased them, calling them 'The Guardian Angels' and they had been delighted at such a title. This, Kendra thought, must have set them off giggling.

'Good-morning, Mr Devereux, good-morning, Mrs Devereux,' they chorused.

Pel raised his hat. 'Good-morning, ladies, I trust you are both well?'

Oh, indeed they were.

Kendra wondered how he could be so amiable when they irritated him so much. Then he said, 'Would you excuse us, please. I see our friend looking for us. Enjoy your stroll.'

Pel waved to an imaginary friend and grinned as they walked away. 'Which person shall we stop and talk to? Ah, here is Lloyd Francis right on cue.'

Kendra was always pleased to see Lloyd but before they reached him a couple stopped to speak to him.

'We will pause to give greetings,' Pel said, 'but we shall not stay talking. I have promised to see Mr Dell at ten o'clock.'

'To discuss card playing,' Kendra said with a sigh. 'Of course.'

The two men met mid-deck and Kendra excused herself.

She stopped at the rail further on. And it was here that the two stepsisters found her. During the days that followed the stepsisters were never far away. Sometimes Kendra was glad of their company, especially at night when Pel was playing cards. Lloyd Francis spoke to her from time to time but Kendra would not walk with him, knowing how Devereux felt. He kept saying cheerfully he had retained ownership of the showboat and lived in hope of getting back the riverboat. Devereux, who seemed to still be on a winning streak never mentioned either.

When Kendra went to bed at night Pel nearly always stayed up playing cards. But when he did come to bed early one evening it was to change her whole life.

The feeling between them had started in the morning when for once Devereux sat in a deck chair beside her. Kendra smiled and asked him why on this particular morning she should be so honoured, and he replied, 'I just wanted to be near you, you flitted through my dreams last night, teasing me, tempting me, just as you are doing now.'

Kendra indignantly denied tempting him. 'I simply smiled at you.'

'Yes, that is the trouble.' Devereux sighed. 'It's your smile that tempts me.' Then he added with a wicked grin, 'At this moment I am tempted to pick you up and carry you below.'

Kendra had to hold herself tense to prevent her from asking him to do so. She forced herself to say lightly, 'And what a furore that would cause.'

Devereux laughed softly, 'It might tempt a few men to carry *their* wives to their cabins—or their paramours.'

'I think it more likely they would control their passions until bedtime.'

'Is that an invitation?'

'Certainly not!' For all her intended sharpness Kendra could not control the tremor in her voice.

'I want you, Kendra.' The lightness had gone from Devereux's voice. 'These past few days have been agony for me. I don't feel that we ever really consummated our marriage, and now I've seen the way other men have looked at you, seen the way you have flirted with them.'

'I have not flirted with any man! That is a figment of your imagination, sir! I have exercised the utmost decorum. Most of the time I have had the step-sisters plaguing me. They are kind in their way, but their talk at times has driven me to distraction.'

'I asked them to keep you company,' Devereux said calmly. 'I thought it would prevent you from getting into mischief.'

'You what?' Kendra drew herself up in the chair. '*You* asked them? How dare you take such a liberty. I may be your wife but am not your property Mr Devereux, stop arranging my life. I shall choose my own company.'

'No, Kendra you will not. You *are* my property, and as such in my care.'

'In your care?' She gave a derisive laugh.

Devereux was beginning to look angry. 'You say you don't flirt, but you do, you do it unconsciously. You look at men from under those long curling lashes and I've seen desire in their eyes, I saw it in Lloyd Francis's eyes. I told

117

him to stay away from you.'

Kendra threw back the rug and got up. 'Lloyd Francis has never treated me with anything but the utmost respect, nor any other man, and I shall speak to whom I please, and flirt if I feel like it.'

'If you do, you shall not be the only one to regret it. Now remember that, Kendra.'

She stormed away from him. The two step-sisters came hurrying up to her but she brushed past them saying, 'Oh, for heavens sake stop pestering me!'

Kendra was still fuming when she reached her cabin. The arrogance of the man. Why did he think he had the right to control her life? She sank onto a chair. But then she had been caught up by her desire to know a different way of life, caught up by Devereux's charm. She could have avoided contact with Mr Bagley—if she had been determined enough. Leonora, she was sure, would have found her a position where she would have been safe. No, she had only herself to blame. Well, from now on, she would start thinking in-terms of being more independent, starting from when they arrived in New York.

She went to the dining saloon for the midday meal, going early to avoid meeting Devereux, who always took his later. The two step-sisters, undismayed by her rebuff, came and sat beside her. Kendra apologised for her behaviour and they beamed at her and said that everyone had an off day and she was not to worry.

Kendra escaped as soon as she could and did not leave their cabin again until she was sure all the passengers would be in the dining saloon for dinner. Then she went up on deck. She stood watching the great paddle wheel turning, the volume of water surging, thundering, spray rising. The lights from cabins threw a warm glow on the water, a vast expanse that gave her a feeling of melancholy. She wanted to be back home with her life as it was, her father loving and caring, talking with excitement of his wins and with so much hope when he lost. Why did he have to die so tragically? Her throat tightened with unshed tears.

'Mrs Devereux, are you all right?' It was Lloyd Francis, he touched her arm. 'Do you feel ill?'

The tears spilled over and it was seconds before Kendra could answer. 'No, I was thinking of my father, of home.'

Lloyd took her hands in his. 'I know what it is to suffer from homesickness. I can promise, as consolation, that it does pass.'

The next moment Kendra felt herself seized and flung aside. Devereux, in a rage shouted, 'So this is what happens when my back is turned, a secret assignation!' He lashed out at the American.

Several blows were exchanged then Kendra, stepping between them screamed, 'Stop it, stop it, do you hear!' A punch intended for the

American caught her a glancing blow on the shoulder.

'Oh, my God,' Devereux said with a groan, and tried to draw her to him.

She pulled away. 'Leave me alone, don't touch me! I hate you.' And with that she ran, stumbling, along the deck.

Once below the tears came thick and fast. Why, oh why had she ever left London, and married the man! All this ill feeling and Lloyd Francis had only been trying to be kind.

Kendra, thinking Devereux might come to apologise and not wanting to see him, locked the cabin door. But no one came. Eventually she realised he must be occupied at cards, and so undressed and got into bed. The vibration of the paddle wheel threatened to split her head open, and so it was a long time before she slept.

Kendra aroused from a nightmare in which Pel Devereux had been trying to drown her. They were in a turbulent sea and he kept pushing her head under the water. He was laughing, his face evil.

She lay gasping for breath, not yet completely out of the horror of the nightmare. Her body was bathed in perspiration. She pushed the bedclothes away from her, then, when she became chilled she drew them up again. She was thankful she had left the lamp on low.

Although she lay with her eyes closed she willed herself to stay awake, afraid the nightmare might recur. Why should she dream Pel was trying to drown her? He would not have such evil intentions. He wanted her alive—to bring him luck. Was it her reaction to his rage when he had found her with Lloyd Francis? His behaviour had been unreasonable. Was he perhaps on a losing streak and he had to vent his temper on someone?

Kendra tossed and turned for a long time then just when she was beginning to feel drowsy she thought she heard a scrabbling noise outside her door. Alert now she sat up. There was something stealthy about the movements. It would not be Pel, if he came he would give a peremptory knock on her door and expect her to jump out of bed and open it.

The door handle turned, then there was a bump against the door.

Heavens! Was someone trying to break in? Kendra's hand suddenly flew to her throat. The jewellery! Had someone found out she was carrying it? Her heart began to beat in suffocating thuds. She got up, intending to get her dresses and put them under the bedclothes when there was a sharp rap on the door. She grabbed her robe, went to the door and whispered, 'Who is it?' and she could hear the fear in her voice.

'Kendra, let me in,' Devereux spoke in a whisper.

'Go away,' she hissed.

121

'Let me in or I shall start banging on your door.'

She opened the door a fraction and he brushed past her. 'Shh!' he put a finger to her lips as she made to protest. 'You had a drunken man trying to get into the wrong cabin. I got rid of him.'

'And what are *you* doing roaming round the ship at this hour?'

'I was on my way back from cards. Kendra, I have to know if I hurt you, it was the last thing I wanted.'

'Fighting over me like a callow youth,' she whispered fiercely. 'I suffered no hurt, now get to bed.'

'Let's stay up for a while, Kendra—' His voice was low, coaxing, seductive. 'I want you, I need you.'

She wanted to say she knew now she did not need *him*, but the words stuck in her throat. He came closer and picking up a strand of her hair he curled it round his fingers. Kendra drew a quick breath, wondering why curling her hair round his fingers should give her such pleasurable shivers.

She was still clasping her robe in front of her. Devereux took it from her and let it fall to the floor. Then, catching all her hair at the back he wrapped it round his hand, tugged at it gently bringing her face up to meet his. Laying his cheek against hers he said, 'I want to feel your body next to mine.'

'No,' she said, 'not now,' then gave a gasp as he began to lift the hem of her nightdress. Pulses were leaping madly. Slowly he went on raising the garment and she stood there, helpless, a prisoner in the throes of her own longing. She must stop him, she must—what he had done before was unforgivable. The nightdress was lifted over her head and she gave a small moan. The garment fell to the floor. Kendra came to life. She backed away. It was wrong, wrong . . .

'Don't fight me, darling—' His words were just a breath. He picked her up and held her above him, then slowly lowered her gently to the floor. The touch of flesh on flesh, the hardness of him, the sensuousness of the action had her aching for him. But still she resisted. 'No, there should be real love between two people who—'

'Live for now, dear heart.' He pulled the bedclothes to the floor then the pillows and lowered her on to them. 'Enjoy it, Kendra,' he pleaded, 'help me to enjoy it to the full.'

He lay beside her moving his fingertips as before over her body, the feather-light touch becoming an instrument of both ecstasy and torture. He pulled her to him, whispering endearments in her ear, at her throat and at her breast. A small, teasing biting of her flesh made her cry out. Pel sounded exultant as he said, 'I shall teach you how to love *me* in time, my darling.'

123

A timid knock on the door had them both tense, their breathing ragged.

'Mrs Devereux, are you all right, my dear? My sister and I heard you cry out. Is your husband with you?'

'Oh, God,' Pel whispered with great feeling, 'what a time to choose. Get rid of her!'

Kendra jumped up and went to the door, saying, 'I'm all right, Miss Baker, I had a nightmare ... Yes, really, I'm fine, I'm feeling sleepy again. Thanks for enquiring.'

'Would you like me to stay with you for a while, dear?'

'No, no, if I have another nightmare I shall call on you, I promise.'

When Kendra was sure the footsteps were moving away she turned and leaned back against the door. Then she felt an hysterical bubble of laughter well up. Pel was on his feet, a sheet wrapped around him at the waist, with the ends thrown over his shoulder.

'You look like a Roman emperor in a toga,' she whispered, then pushed a fist against her mouth to stop herself from giggling.

'I don't find it at all amusing,' Pel said stiffly. Then, obviously affected by Kendra's stifled giggles he began to laugh softly.

He caught hold of her and drew her to him, saying, 'You know what happened to the slaves of the Roman emperors don't you?' Pel tried to pull her to the floor but Kendra shook her head and pushed him away.

124

'No, I couldn't. I wouldn't be able to stop laughing. It would spoil everything.'

Pel was smiling. 'Think of all the pleasure we can have, all the nights, the many nights when I can initiate you into the art of lovemaking. After all, you want me as much as I want you.'

He reached out for her again but she picked up her robe and put it on, tying the sash tightly. 'Yes, but you have yet to find that out.'

Pel grinned suddenly. 'You will never be able to sleep after for thinking about what you have just missed.' He gave her a chaste kiss on the brow as she got into bed. Kendra thought she could hear him laughing softly to himself as he moved away to get undressed.

She ran her hands over her body. She wanted to be initiated into the art of lovemaking. The incident with Pel, the broken sleep, the nightmare, had Kendra wide awake and cold. She found herself moving against him to curl up against his warm body, and lived again the mastery of him catching hold of her hair and tugging her head back to receive his kisses. She wanted to be mastered. Yes, she did, and with that thought she fell asleep.

* * *

The following evening Pel was in a foul mood. Kendra assumed he had lost at cards, worried that if he kept on losing he would no doubt discard her. The thought disturbed her, knowing she would miss him terribly if he went out of her life. In spite of his moods he had coloured her life, roused her to know the emotion of wanting a man in a sensual way, and giving her a desire to share his life, to love him in a more gentle fashion—to care for him, to commiserate with him over losses, as she had done with her father, share the excitement of his wins. But would she be able to hold him?

During the following days Kendra found it difficult to assess Devereux's attitude. He would tease her on occasions, admire certain gowns she wore, be in a mood when he would hardly notice her. He would play cards all night, escort her to breakfast the next morning, take her strolling on the promenade deck then leave her and she would not see him again until dinner. She came to depend on Lloyd Francis for company and although Devereux knew they were meeting he made no objections. It was all so puzzling.

Yes, Lloyd Francis said to her questioning, Mr Devereux was still on a winning streak. Oh, yes, there had been setbacks, but not serious ones. He himself had refrained from joining in any games. Then with a broad smile he had added, 'I'm determined to keep my showboat and I know I would lose a half-share or perhaps the whole ownership if I attempted to play.'

'Tell me about the showboat,' Kendra said.

He described it in glowing colours, the size, the decks, the theatre. 'It seats eight hundred

126

people.'

'Eight hundred?' Kendra looked at him in astonishment. 'I imagined an audience of about fifty.'

'Oh, no, some seat a thousand.' His eyes took on a far away look. 'My grandfather owned it, when my father died my mother took me on the boat and we travelled on it for a year. It was a wonderful experience, an exciting life for a boy, the players, doing Shakespeare, the melodrama, the magnificence of the voices of the actors, the richness of their costumes, the colour. The audience were spell-bound. Most of the people were poor, the showboat was the highlight of the year. I can see them now hurrying along the levee their cents clutched in their hands to book seats for the evening's performance. It was beautiful and sad. I had never witnessed poverty until then. The people lived in wooden shacks, had little food. They still live in wooden shacks and have little food. When I was a boy I vowed when I grew up I would do something to ease their lot.'

Lloyd raised his shoulders. 'I inherited three fortunes and did nothing. That is the way of people. Sometimes I feel ashamed.'

'I hope to see the showboat,' Kendra said.

'So you shall. It will give me pleasure to show you round.'

When Pel next escorted Kendra on their stroll round the promenade deck she mentioned her talk with Lloyd Francis and he seemed interested. 'There is something fascinating about them. I rather fancy myself as an impresario.' He gave a quick nod. 'Yes, I think I shall have to persuade our Mr Francis to join us in a game of poker one evening.'

'No,' Kendra said sharply. 'Let him keep his showboat. He appreciates what it does for the people on the riverbanks.'

Pel's eyebrows went up. 'And you think I wouldn't?'

'I know you wouldn't. You would see only the profits to be made.'

'So do the owners of showboats. They would not exist without profits. Do not let Lloyd Francis pull the wool over your eyes, my dear Kendra. Why do you think he plays cards?'

'He is not so obsessed by them as you,' she retorted. 'He has refrained from playing for a number of nights.'

'But not for much longer. I've seen the look in his eyes, the haunted look. Tomorrow night, or the next, he will be sitting in on a game.'

Kendra gave an exasperated sigh.

CHAPTER SIX

The next morning Pel and Kendra were strolling on deck. He raised his hat to a passing elderly couple. 'Good-morning, sir, good-morning, ma'am, a lovely day.'

'Indeed yes,' replied the man, 'although I understand there are squalls to come.'

Squalls to come? As Kendra repeated the words to herself Pel spoke them, a teasing in his eyes. 'Do you think it describes our marriage?'

'I could not imagine it to always be plain sailing.'

'I should hope not, how dull life would be.' He laughed softly. 'If we never had words there would be no making up and reconciliations can be most rewarding. Now, what shall we quarrel about?'

'I think we can save that for when we've been married a little longer.'

'You spoiler of fun! Still, I can wait.'

Splendid for him, Kendra thought, as tremor after tremor went through her, imagining him making love to her again.

The following day the Statue of Liberty came into view and there was great excitement as everyone rushed to the rails. Pel had talked about it and the size but Kendra had not imagined it so large, or so beautiful. She felt emotional and stood with the crowd, watching it. But when they eventually docked at New York she was greatly disappointed.

Perhaps because of crossing an ocean she had expected to see a magic land, and instead found disembarking little different from embarking at London docks, with its noise and bustle, ships being loaded and unloaded. Some drunken men were chasing a few squealing pigs, painted women flaunted their 'charms' as they hung on the arms of sailors. Black-clothed immigrants huddled together, waiting for guidance or for friends or relatives to meet them. Babies wailed, frightened children clung to the skirts of their mothers. All around was a babel of different tongues.

'Come along,' Pel said, taking her arm, 'I have a carriage waiting.'

He took her to friends living in an imposing house on Fifth Avenue but Kendra could not rid her mind of the poverty she had seen on the way, tenements teeming with ill-clad people. How many of them she wondered had come to this new land with hopes high and become disillusioned? Kendra felt she was lucky indeed to have married a man who, for the time being at least, could offer her a more luxurious way of living.

Afterwards Kendra was not quite sure when the change came in her husband, she only knew when they were on the ship to take them to New Orleans for a proper honeymoon, and the steward was showing them to their cabin, that Pel had gone quiet and was deep in thought. 'What is it?' she asked.

He pulled out his gold pocket watch, stared at it for a moment then replaced it. 'Kendra, I have to go ashore for a while, but I shall be back in plenty of time for sailing. You are not to worry.'

'Where are you going, why are you leaving,

surely nothing can be so important as to—'

'It is important. I must go.' He kissed her in an abstracted way and left, leaving her utterly bewildered. What on earth could have taken him away at such a moment? If it was business why had he not dealt with it during the past three days?

Kendra's worry increased as the time passed and her husband had not put in an appearance. What would she do if sailing time came and he had not returned? She would have to go ashore and wait.

The feeling of being friendless in a foreign country was never more strongly felt than at this moment. There was not even Lloyd Francis she could contact. He had told her the night before they docked he was planning to spend some time in New York but promised to see her the following morning to say his goodbyes. But in all the bustle, the crowd of passengers, she had not seen him. She could of course go back to Pel's friends, but she felt she would be imposing on them, after all she had been a stranger to them when they first met.

Kendra cast her mind back to their journey to the docks. Something, she felt sure, had happened on the way to bring about the change in Pel. But what? They had discussed the promised honeymoon, Pel's manner teasing, and talked about the kindness of his friends. Then she remembered that a carriage had passed them and he had looked round quickly,

131

as though recognising someone in it. Was it then his manner had changed? But if so, why? Who had been in the carriage that he would have wanted to see with such urgency?

Kendra felt a sudden chill. Had it been Eleanor? It seemed the only answer. Would he come back, or would seeing her make him regret marriage to Kendra?

When Devereux had not returned by eleven o'clock, an hour before sailing time, she was nearly frantic. It was easy to say she would leave the ship and wait for him but for how long and what if he never came?

While these thoughts were chasing through her mind a note was delivered to her. She tore it open and read:

'Dear Mrs Devereux, your husband has been unavoidably delayed. You are to stay on the ship and go to New Orleans and wait for him there. This, he says, is an order. He will follow in three or four days' time. You are to contact a Mr and Mrs Gerald Kistarne who are travelling on the ship. They will chaperone you.'

It was signed, 'your obedient servant, George D. Daler.'

Kendra, her heart beating in slow, painful thuds, read the note for a second time. Why had Pel not written the note himself? Was he ill, or hurt, had he been in a fight, or a duel? Or was he in prison for some previous misdemeanour? He *had* been in America for some time before returning to England. But then, he said he would follow her in three or four days' time. Was it something perhaps to do with card games? He had played each night since coming to New York.

The questions were to plague Kendra many times during the following days. She had not bothered to contact the Kistarnes, but they contacted her, and could shed no more light on Devereux's disappearance than Kendra. They were a middle-aged and warm-hearted couple who, although chaperoning her, did not intrude.

The voyage, which should have been so beautiful, their honeymoon, was something to be endured for Kendra. The days were endless. The only thing in the journey's favour was travelling under sail, she felt she could not have stood the constant juddering of a paddle wheel. At times she brought out the sailor-man and set him dancing and it would make her smile, but more often than not she ended up in tears.

At last the day came when they were in sight of New Orleans. Although there was all the excitement of disembarking for other passengers, Kendra could only think of being reunited with her husband in a few days' time.

When they arrived at the hotel where they were to stay and Kendra was following Mr and Mrs Kistarne she stopped abruptly and stared in utter astonishment at the figure who was coming towards her.

Lloyd smiled gravely as he held out a hand and greeted her. Kendra felt more bewildered than ever. 'How did you get here, Mr Francis? Have you seen my husband?'

'I left New York the day before you.' He looked beyond her. 'You asked if I had seen him. Is Mr Devereux not with you?'

'No—' Kendra, seeing that the Kistarnes were waiting for her said, 'I must talk with you. If you would just excuse me for a moment—' She explained the situation to her chaperones, was told they had booked her in and that she was to come up when she was ready, and left her.

'Now,' Lloyd said, 'why are you travelling on your own?'

When Kendra told him the story he said, 'I feel there will be quite a simple explanation. Perhaps your husband had a fall, injured himself in some way, and needed medical attention.'

'But why did he not suggest my waiting with him and travel on another ship?'

'Mrs Devereux—' Lloyd spoke gently, 'I know your husband and feel quite sure he had a good reason for everything he has done. You will know in a few days' time when he comes, so why not try and settle your mind. I would be pleased to show you New Orleans.'

Kendra thanked him but refused, wanting to

be in the hotel when her husband arrived. 'He could arrive tomorrow,' she said. 'Mr Devereux is most unpredictable.'

But after spending two days on her own, with the Kistarnes away visiting friends, Kendra worked herself into a temper. She could be waiting for weeks, he might never even arrive. And so she had a message delivered to Lloyd Francis's room saying she would be pleased to have his company.

He took her driving round the French part of the town and Kendra was charmed by all she saw, the blocks of houses, their plaster facades stained by time and weather to warm, variegated tones; the balconies, running the length of the houses with each house having its own cipher or monogram in the centre, a delicate filigree cobwebbing of intricate designs. And she loved the music in the French quarter.

She loved hearing the soft Southern drawl, and was fascinated by the different shadings of the skins of the people in this part, remarking on the beauty of some young girls with pale yellow skins. Lloyd spoke of quadroons and octoroons, explaining they were the children of mixed blood, octoroons having one eighth negro blood, and who were the offspring of a quadroon and a white.

They went on foot to a square where vendors offered them pies, ginger beer, or lemonade. One man, white teeth flashing, informed them he had very nice grass-hoppers, well dried. When Kendra pulled a face Lloyd said laughing they were delicacies for pet birds.

In the afternoon he took her to see the riverboats leaving. Kendra was not only astonished at the number, but how ornate most of them were. There was a long rank of boats which stretched for about a mile, their tall twin-stacks belching forth smoke. A pall of it hung over the town. A crowd of people was waiting to see them leave. The noise was deafening, and yet Kendra found herself catching her breath in the excitement of movement, of people chattering and shouting. Processions of freight barrels and boxes were being constantly swung on board, belated passengers were rushing and dodging cargo to reach the forecastle companionway. To add to the general distraction drays and luggage vans were getting jammed, wheels locked together. Windlasses kept up a deafening whizz and whir.

Lloyd pointed out various decks on the boats and when the hurricane and boiler decks were black with passengers the 'last bells' started clanging, a continuing sound right down the line. Then, with the last planks hauled in the steamboats began to move away in a colourful stately procession to the accompaniment of whistles and blasts from the funnels; every blast, it seemed, having a different tone.

She had asked previously if the *April Queen* was among them and was told by Lloyd it was under repairs but would be ready in a few days' time. He added that the showboat was, at the moment at Memphis.

Kendra found Lloyd Francis peaceful to be with, not like Pel who wanted always to be on the move. And yet, she longed to see her husband, longed to feel his arms around her, his lips on hers. What if he did not return? She could not now imagine her life without him.

That evening Lloyd was dining with friends and although he had asked her to come with him, Kendra had refused. It was kind of him to ask but she had several things she wanted to sort out.

Kendra suddenly remembered the gift that Leonora had given her on her wedding day. She had said, tearfully, when they were ready to leave the house to go to the registry office, that she wanted her to have something special, then had handed her a small valise.

'I shall miss you terribly, Kendra, but I want you to accept a small gift. And, I want you to promise you will not look to see what it is until your wedding night.'

Kendra had smiled through her own tears, and promised.

Mr Garfield had pushed some money into her hand and whispered, 'And this is from me, buy something you particularly want.'

Such lovely people. She had spent some of the money on buying a nightdress and a robe in New York, and had worn both.

The valise was brought out and when she opened it and saw the flimsy chiffon nighties and the matching negligés she remembered her wedding night; and wanted to wear them again.

She walked up and down in her room, the negligé floating behind her, and decided to wear the white nightie and matching negligé to cheer herself up.

The rest had been hung in the wardrobe and Kendra had yawned and felt she was ready for bed when the door was flung open and Pel stormed in, his eyes blazing.

'So—who are you preparing to receive, your lover?'

Kendra was so astonished she just stood staring at him.

'Oh, yes, I've heard all about our American friend escorting you around town. It's a wonder I didn't find the two of you in bed. Perhaps I was just a little too early.'

Kendra went up to him and struck him across the face, then, picking up the thing nearest to her, a silver candlestick, she held it aloft.

'You dare touch me and you will feel this on your head! How dare you accuse me of infidelity, you who left me stranded and sent a note, written by *someone else*, to say you had been unavoidably detained. Who detained you, some whore, or did you have a card game to finish? Or is it Eleanor you have been entertaining?'

He looked at her startled for a moment then said, 'I had some business to attend to.'

'I cannot imagine any business being so important that a man would leave his young wife alone.'

The fire had gone out of him and Kendra saw a familiar look in his eyes, a wanting.

'Put that candlestick down, Kendra, and come here.'

'Oh, no, you are not going to win me over with your soft talk. Have you any idea of the humiliation I suffered on the ship, the pity of the women? "Poor Mrs Devereux, her husband has not sailed with her. Where could he be?" Can you imagine the speculations?'

'I care nothing for their speculations. Is it not enough that I am here now?'

'No, it is not enough. The moment you arrive you burst in and accuse me of having an affair with Mr Francis. You will need to apologise for that for a start.'

'I am doing no apologising. Now put down that candlestick, Kendra, and get into bed.' When she made no move he wrenched the candlestick from her then gripped her arms. 'You better take care, Madam. I am normally an easygoing man, but when my wife refuses me my rights—'

Her head went up. 'If you touch me I shall scream.'

'If you do I shall give you good cause for screaming. You will beg me for mercy. And

139

when people arrive to see what is happening I shall explain that you ran away from me, took a lover and are now refusing me my conjugal rights. The men will applaud me for beating you, and so will the women.'

'Beating me? You wouldn't dare!'

'Oh, wouldn't I?' He tore her negligé from her, then her nightdress, and gave her a sharp slap on the buttocks. 'That is just a taste of what you will get. Now, are you going to get into that bed?'

Kendra was furious. She shouted, 'That was my nightdress and negligé that Leonora gave me for my wedding night. You've ruined them. I hate you, you have no feelings! You're just a clod.'

She walked across the room and climbed into bed. 'But if you insist on your rights you can have them. Only don't expect me to pleasure you.'

Pel, eyeing her, undressed and got into bed beside her. She lay rigid, determined not to give into him in any way.

He leaned up on his elbow. 'Kendra, you can get pleasure out of this, or pain.' His voice was surprisingly gentle. 'But I am going to have my rights.'

'Go ahead. You've already given me pain. I don't care. You won't get much pleasure out of it. You haven't even told me what business it was that kept you away.'

'Nor am I going to discuss it.' His fingers

traced a circle round her breast. 'So why did you wear the nightdress and negligé tonight?'

'Because I thought you might be home. Not for Lloyd Francis's benefit as you so crudely stated. I am not a whore.'

Although Kendra hated to admit it the slap had aroused something primitive in her. His touch was adding to the desire to turn to him. She would suffer if she resisted him, yet if she gave in to him he would expect her to be always submissive to him.

'Well, *which* is it to be?' His tone was now coaxing. 'After all, this *is* the start of our *real* honeymoon. Make up your mind, my patience is running out. I want you and I'll take you if you don't submit.'

'I don't want to be hurt,' she said in a small voice. 'I'm hurting now, your hand was hard.'

He pulled her gently to him and ran his fingers over the heated flesh, moving them in a circular motion that roused her more than any other caress could have done.

'Give yourself wholly to me, my darling,' he coaxed, 'don't hold back, it will make it easier for you.' Kendra told him she wanted to please him but was not sure how. Pel went on talking in a soothing way while his hands and lips did the explaining.

She had experienced a small, but very pleasurable taste of Pel's touch but had not imagined anything so exquisite as the feelings roused in her. She would never have imagined

141

sensations to spring from a kiss in the space between her shoulder blades, even his lips on the palms of her hands sent fire through her veins. She discovered a rhythm in her limbs that responded as though to music, movements that matched those of Pel. He praised her in a low, impassioned voice, said she was learning and now she was to touch him.

As he held her above him, her breasts lightly touching his warm flesh, she explored his body, experiencing an awe and an excitement as she moved her hand over his tautened belly and down his thigh. 'Go on,' he urged.

Afraid of making the final onslaught her fingers explored the muscles of his thighs and she exulted in his strength. This was her man, it would be a delight to pleasure him.

But even then Kendra hesitated and she closed her eyes before she made contact with the most sensitive part of her husband's body. His response excited her, made the blood pound in her veins. A few months ago she would not have thought herself capable of behaving in such a way.

'Oh, Pel, I want you,' she whispered.

But Pel did not take her then, there was more love-play, more touching, teasing, she would never have imagined how the tip of a tongue could send every nerve in her pulsating. Then when she was almost whimpering with the need for fulfilment Pel took her, gently at first, then with a passion that she was able to match.

When the throbbing of fulfilment died away they lay languorous in each other's arms, with Pel whispering his admiration for her response.

He nuzzled his cheek against hers. 'Now you understand what I meant by giving of yourself, my darling.'

'Oh, yes, I do,' she whispered. 'I want more, more.'

He laughed softly. 'Hey, give me five minutes. I promise you this, the next time will last longer. All night, as a matter of fact.'

She snuggled into him. 'Lovely.'

He knuckled her under the chin. 'And you were the one who was going to hit me with a candlestick if I as much as touched you.'

She said pertly, 'When I was naughty as a child and my nurse beat me it only made me more rebellious, so do not get the idea that beating me will make me your slave.' She smiled up at him. 'The answer is that I was wanting you to make love to me, longing for it, but I was so furious at the way you came bursting in—you still haven't told me what the business was that kept you away from me.'

'Nor am I going to now,' he said softly. 'I have more important business here—right now—'

'Pel—not already—I—' His mouth covered hers.

It was eleven o'clock the next morning when they got up and even then, when she was getting dressed, he was looking at her, smiling and with desire in his eyes. When he started to come towards her she laughed and darted away. 'No, Pel, not now. I do not want any more lessons. In fact, I doubt whether there is anything else you could teach me.'

'Oh, yes, there is, my darling, you have had only the first lesson.'

He was using stalking movements and she began to laugh helplessly. 'Now no, Pel, no, really.'

He caught her and held her to him, with her thumping his chest feebly with clenched fists. 'We must have something to eat and you promised to take me to see the *April Queen*.'

A knock on the door had them springing apart. It was Lloyd Francis. Oh, no, Kendra thought, expecting trouble, but Pel greeted him brightly, 'Come in, come in.'

Lloyd greeted Kendra without any sign of embarrassment then said to Devereux, 'I heard you had arrived. I wondered if you would like to look over the *April Queen*.'

'That was our intention. I was going to contact you. We have overslept so have not had breakfast yet, perhaps in an hour.'

'Yes, that would suit me fine. An hour then.'

Lloyd was at the door when Devereux said, 'By the way, my thanks for taking such good care of my wife. I really am grateful.'

There was no hint of any unpleasantness in his voice. He really did sound sincere. And

144

apparently, he was sincere, because when Lloyd had gone he said to Kendra, 'If anyone had to escort you I would want no man better than Lloyd Francis.'

She stared at him. 'Last night you accused me of having an affair with him.'

'Yes, I did, in the heat of the moment. You can imagine how I felt, arriving and being met with the story of you driving with him, dining with him.'

'So what made you change your mind about me?'

'It was not only your indignation, your anger, but—a sort of innocence about you, Kendra. I don't think you could deceive me.'

'Don't be so sure about that,' she teased him. 'I might run away with a man less lustful.'

'And you would soon come running back to me, my darling. You are as passionate as I. Shall we forego breakfast?'

He fingered the top button on her bodice and she slapped his hand away. '*You* might be able to live on love alone, my husband, but I have a very healthy appetite—for *food.*'

'Shame on you,' he chided.

When they boarded the *April Queen*, Kendra, who had been astonished at the ornateness of those she had seen the previous day, was overwhelmed with what she saw now. It was like stepping into a new and wonderful world. On the decks alone there was beauty, the pilot house, the decks decorated with white wooden filigree work of exquisite patterns, gilt acorns topped the derricks, and even a picture painted on the paddle box.

When Kendra exclaimed her delight Lloyd said, 'Wait until you get below, Mrs Devereux. It is a floating palace.' She thought she heard a wistfulness in his voice, and knew why when they did go below. The loss of such a boat must have hit him hard.

There was such elegance, beautiful chandeliers, carpets of rich blue, porcelain knobs and a picture painted on each cabin door. It was like going on along a beautiful tunnel with the white filigree overhead touched with gilt, and lovely rainbow light fell from the coloured glazing of skylights. The ladies' cabins were carpeted in deep rose Wilton and the bridal chamber was a dream with its tester bed, its lovely chairs and porcelain hand basins. The saloon was decorated in shades of red. It was a vast room, with a grand piano and furniture of rosewood; elaborately carved and upholstered in satin damask. Here too were chandeliers, and there were gilded mirrors, moulding, fretwork and marquetry.

Lloyd took them to their state-room, which was spacious and luxurious. There were comfortable chairs, a desk in walnut, a wardrobe with a mirrored door, a double bed with spotless linen laid out and a quilted cover in damask.

Kendra said, her eyes shining, 'Oh, Pel, I

cannot believe it.' She turned impulsively to Lloyd. 'How you must grieve to have lost the *April Queen*, Mr Francis.'

He bowed and said gallantly; 'It makes my loss easier knowing it will be graced by your lovely presence, Mrs Devereux.' Then he added, 'And of course, I still have my showboat as consolation. I do hope that both you and your husband will honour my boat with a visit.'

'We shall be delighted,' Devereux answered graciously. Then spoilt it by adding, 'That is, of course, if it is still in your possession, Mr Francis.'

'Yes, it will be, Mr Devereux, because I am determined I will not gamble it away.'

'We shall see.'

Kendra said to Devereux when they were alone for a few moments, 'That was a dreadful thing to say to Mr Francis. Surely you must know how he feels about losing the *April Queen* without making unpleasant remarks.'

'Unpleasant?' His eyebrows went up. 'I made a statement, which was true. Knowing Lloyd Francis he will lose the showboat, and I hope I shall be the one to win it.'

Kendra's head went up. 'I hope he keeps it, I feel sure he will.'

'You seem to know more about our American friend than I do, Mrs Devereux.' The coldness of his tone warned Kendra she must be more careful of her words in future.

She linked her arm through that of her

husband and smiled up at him. 'What I do know is that the loser always gains sympathy. You must agree with me on that.'

'Indeed I do, my darling.' With his good temper restored he put his lips to her cheek. 'I only hope if I happen on a losing streak—which heaven forbid—you will console me with your wifely ministrations.'

She gave him a pert smile. 'My wifely ministrations are available to you at any hour of the day—*or* night.'

'Stop looking at me in that way, Madam, or I shall pick you up and carry you into the bridal chamber.'

'There is a cabin nearer.'

'If you persist in tormenting me I shall not even bother with the use of a cabin—'

'Mistress Devereux!' Kendra laughed in delight at all this love-play, feeling she had never been so happy in her life.

Lloyd Francis called, 'The captain is aboard, Mr Devereux. I thought you would like to meet him.'

'Coming.' Devereux drew Kendra to him, kissed her passionately, and released her, leaving her weak with desire and loving her husband so much at that moment she felt willing to die for him if needs be.

Then, as they went up on deck the sun went in and a sudden chill gust made Kendra shiver. She had a swift feeling of apprehension. Was this a warning? Had she been too happy?

Devereux held out a hand and led her towards a stockily built man on deck who greeted them unsmiling.

'Captain Craig,' Lloyd Francis said.

The captain acknowledged Devereux as the new owner, but although showing him respect his manner remained aloof. With Kendra, however, he unbent, asking her smiling if she had done the journey on the Mississippi before and offered to show her anything she wished. She could see her husband was not pleased at this, but he said nothing until they returned to the hotel, then he accused her of once more exerting her charms on a man.

Kendra, who had been so happy was distressed by this accusation. 'You are wrong, Pel, I did not, and never have attempted to play the coquette. In fact, I would not know how.'

He touched her cheek and said gently, 'I don't think you would, Kendra, and don't learn to be the coquette, I like you the way you are.'

She stood looking at him. Was it only liking that Pel felt for her? Why could he never say he *loved* her the way she was. Perhaps later.

But later Pel told her he was going out for the evening and when she remonstrated with him about leaving her on her own he became a little impatient, reminding her that she knew about his gambling habits before she married him.

He dropped a kiss on her brow and grinned. 'Keep the bed warm for me.'

149

With that he left, closing the door quickly with a soft laugh as a cushion was aimed at him.

'Wretch!' Kendra shouted after him and retrieving the cushion threw it on the settee. Was she to spend the rest of her honeymoon minus a husband? 'I hate him,' she informed the empty room.

Dawn was breaking when Pel returned. He made enough noise to rouse her and everyone near. 'Miss me?' he asked.

'Not at all,' she replied sleepily.

He laughed. 'You might be interested to know that I won back the half-share in the showboat.'

'What?' Kendra, wide awake now, sat up. 'Oh, poor Mr Francis, I feel sorry for him.'

'Sorry for him, the man is a fool, he came into the game at two o'clock, bet recklessly, and this is the result. It seems he will never learn.'

'And you were determined to get back that half-share, weren't you? You are never satisfied with what you have.'

'God, I'm tired.' He shed his last garment, pulled back the covers and got in naked. 'Oh, you are lovely and warm.' He drew her to him.

'And your feet are like ice.' He rubbed the sole of his foot up her leg, laughing softly. Then he stifled a yawn.

'Do you know, it really is good to come back and have your wife warm the bed for you.'

'So now I'm a bed warmer!' Kendra tried to still the tremors the touch of his body had roused.

'Lovely and warm—' he stifled another yawn. 'So tired—'

He nuzzled her neck. 'Darling Kendra. Put your arms around me.'

Before she could do so he was asleep. So, she said to herself, the life of a gambler's wife!

CHAPTER SEVEN

It was late when Pel roused and he was not in a good mood. He said that something he had eaten the night before must have disagreed with him, but Kendra thought he had probably drunk more than usual. They boarded the *April Queen* at midday, and Devereux was still in a bad mood. Then they met the pilot William Cartwright and Devereux became affable.

Mr Cartwright, a tall thin man, with spiky grey hair, a receding chin and an amiable smile showed just the right amount of deference towards Devereux to flatter him. They were invited into the wheelhouse and Kendra was surprised to find it carpeted and with two Windsor chairs and curtains at one window. 'Sit down, Ma'am,' the pilot invited, drawing up one of the chairs. 'I'll see about getting some coffee soon, the Cap'n will be coming aboard any minute.'

Devereux's face took on a closed, cold look

at mention of the captain and Kendra's spirits sank.

'Not a very forthcoming man your captain, Mr Cartwright,' he remarked to the pilot.

'Well now, depends on how you handle him, sir. Couldn't rightly get on with him myself at first, but we have the measure of one another. A good man, knows the river like he knows his own face. And you've got to know her. Captain never married and this river is wife, child and mother to him.'

'I know how he feels,' Devereux said softly. 'I was just beginning to get to know it when I had to leave. It has so many moods.'

'Yes, it has, Mr Devereux,' said a voice from the open doorway. The Captain stood there, unsmiling, but there was a warmth in his voice and a light in his eyes. 'Glad you feel that way about the river, sir.'

They talked about it as though it were a person, and at times Kendra wondered how they could become so poetic over a river that was a muddy yellow. But she was pleased there was this feeling between the three men.

By early evening a number of passengers had come aboard, intending to sleep on the boat overnight. It was not leaving until the next day. Loading had started too.

When they went into dinner they found the tables laid with snowy cloths, crystal and fine china. Stewards, in white starched jackets waited on them. Dinner was a pleasant affair,

152

the food excellent and everyone in a sociable mood.

'Well, Kendra,' Devereux said when they returned to their room, 'how do you think you are going to like living on a riverboat?' He held her by the wrist, smiling into her eyes.

'I know I shall like it, it's different, and there is so much to see.'

He drew her to him, giving playful little bites on her neck. 'I could gobble you up.'

'What, after that huge meal you had?' she teased, happy again as she wondered how she could ever have been annoyed with him.

'Ah, but this is *different* food; warm, tempting flesh. I shall take my fill later, but at this moment—' he pulled away from her, 'regretfully I must leave you once more.'

'Oh, Pel, you are always leaving me! Cards again, I suppose.'

'Of course, I want to win the other half of the showboat. Lloyd Francis came aboard twenty minutes ago. He will be travelling as far as Memphis, expects to board his showboat there.' Devereux gave a wicked grin. 'I have a feeling I will have whole ownership by then.'

'Oh, I hate you!' Kendra exclaimed, 'hate your attitude. You are always wanting more.'

He drew her fiercely to him. 'I want more and more of my wife and Lloyd Francis out of the way. He's a threat to me, a threat to our happiness. I know how he feels about you.'

'Our happiness, did you say? How could we

be happy with this vicious streak in you. Mr Francis is no threat and you know it. I hope he wins back *your* share of his boat, *and* wins this riverboat back too. It would serve you right.'

'Kendra, take care—'

'Very well, I shall say no more. And now, if I may be excused, I shall tidy up and meet some of the ladies in the saloon. I was asked to join them and I did say yes, anticipating you would be playing cards.'

'You may go, you have my permission.' He tilted her face. 'Just see you behave yourself, and tonight when I come to bed be prepared for another lesson.' He was smiling, but Kendra responded by saying all he thought of was cards and bed. He replied, 'What else is there?'

Kendra did not get another lesson in lovemaking that night. The next time she saw her husband was when he came to escort her to breakfast the next morning. He had washed and shaved, and looked surprisingly fresh, too fresh to have been playing cards all night. Kendra wondered uneasily if he had slept in some other woman's bed.

Kendra's fears about Pel having spent the night with another woman were allayed when the eminent judge sitting next to her at breakfast said with a wry smile, 'Your husband took me for a cool thousand dollars, Mrs Devereux, and this at five o'clock this morning. I marvel that I can summon up any appetite at all.'

'A thousand dollars is a lot of money, sir.'

'Not when playing with experts like your husband, Ma'am. It's a pleasure to play with him.'

Kendra, seeing that Pel was talking animatedly to the woman on his left, said in a low voice, 'Can you tell me, sir, how Mr Francis fared in the games last night? I understand he has had a run of ill luck.'

'He held his own, a nice fellow, but rather reckless. Has too open a face. Gets excited when he has a good hand. Gives himself away, should never play cards.'

Kendra looked for Lloyd Francis that morning but he was nowhere around. Sleeping perhaps. Later she went on deck and stood at the rail, watching all the preparations for leaving. There was the usual frantic activity of loading, and passengers coming aboard. The roustabouts, stripped to the waist, sang as they loaded, their black bodies glistening with sweat. There was the strong smell of burning resin and pitch, soon black columns of smoke would rise from the pipe stacks of the three boats which would be leaving.

Pel, who had come up to her, laid an arm across her shoulders. 'I like this time, always have, there is something reminiscent of my childhood, when we would spend summers at our house in Dorset. It seemed that half our household goods were stacked on wagons, very exciting. I loved those early summers—' There

155

was nostalgia in his voice. The next moment he was smiling at her. 'Happy, Kendra?'

'Y-yes.' She could hear the doubt in her own voice and Pel took it up.

'You sound unsure.'

'It's just that I feel upset when I realise just how much gambling means to you.'

'You knew that when you married me.' There was an edge to his voice. He drew his arm away. Kendra, realising they would never know any happiness together if she was constantly on to him about his gambling, changed her tactics. She linked her arm through his.

'Yes, I did, and I must accept it. I adjusted to the life my father led, so must now adjust to that of my husband.'

'A most satisfactory attitude, Mrs Devereux.' A warm smile and her husband's arm going round her waist and drawing her to him was Kendra's reward for attempting to cope with the problem in a sensible way. She was learning.

They stood at the rail together again later when departure time came. The river at this point was a mile wide and according to Mr Cartwright very deep, which made navigation easier. On the river were little trading scows and a number of timber rafts. Kendra once more found herself caught up in the sounds of departure, whistles, bells clanging and deep-throated blasts from the stacks. The paddle wheel began to turn, churning up the water, sending the boat vibrating, but this Kendra no longer minded. She had a sudden feeling of pride. This was her husband's boat, he had won it fairly, as the judge had so rightly said at breakfast time, Lloyd Francis was the fool for gambling when he had no control over his emotions.

On both sides of the river timber had been cleared, showing a continual stretch of sugar plantations. Pel said they stretched for many miles before forest land appeared again.

They came up on deck once more when it was dark. The forecastle was lit up by torches in their baskets, the lights flickering and smoking and the pitch dropping. They gave an atmosphere to the scene. Ahead lay a darkness so intent Kendra marvelled that the pilot could find his way without the aid of buoy or lighthouse. When she mentioned this to her husband he said this was why it was important to know every inch of the river, to know every sand bar, know when what appeared to be a sand bar turned out to be a pile of logs. Then he added the information it was easier to see a black log in the darkness than a white one.

Kendra was initiated into so many aspects of the river she began to realise why the men thought of it as a person. She found herself interested in getting to know all its moods. There was something else too she wanted to know, why her husband had stayed behind and left her to start their long-awaited honeymoon alone. Perhaps she would be able to coax it out of him during their long journey ahead to St Louis. Perhaps, when he was giving her one of his lessons in lovemaking. She felt a stirring of desire. She moved closer to him.

'Are we going below?'

By the light of a torch she saw the response in his eyes.

'Yes,' he said softly, 'when you look at me like that how could I refuse?'

But the pleasure, the ecstasy Kendra expected was denied her. Devereux, without properly undressing, took her with an urgency that left her gasping. Then, with only a brief apology for his haste (blaming her for exciting him) he left for his inevitable card game.

She lay with her fists clenched vowing she would never let him come near her again, yet knowing even as she vowed it, she would never deny him her body. And she wept for her weakness in loving him so.

* * *

Kendra had made up her mind she would say nothing to her husband about his behaviour but when, the following morning, he arrived just in time to escort her to breakfast she found it difficult to be civil to him. She said, 'I thought you would have been more interested in sleep than food.'

158

'And what ails you this morning, Ma'am?' he demanded.

'Your treatment of me last night before you rushed away to play your games.'

He eyed her in the amused way that annoyed her. 'My dear Kendra, you would not expect a musician to compose a symphony every evening.'

'Indeed no, but it might be interesting to learn how you would describe your performance last night. To me it was all discord.'

'Ah, but you are not attuned to the melody. There are many nuances in music. You must learn to know them, and respond. Then you will be able to appreciate the full score. If you are ready, my love, we will go and have breakfast.'

Kendra picked up her shawl and said sweetly, 'But if the teacher has not the time to teach the pupil all the rudiments of the music how will she ever learn to appreciate the whole symphony?'

'That is a point, and one we must rectify.' He placed the shawl about her shoulders, dropped a kiss on the back of her neck then held out his arm. Kendra shook her head in a despairing gesture. How could one deal with a man like this?

Devereux was animated at breakfast, seating himself next to an attractive woman, as usual, but afterwards he looked jaded. He said, 'Can I leave you to your own devices for an hour or so, Kendra, I must go and rest.' She started to say yes, of course, but was interrupted by her husband hailing Lloyd Francis.

'Ah, Mr Francis, just the man I was looking for. Can I leave my wife in your care for a while? I must catch up on my sleep.'

'Indeed, yes, I shall be delighted.'

She wanted to say that if Mr Francis had been up all night he too would be wanting to catch up on his sleep, but there was no opportunity, Devereux was away with a wave of the hand. She turned to the American. 'Mr Francis, I really am sorry about this, you being saddled with my company.'

'Saddled? My dear Mrs Devereux this is a pleasure. I always enjoy your company. Shall we go up on deck?'

There were not many passengers who had come up as yet for their airing and Kendra had a sudden feeling of peace with this restful man. She stole a glance at him. He looked quite fresh, and his eyes seemed more blue than ever in the openness of the river.

'Did you sit in the card games last night, Mr Francis?'

'Yes, I did, and held my own.' He smiled down at her. 'What did you think of your husband winning a house and a plantation?'

'A house and—' Kendra's heart began to beat in slow thuds. 'He never mentioned it.'

'Oh, I'm sorry, perhaps he was keeping it as

160

a surprise.'

'Yes, that must have been the reason. Where is this house?'

'At Memphis. Perhaps you will have a chance of seeing it when we arrive and I hope too that you and your husband will come and see the showboat.'

'I hope so. Who owned the property my husband won?'

'A Mr Lamartine.'

'He must be feeling sore at losing his home.'

'He does have other property, but I feel he will regret losing this one, because it was to have been given to his daughter on her next birthday. Mr Lamartine was not playing recklessly—' Lloyd smiled wryly. 'Not like me. He did have good cards, a full house, Queens up. It just so happened your husband also had a full house, Kings up.'

Kendra shrugged. 'What can I say except, the luck of the draw.'

Lloyd nodded. 'True, but your husband is always so cool. He really is an excellent player. I should never play against him but I cannot resist the challenge.'

When Kendra said she was sorry that Pel had won back the half-share of the showboat Lloyd laughed and said she had better not let her husband hear her say that.

'I feel there is a greed in always wanting more,' Kendra said. 'Perhaps I am wrong, I cannot understand the compulsion to gamble,

161

in spite of my father being a gambler. It alters people's lives, and destroys marriages.' When Lloyd Francis smilingly pointed out she had married a gambler she said, in a helpless way, 'Yes, why?'

'Because you love him,' he replied simply. 'Your husband is a very lucky man, Mrs Devereux. I think I shall have to give up gambling and settle down. It will not be easy, gambling is in one's blood. A disease.' He grinned suddenly. 'But it's such an exciting disease to have. One is never bored. Life is never dull, there is always the hope of a big win—'

Kendra had to admit that life had not been dull since meeting Pel Devereux, but what would it be like if he was ever to lose everything? There would be no living with him. Poverty, she felt, was something he had never experienced.

Devereux slept until late afternoon, and when he was up and dressed Kendra mentioned the house and plantation he had won, and saw him tense. She asked him why he had not told her about it and he dismissed it with a shrug. It was not a house he was particularly interested in and therefore unimportant to him.

In spite of his off-hand manner he was still tense and Kendra wondered why. She did not press the point, knowing she would get no satisfactory answer. She had yet to learn the reason for his leaving her when they arrived in America. It still rankled, more so when something like this house and plantation cropped up. There were becoming too many mysteries in her husband's life.

The odd thing was that since winning this property he did not make love to her again. Their days followed the same pattern, breakfasting together, Devereux going off to bed afterwards to catch up on his sleep, meeting for dinner and then she was alone once more when he went to play poker. She had been invited to join a small group of women in the saloon in the evening, who were also 'poker widows'. Kendra became interested in their lives, finding them all philosophical about their husbands' gambling habits.

Mrs Dawson, the eldest woman in the group said to Kendra one evening, 'You too will become philosophical, dear Mrs Devereux. You will find you have to. Sometimes you might feel you want to run away, but few gambling wives do because they know they are needed.' Mrs Dawson's eyebrows went up in a quizzical lift. 'Now how many wives can say such a thing? In many marriages wives are treated as chattels.'

Kendra looked round the group of women. They were all beautifully dressed and all looked happy. But was there one among them whose husband had married her because he regarded her as a good luck charm?

Mrs Dawson said in a gentle voice, 'Take my advice, my dear, and just be there when your husband needs consoling after a run of bad luck. His gratitude and love will be your reward.'

Kendra, remembering the times she had consoled her father after heavy losses, and knowing how much he had appreciated her being there, decided she must try and take a more philosophical view of her marriage to Pel Devereux. He was on a winning streak and his whole concentration must be lavished on his games. One bad night and he would have need of her.

But in spite of her good resolution she was unhappy most of the time. She would slip away to go up on deck and if Mr Cartwright was on duty he would invite her into the wheelhouse. And through him she began to get to know the river.

'Always shifting,' he said, 'always changing. One time you'll see an island and the next time it's gone.' He would swing the big wheel bringing the boat close to the shore to avoid 'wicked' currents, and in another part keep it 'plum' in the middle.

Once there was the strange sensation of the paddle wheel 'walking' over a log and another time everyone experienced the harsh juddering of the boat meeting logs full on.

Mr Cartwright's eyes crinkled at the corners. 'Keeps 'em up her sleeve, does old Mrs

164

Mississippi, just to make sure we stay awake. She's a wily lady.'

The scenery changed as they neared Baton Rouge, it was all forest land along the banks. At Baton Rouge bales of cotton were hoisted aboard, so many Kendra wondered how they had room for them all. She was at the rail alone watching the activity when her husband came up to her. He said, in what she thought was a forced jocular tone, 'I'm afraid I've been neglecting you.'

She turned her head and met his gaze squarely. 'I would say so, considering we are on our honeymoon and my husband sleeps alone.'

'You might not understand this, Kendra, but what I am doing now is to benefit both of us in the future.' He sounded so earnest, so sincere she wanted to believe him.

But when he went on about needing all his wits about him, needing all the rest he could while the cards were running for him, she moved away from him saying, 'I refuse to believe you could not sacrifice *one* night to be with me.'

He followed her, caught her by the arm. 'Try and understand. One night might break the run of luck. This is what happens.'

'I would not appreciate another "attack" on me, but that one took no more than minutes. You desired me before but that desire seems to be gone. And I feel fairly certain it has nothing to do with needing concentration for gambling.'

The next moment when a few couples came up to ask if they were going ashore with them Devereux said at once, 'Yes, of course,' and was all amiability.

Although during the next stage of the journey Devereux did spend a little more time with Kendra their relationship changed in no way. She tried many times to find a reason for the change, but could think of none.

She began to feel that Lloyd Francis was aware of her loneliness because often when she was on her own he would come to her. Once they watched the sunset together. The river changed from blood red to gold, there were tumbling rings of water, tinged with both shades. Kendra had come to know that these rings indicated a dissolving bar of sand. At either side of the river, trees made deep shadows on the water. They gave a melancholic air to the scene.

Lloyd Francis said softly, 'The sunrises are even more beautiful.'

She wanted to say she was free to see one with him, but instead found herself asking him if he were married. 'I took it for granted you were a bachelor,' she said, 'because you never mentioned a wife, but—'

'Alas the girl I was in love with married someone else, and so far I have not met another to match up to her. At least—not a lady who is available.' He glanced quickly at

166

her and away.

'Is this the reason why you gamble?'

He shook his head. 'No, I gambled before I met her. I told you, it is in my blood. But these past few nights I have managed to curtail the urge.' He smiled. 'Who knows, I might overcome my obsession.'

The day before they were due to arrive at Memphis one of the women in the group Kendra was friendly with said, 'My dear, your husband tells me you sing. You must sing for us, we have an excellent accompanyist in Miss Mason.'

Kendra, her colour high, protested that the only singing she had ever done was for her own pleasure. But they would not accept this as an excuse. They needed to be entertained. And so, very reluctantly, she agreed to sing 'Greensleeves,' which was a favourite with her.

She was nervous at first but then forgot it in the beauty of the words . . .

> 'Alas, my love, ye do me wrong,
> To cast me off discourteously:
> And I have loved you so long,
> Delighting in your company!'

There was not only tremendous applause and encores for more but several young men came up to congratulate her. A little flushed with her success Kendra agreed to another song, and another, and then her husband came up and escorted her back to her seat. 'Excellent, Kendra, but that is enough for one evening. We must not spoil your audience. I heard a fellow remark beind me that he could get you many engagements in New Orleans, and in New York, if you were interested. If any man approaches you on this subject refer him to me.'

'But of course,' Kendra murmured. 'Perhaps you could sell me and get a good price.'

He raised his eyes. 'What have I done to deserve such an unkind remark?'

Kendra decided to change the subject. 'When we reach Memphis tomorrow will we have time to visit the house you won and also see over the showboat?'

Devereux was suddenly tense again. His hands were clenched so hard his knuckles showed white. 'I doubt whether there will be time to see both. I suggest you go with Lloyd Francis to see the showboat and I shall go to the house and look over the plantation.'

On an impulse she said, 'I think I would rather come with you to see the property.'

'No—' he spoke sharply. 'There will be business to conduct.' At Kendra's prolonged searching look he added in quieter tones, 'I feel sure you would find more interest in the showboat, and I would feel freer if you were not there when I do business.'

She said, very well, but she was greatly disturbed to know why he did not want her at

168

the house. Had he had dealings with Mr Lamartine in the past and there was something Pel did not want her to know, something unpleasant?

Kendra was quiet when Lloyd Francis came to take her to the showboat. She explained her husband's non-appearance and Lloyd accepted this. He was full of praise for her singing, said he could not get near afterwards to congratulate her, then suggested she might sing on the showboat, adding, 'I am of course, just jesting.'

'If my husband has a run of ill luck,' she answered lightly, 'I may be more than willing to take you up on your offer.'

They took a carriage to where the showboat was moored, and at first sight Kendra was disappointed. The paintwork, which must at one time have been rich blues, reds, greens and yellows, was badly faded. All the gilt touches were dulled, and the white paint of trelliswork now dirty. Lloyd Francis, she could see, was disappointed. There was a big change in it, he said, since he had last seen it.

As they came nearer Kendra could see where someone had started to repaint the letters on a big board proclaiming, 'COLONEL LLOYD FRANCIS'S FLOATING PALACE, THE MARY LOUISE'.

'He was my grandfather,' Lloyd explained.

An elderly man, carrying a paint pot, came on to the deck. He peered at the two visitors

169

approaching, then his rheumy eyes lit up. 'Why, Mr Francis—'

Lloyd raised a hand. 'Hello there, Mr Beakin.'

The muddy banks of the levee had been covered with cinders and ashes, and over this gangplanks took them on to the foreward deck. The elderly man was there to meet them. Extending a hand, he exclaimed 'What a welcome surprise, sir! We wondered when you would come. Funds are low, had to release the players, but they will be back as soon as I give them word you are here.'

Lloyd introduced Kendra to Mr Beakin, explaining he was the support of the company, without him they would flounder. To which Mr Beakin, looking pleased, said, 'Oh, shucks, an exaggeration.' Then he added, 'But come along, come down to the kitchen. I can offer the young lady some tea.'

The boat had the feeling of a house at first, there was a porch, a door that led into an entrance hall, and more doors that led to a stairway. Then the boat became a theatre with a balcony and upper boxes, an auditorium, the orchestra pit, the stage, the stage boxes with their shining brass rails and red plush seats. Lloyd, his tone apologetic, said it all looked a little depressing, but at night, with a hundred lamps lit and the theatre full of animated, chattering people, with the band playing—he paused and added with a rather shy smile,

170

'Then it has a magic, it really has.'

Kendra nodded slowly, 'Yes, I can believe it.'

The way to the kitchen was through a low door in the orchestra pit. There was a dining room and a cook's galley under the stage. Lloyd had to stoop to avoid the low beams. There were dressing rooms and tiny bedrooms and a wardrobe with a fascinating selection of costumes, Shakespearean, Elizabethan— Kendra said, feeling somewhat wistful, that she used to like dressing up as a child.

'You can dress up again,' Lloyd teased, 'if you take me up on my offer.' He explained to Mr Beakin about Kendra's excellent singing voice and Mr Beakin remarked they could do with a good singer to take part in the concerts after the plays.

They had tea and then Lloyd showed her more rooms in the balcony area. When Kendra looked down on the auditorium she was lost in imagination for a few moments, seeing herself on stage, singing to an audience of over eight hundred people, hearing their applause. It was a heady thought.

Lloyd showed her over the rest of the boat and the more Kendra saw the more she was attracted to this 'floating palace' rather than to the *April Queen*, with all its luxury. She had a feeling of belonging and had to shake herself free of wanting to stay there.

When they eventually returned to the *April Queen* there was all the usual activity of

171

loading, of passengers boarding, of sightseers milling around. Kendra looked for her husband but he had not yet returned. Would the house give him the feeling of wanting to settle down? He had said it was not a house he had particularly liked so therefore unimportant to him. In that case why had he bothered to go and see it? After all, he did own a half-share in the showboat and had talked about seeing himself as an impresario. He seemed to have forgotten all that. There must be something about the house that drew him, in spite of trying to make out it was unimportant to him.

It was an hour before Devereux arrived. He came in a carriage, seated opposite an elderly white-haired lady and a girl. The girl was one of the most beautiful Kendra had ever seen. She was wearing emerald green which emphasized her luxuriant dark chestnut hair and magnolia skin. Her parasol was also green, edged with navy blue. She had a regal air and offered her hand to Devereux to kiss when he alighted, as a queen might have done. He even backed away as a subject would. He straightened, came up the gangplank then turned to raise his hand in farewell. The girl inclined her head, acknowledging it, then suddenly gave him a dazzling smile. The man behind Kendra exclaimed, 'By heavens, what a smile, who is the beauty?'

'Lamartine's daughter,' said his companion, then added with a laugh, 'But don't get ideas

172

about her. Eleanor has about fifty beaux dangling on strings.'

Eleanor . . . Kendra's mouth had gone dry. So this was why her husband had refused to discuss the property he had gone to see. Eleanor, the woman who had haunted his dreams. She gripped the rail. What had happened at the house this afternoon? Eleanor Lamartine's dazzling smile did not indicate she had been deprived of a house and plantation, due to be presented to her on her next birthday.

The carriage was leaving. Devereux stood and watched until it was out of sight, then he came on slowly up the rest of the gangplank and in his eyes was a look Kendra had never seen before.

The look was of a man who had glimpsed paradise. She turned and hurried away, feeling as though her heart was breaking.

CHAPTER EIGHT

Kendra went down to the cabin with a terrible coldness in her. She needed something to do to stop her from thinking of what had happened. She smoothed a hand over an already smooth bedcover, plumped up cushions on the sofa, took a dress out of the wardrobe, held it unseeingly before her, put it back and was

173

standing with it in her hands again when her husband came in. She tensed.

'Why—hello, Kendra, you are back early.' There was a wariness in his tone. 'Did you enjoy your afternoon? How did you like the showboat?'

Kendra's hurt suddenly changed to anger. She turned on him. 'I might ask *you* how you enjoyed your afternoon with Eleanor Lamartine.'

There was a moment's silence then he said, 'Who told you?'

'I saw you arrive with her. So did a lot more people. I also heard comments that Eleanor Lamartine has about fifty beaux dangling on strings. Where in the line do you hang?'

His expression changed, became cold. 'I will not have you speaking to me in this way, Kendra.'

'Indeed. I have a great deal more to say. How dare you bring your mistress here.'

Devereux flared. 'She is not my mistress and never has been.'

'Then what is the relationship between you? She certainly did not behave as a woman who had been deprived by you of her inheritance. When is she moving out of the house, I should like to take a look at it.'

There was another silence, a longer one this time. Devereux ran the palm of his hand over a chair back, then his head went up. 'She will not be moving out, neither will her father.'

174

Kendra hung up the dress and slammed the wardrobe door. 'Oh, I suppose you are going to let them go on living there—rent free.'

'If you must know I have transferred the house and plantation back to Mr Lamartine.'

Kendra stared at him. When she spoke her voice was little above a whisper.

'So he can give it to his daughter on her next birthday—as planned. How could you, how could you humiliate me so?'

'I see no reason for you to be humiliated, no reason at all. The transaction has nothing whatsoever to do with you. I told you once and I tell you again, I will not be criticised.'

Kendra picked up her shawl, put it round her shoulders and walked to the door. Devereux demanded to know where she was going but she found it impossible to answer for the tightness in her throat. She went out.

Her first instinct was to go on deck into the air then she knew she must find somewhere quiet. The saloon. It would be deserted at this time of day. She made for a corner behind the piano.

In the evening the room was alive with colour and noise. Now, with the chandeliers unlit and deserted there was something terribly depressing about it. In spite of the saloon being thoroughly cleaned and polished every morning the smell of spirits and stale cigar smoke still lingered. Kendra stared at the red bobble-fringe on a tablecloth. Eleanor

Lamartine's face intruded. Determinedly Kendra's gaze went to the bamboo screens dividing the section where the men played cards.

Gambling—the root of so much trouble, so much unhappiness, tragedy. Kendra put her hands to her face. Why had Devereux allowed Eleanor Lamartine to come to the boat? Had he wanted to show the other passengers he was acquainted with such a desirable woman? When he had won the property and land had he intended then to return it to her father—so it could be handed on to his daughter? The property and land must be worth a king's ransom. No wonder Eleanor had bestowed her dazzling smile on him. How much did that smile promise? Probably nothing. Pel was a fool. He must be obsessed by her, but then why had he rushed into marriage? Had he realised she would not marry a gambler and he was hoping to win her favours with the gift?

'Kendra—where are you?' Hearing her husband calling, Kendra let her hands fall to her lap and sat up straight. He came into the saloon, looked about him then, seeing her, came over, his face set, a determination in his stride. He pulled out a chair and sat opposite to her.

'Now listen to me, we had better get certain things straight. You are my wife and I will not have you running out on me.'

'No, because then you would not have your

"good luck" charm and, if you happened on a losing streak you would not be able to hand over expensive gifts to Eleanor Lamartine.'

'Stop it, stop it at once, do you hear?' Devereux slapped a palm on the table top. 'Eleanor did not expect gifts. You are my wife and I repeat I will not have you running out on me.'

'I had no intention of running out. I wanted to get away from you, from your arrogance, your lack of understanding.'

'There is nothing to understand. I repeat also I made a transaction which has nothing to do with you.'

'Eleanor Lamartine has.'

'In what way? Go on, tell me. How does she affect you, how has she changed your life?'

'When you knew you might be seeing her at Memphis you stopped making love to me.'

'What nonsense!' Devereux threw up his hands. 'Do I have to give an account of my sexual feelings? You do realise that a man who has been playing cards all night needs some sleep?'

'You've played cards all night before but still found time to make love to me.'

'That was in the first flush of our reunion. You expect too much, Kendra. I might have felt differently had I really been in love with you, but—'

'I thought you did have some affection for me,' she said in a low voice.

177

'I do, I'm very fond of you and if you are really in need of me, I could, I suppose, sacrifice an hour of my card playing.'

Kendra laughed and she could hear a note of hysteria in it. How could anyone be so condescending? The ego of the man.

'No, sir,' she said, 'I am not in need of you. You play your cards, stay up all night and if you have any desire to be with a woman then seek out Eleanor Lamartine. She owes you a great deal.'

Devereux jumped up. 'That is enough, Kendra. I will not have you insult a woman who has done nothing to you and who is certainly no whore to come to my bed to pay a debt. The subject is closed, I don't want to hear another word about it.'

'Not entirely closed, there are questions I want to ask. When we were in New York and on our way to the docks a carriage passed, in which you showed great interest. Was Eleanor Lamartine in that carriage?'

'No—her father, I was surprised to see him. I had no idea he was in America, and as I was not aware of how long he might be staying and he owed me money, a large sum, I decided to try and collect it.'

'And you were hoping, of course, that his daughter was with him and—'

'I was hoping nothing,' Devereux snapped. 'Now will you please let the matter rest?'

'One more thing. Why did you get someone

178

else to write the note that was brought to me on the ship? Why didn't you write it yourself? Have you any idea of the worry, the agony, I went through—imagining all sorts of things happening to you?'

'You would have worried more if you knew what *had* happened.'

'I would be interested to hear it.'

'A man accused me of cheating, he attacked me. I have never cheated in my life and would never stoop to such a low action. I knocked him down, broke his nose. He shouted for help, and as ill luck would have it a constable was near, and knowing the delay it could cause, if I were apprehended, I ran. Two louts barred my way and after having engaged with them in fisticuffs and knocking them to the ground, it seemed that every man in the area was after me. I was forced to seek sanctuary with a friend, George Daley, the writer of the note. I found it impossible to hold a quill.'

'But why on earth didn't you explain all this when you arrived in New Orleans. You made such a mystery of it.'

'Because we were still only newly married. There's a stigma to the word cheat, and I felt if I told you then you would have been wondering if the man was telling the truth.'

'I find it hard to accept you did not want me to think badly of you over that incident, yet were so uncaring about my knowing of your relationship with Eleanor Lamartine. You do realise that once it becomes known you handed back property and land to her father, tongues will wag. I will once more become the "poor Mrs Devereux" the wronged wife.'

'Kendra—' he said through clenched teeth, 'if you persist in harping on this subject I shall move to another cabin.'

'Good. It will be a treat not to have you come to bed in the early hours and put your icy feet on me.'

A slow smile suddenly spread over Devereux's face. 'And do you know, my love, I would miss your warmth.'

Kendra was not willing to be appeased too easily, but because she loved him, wanted him, in spite of what had happened she gave in. By evening a truce had been established between them, although on Kendra's part it was with some reservation.

She would have been willing for a full reconciliation had he sacrificed an evening to be with her, or even had he come to bed earlier after his game, but he arrived at breakfast time as usual and she wondered, with a feeling of bleakness, if this was to be a pattern of their lives from now on.

Just before the boat was due to sail a man called Bo Burford came aboard. He and Devereux knew one another but although outwardly affable, Kendra sensed an animosity between them. She disliked Burford on sight. He laughed a lot, guffawed, but the small eyes

180

in the florid face were mean, his glance sharp. He had a fat cigar between his thick lips which he rolled constantly from side to side.

He boomed a greeting to Kendra when introduced and gave her an exaggerated bow. 'My pleasure, Ma'am. I had no idea my good friend had launched into matrimony. We must get better acquainted.' His gaze was on her bosom. 'Looking forward to a game with your spouse, Ma'am. A man of my own calibre. Cleaned him out the last time we met, that right, Devereux?' He roared with laughter as though it were some huge jest.

'But not this time,' Devereux said, his tone lazy, his eyes cold. 'The circumstances are somewhat different.'

Burford gave a knowing wink. 'Heard you'd come into a fortune. Soon relieve you of that, ha-ha. Heard a few more things about you too, but they can wait.' More laughter.

Devereux put a hand under Kendra's elbow. 'We must go, if you will excuse us.'

When they were out of earshot Kendra said, 'What a dreadful man.'

'Dreadful is too mild a word. I have yet to meet a man who has anything good to say about Burford. He has an infuriating habit of making a losing opponent feel a fool. Someday he will get a knife in him, I'm sure.'

'He seemed to expect you would be playing with him.'

'And, of course, I must. I want to get my own

181

back.'

'But you could lose everything you have to him.'

Devereux gave Kendra a teasing smile. 'Not if you strengthen that good luck "influence" of yours.'

'Oh, Pel, it's wrong to depend on such a thing. If you lose I shall feel responsible.'

He laughed and assured her that if he did lose he would not throw her to the fishes. After that he remained in a determinedly cheerful mood, declaring he was looking forward to a game with Bo Burford. Which, as Kendra had to admit, was the right attitude.

When he was ready to leave to play, immaculate and still confident, Kendra, on an impulse, stood on tiptoes and kissed him on the lips. He held her close for a moment and she felt there was a greater rapport between them than there had been for some time.

He drew away. 'Well, into battle we go!'

Kendra asked if she could watch the game but he gave her a definite no, it would put him off, lose concentration. He knuckled her under the chin. 'See you in the morning. Keep the bed warm.' Her pulses leapt in response to what she took to be a promise to make love to her.

'I will,' she said softly.

When later Kendra sat with the other gamblers' wives their talk was all of Bo Burford. Not one of them had any time for him. 'A most detestable man,' Mrs Dawson

182

said. 'He usually has a woman with him, but if not he very quickly finds one once he is aboard. You beware of him, Mrs Devereux. I noticed him watching you closely at dinner. I have a feeling he fancies you and if he does he will pester you.'

'He pestered Bella Harvey last year,' one of the other women said, 'and she eventually went off with him. I don't know where his charm lies. Perhaps his money. I'm told he's generous that way to women, but brutal with them.' She shuddered.

Mrs Dawson said, 'He looks a brute, but there, let us talk of something else. Do you think there is anything in all this talk of war?'

The women decided it was no more than 'man talk' and they got on to the subject of clothes.

Several times Kendra's gaze went to the bamboo screens and she wondered how her husband was faring in the games. He had not yet encountered a losing streak since she had known him so she had no idea of how he would react. Well, she would know the worst, or the best, the next morning.

Kendra was up and dressed when her husband came in. He was quiet, thoughtful. Her spirits sank. 'Did you lose, Pel?'

'What—no, no, I held my own, but Frank Dawson had heavy losses.'

Devereux rang for hot water to shave and wash. He was silent and Kendra waited, afraid to speak. But at last, unable to bear the silence any longer she said, 'Why don't you give up gambling, Pel. You spoke at one time of settling down.'

He drew the razor up under his chin, wiped the soap on a cloth then turned and looked at her as though she might have suggested he go and drown himself.

'If you cannot offer anything more intelligent in the way of conversation, Kendra, then say no more.' His tone was so scathing she flared.

'Why don't you admit that you too, have had heavy losses? Your whole attitude announces it.'

'Oh, of course, I forgot, you have had so many experiences with men who gamble.' He turned back to the mirror and continued shaving.

'Yes, I have,' she said, 'and I know all the signs, the silences, the reluctance to admit losing. When you win, of course, the whole world knows it. Look how clever you are, you have beaten your opponents. Triumphant, the gladiator!'

He closed his eyes. 'Kendra—will you either stop talking or get out of here!'

'I shall stop talking.' She sat, prim, hands crossed on her lap, bursting to lash out at him again. If only the foolish man would realise it would help to talk. After all, this was what a wife was for—well, partly. She simmered down, realising she was not carrying out her wifely duties by rubbing salt into the wound. It would be bad enough to his pride to have lost to Burford, a man he had already disliked when he came aboard.

He was still quiet when they went into breakfast, but he was courteous to her, attentive. He spoke to his table companions but did not, as usual launch into discussions. Kendra became worried about him. How much *had* he lost?

When they went up on deck for their morning walk he said it must be short, he was unusually sleepy. He saw her settled in a deck chair with congenial company, then left. Kendra talked to the young couple next to her but after a while, feeling restless, she got up and said she thought she would take another turn around the deck. Pel would not like her being on her own, but there were one or two women who were unaccompanied.

Kendra realised then just how much she missed Lloyd Francis, not only his pleasant company, but to have a confidant. He was so easy to talk to. Kendra stopped to watch the big wheels. She was used now to the vibration and had come to find something awesome in the power of the wheel and the way the water surged, cascading, driving the boat along, leaving a wake of creamy foam.

'Good morning, Mrs Devereux.'

Kendra's heart began a quick beating as she

turned to face Bo Burford. He swept off his hat. 'All alone, dear lady. Is your husband indisposed after the trials of the night?'

His smirk incensed her. But she managed to say calmly, 'Not at all, Mr Burford, I left him discussing with friends the perils of a possibility of war.'

'Oh, it will come, Ma'am, it will come, as sure as birds lay eggs. Would you care to walk, may I escort you?' He rolled his cigar from one side of his mouth to the other. 'Took to you the minute we met, Ma'am. Would like to get to know you better.'

'Well, I—as a matter of fact I'm expecting a friend to join me.' And, catching sight of Mrs Dawson she waved to her. 'And here she is now.'

Burford glanced over his shoulder then said, 'Well now, seeing that the lady in question seems to have been detained perhaps you will tell me all about yourself.' He laid a hand on her arm.

Kendra soon discovered that Bo Burford had the same hateful habit of touching that Mr Bagley had. Burford did not attempt to touch her breasts, but he made a pretence of straightening the lace collar on her dress, flicked an imaginery piece of fluff at her waist, and pressed himself against her as three people passed, in spite of the fact there was plenty of room for them to pass. To her relief she saw Mrs Dawson hurrying towards her.

186

'Oh, here is my friend now, Mr Burford. Do please excuse me.' She hurried away.

'Kendra, are you all right, that dreadful man.'

'Let us get right away from him, he really is hateful. He wanted me to walk with him. I tried to be as pleasant as I could on account of my husband, but it was certainly not easy.'

Mrs Dawson sighed. 'The problems of having gambling husbands deprives us of their company, just at a time when we need it. My poor husband had a disastrous time last night. We are not exactly bankrupted, but—' She gave another sigh. 'Still that is the luck of the game. And he does have time to recoup his losses. How did your husband fare, Mrs Devereux?'

'He said he—held his own.'

'Oh, good, perhaps tonight—'

They were joined by two more of the women and talk became general.

Kendra had cause for more worry than just her husband's quietness during the next two days. He looked so strained she felt sure he must be losing, and heavily, but he still insisted he was holding his own. Kendra's other concern was Bo Burford pursuing her wherever she went. For two days she had managed, by devious means, to avoid direct contact with him, but on the third morning he caught her and grabbed her by the arm.

'Not so fast, Ma'am. I know you've been avoiding me, but I'm going to get you. I want you and no woman I've ever wanted has escaped me for long.'

'Mr Burford!' Kendra, shocked by his manner and the lascivious look on his face tried to free herself, but his grip tightened. 'How dare you hold me. If you don't release me I shall call for help.'

He rolled the stub of his cigar between his teeth and moisture dribbled from the corners of his mouth. 'I'll let you go for now, but you stop avoiding me in future, or else—'

'I shall tell my husband of your behaviour,' she said. 'He will know how to deal with you.'

Burford laughed. 'Save your breath. He'll not do anything, I've got him where I want him.'

A group of people came up and Kendra hurried away, her heart pounding. She went straight to the cabin. She must tell Pel, even though it meant rousing him from sleep. She tried not to think what Burford had meant by saying he had Pel where he wanted him.

She opened the cabin door, then stood, and stared—aghast. The bed was empty, and so was the wardrobe. Every garment she possessed lay strewn on the floor.

Even before Kendra made the search she knew she was wasting her time. Every piece of jewellery had gone from the secret pockets in her dress.

She sat back on her heels, her hand to her throat. Pel was the only one who could have taken them. How could he do such a thing! It was the pieces his mother had willed to his bride on her wedding day. If he would stoop to steal these, then he must have gambled away the rest of the jewellery. She got to her feet, still feeling numb with shock. Then she sank on to a chair—to wait.

Kendra's thoughts kept returning to Pel's refusal to say whether Eleanor Lamartine had been with her father in New York. She must have been, they must have spent a great deal of time in one another's company, so much so he had not had time to write a note himself. Eleanor Lamartine was at the root of all the trouble. No doubt Pel was trying to amass more wealth to impress her, and this was why he had been gambling recklessly . . .

Kendra lost track of time, she only knew that when she heard Pel whistling outside the door, and she got up, she was stiff and bone-weary. Even his whistling was a lie, to cover his guilt.

He came in, stopped and looked about him then stared at her.

'Kendra, what is going on? Why are all your dresses on the floor?'

'They were there when I came in, and you were gone from your bed, so was all the jewellery from the secret pockets in my dresses.'

'What? You mean—stolen?' He seemed genuinely shocked but Kendra reminded herself that liars have to be good actors.

'Why pretend, Pel, you know you took it.'

'I? Do you realise what you are saying, Kendra?'

She gave a despairing sigh. 'You've been losing steadily at cards. How much have you lost? Do you still own the riverboat and the half-share in the showboat?'

'Of course I do!'

'And the rest of your mother's jewellery?'

His mouth set in a tight line. 'Why this inquisition? How dare you accuse me of theft. We would be much better employed in trying to find out who has robbed us. The thief will be on board. I must see the captain.'

'Don't make a fool of yourself,' Kendra said quietly as he started towards the door.

His eyes suddenly blazed. 'You must have a very low opinion of me, I treasured those pieces. I would never have parted with them, not even if I were destitute.'

She met his gaze steadily. 'May I remind you that only days ago you made to strike me when I refused to tell you where the jewellery was hidden.'

She expected him to flare up. Instead he looked at her with eyes so full of reproach she wondered if she had made a dreadful mistake.

'You have little faith in me, Kendra, I'm sorry.' He left.

Kendra pressed her palms together, agitated now. It was a terrible accusation to make against one's husband. But who else could have stolen the jewellery? Pel would tell no one about it and she had not told anyone, only— she went suddenly cold as she remembered mentioning the jewellery to Mrs Dawson, when they had been talking about valuables, and Kendra had been so proud of her secret pockets. Mr Dawson had lost heavily at cards— no, she must stop trying to find someone to blame, it was wrong. She must wait and see what action the captain would take.

But no action was taken and Pel refused to talk about it. He said he had his own methods of dealing with the thief and time would prove to her that he was not the culprit.

* * *

From then on there was a barrier between them that Kendra felt would never be broken. Devereux talked to people, smiled, made jests, was attentive to Kendra in company, but icily aloof when they were alone. She ached for him to put his arms around her and hold her close and was often tempted to make an approach to him. Then she would think of Eleanor Lamartine and knew that her image would always be between them, even if Pel did in time forget she had accused him of theft.

He still played cards and so did Mr Dawson, and although neither man showed the animation of having had a good night, neither showed the strain of being on a losing streak.

Mrs Dawson said nothing about her husband's finances and Kendra would not ask.

When the women left the saloon to go to bed Kendra left with them, but being unable to sleep if she went to bed early she had taken to going up on deck. There were always plenty of people on the three decks, mostly couples, but unless she got into the glare of a torch basket the fact that she was unaccompanied would pass unnoticed in the blackness of the night.

Sometimes she went up on the boiler deck for comfort, making sure she remained well back. This deck was always full of people, many of them deck hands, firemen and roustabouts. The boilers were a big attraction with the glow and fierce heat from the row of furnaces. Many cords of wood were taken aboard to feed the hungry maws of the furnaces.

There was plenty of noise here, bells clanging, orders being shouted; but the sounds Kendra listened for were the more intimate murmurings of young couples, the subdued laughter. According to Mr Cartwright many mothers ignored the fact their daughters had secret assignations, wanting them to find husbands.

Kendra walked to the rail. The water had such a stillness had it not been for the noise, and the black outlines of trees slipping past, one could have imagined the boat was not moving.

She found herself longing to be single again,

free to enjoy the flattery of men, to go to parties, to be waiting for her father to come home from his card games, to share in his life. At the moment she felt she was waiting for something to happen.

When something did happen it was unexpected. She had gone to bed early, with a headache threatening, but was lying wide awake when there came a hurried knocking on her door, and Mrs Dawson's voice calling, 'Mrs Devereux—Mrs Devereux—'

The urgency in Mrs Dawson's tone had Kendra out of bed and dragging on a robe in seconds. When she opened the door Mrs Dawson rushed in, a look of distress on her face.

Kendra, sure that something terrible must have happened to her husband put a hand to her throat. 'What is it?'

'Oh, Mrs Devereux, you must come at once. A big game is going on, with very high stakes. Your husband wants you, he's unable to meet Mr Burford's bid. Mr Burford has offered to accept *you* as collateral if you are willing.'

Kendra stared at Mrs Dawson, shocked, unwilling to accept the implication of the words. 'Accept *me*? Did my husband suggest this?'

'No, Mr Burford offered. Your husband has lost a great deal of money, he's put up the riverboat and a half-share in a showboat in this game. He must have a winning hand or else he

193

would not—'

'Mr Burford must think he has a winning hand too,' Kendra retorted. She began to get dressed. 'The game must be stopped.'

When they reached the saloon Kendra could feel the drama. Most of the people had congregated in the game section. A thick haze of cigar smoke hung over the area. People spoke among themselves in low voices. Mrs Dawson gripped Kendra's hand. 'Try and keep calm.'

Keep calm? Her heart was beating at such a rate she could hardly breathe and her legs felt as though they would buckle under her.

When she appeared round the bamboo screen there was a sudden hush. All eyes were turned on her. Her husband looked a little paler than usual but his expression was inscrutable.

'Kendra—Mrs Dawson has told you the position?'

'She has.'

Bo Burford flicked ash from his cigar with a crooked finger and gave her a broad grin. 'Nice to see a stake in the flesh. We could be making history tonight, the sensation of the year. Wife put up as collateral.'

'It would be the sensation of the century,' Kendra corrected icily, '*if* the game progressed, but as I refuse to be part of this conspiracy—'

'Your husband has the right, you are his property.'

'I am his wife, Mr Burford, not his chattel. And if this persists I shall ask the captain to put me ashore.'

There were quick nods of approval from the women, but the men looked disappointed, hating to be deprived of what could be a talking point for years.

'The choice is yours, Kendra.'

She turned to her husband. His eyes were veiled and she still found it impossible to read his expression. Mr Dawson had once said that Pel had the perfect poker face. Was he so sure of winning he was willing to risk his reputation? If he did lose, his name would be discredited the length and breadth of the Mississippi—and beyond. Even if he won there would still be the stigma of a husband putting his wife up as collateral in a game.

Kendra suddenly felt a wave of despair. Was that all she meant to him, just someone to be handed over to a man like Bo Burford? Did it matter any longer who she was with? She could certainly never have any respect for her husband again. Pel was staring straight ahead. A silence had fallen over the watching people. Burford's mean little eyes were regarding her in a speculative way.

For the first time Kendra looked at the cards. Mrs Dawson whispered, 'Deuces are wild. Both men took a card each.'

Out of the five cards in front of each man the two cards, face up, were a couple of deuces.

Kendra's heart began a slow thudding. With deuces wild they could make anything they liked. What other cards did the men hold? With such big money at stake they must surely be going for five of a kind. Or were they bluffing? But would they bluff with such big sums? She remembered then her father once telling her of a friend of his who won a huge pot with a couple of pairs.

She also remembered her father's words that one must take chances in life as well as in cards. She squared her shoulders. 'I accept the challenge.'

There was a long sigh as though breaths had been held and released. A buzz of chatter broke out. A voice called, 'Silence!' and the chatter ceased.

There was still no expression on Devereux's face, but Burford, who had lit another cigar blew out a smoke ring and smiled.

Devereux sat up. 'And so, Burford, you accept my wife as collateral.' The words were clipped.

'Yes, I do.' He tapped the end of his cigar and looked about him with a smirk, as though mightily pleased with himself.

'Then I raise you ten thousand, Mr Burford.'

There was a gasp from the crowd. Burford was still, and Kendra saw beads of perspiration spring to his brow and upper lip. She guessed he had expected Pel to match his bid, but not to raise it. She sensed too that he was beginning to realise he might have a winning hand against him. So now he either threw his hand in, matched Devereux's bid or raised it further.

The cigar was rolled from side to side of the thick lips several times then he clamped his teeth on it and sat staring at the green baize of the table.

There was no sound in the saloon, even the chink of glasses had ceased. The only sign that Devereux was tense was a pulse beating in his throat. The palms of Kendra's hands were sweating. She wanted to grip the back of a chair to give her support, but dare not move.

At last Burford gathered chips together to the value of ten thousand and pushed them to the centre.

'I'll call you.'

There was a sudden hush in the saloon again and when someone gave a small cough it had the effect of a pistol shot. The gaze of all was on Devereux's cards. Kendra was holding herself so tight her body ached.

Devereux turned his cards face up on the table.

'Five Kings,' came a soft chorus of voices. Eyes went to Burford.

Burford was smiling. Kendra gripped the back of a chair. Oh, God—she felt physically sick. He must have five aces.

He ground out his cigar then, getting up he waved his hands towards the chips. 'It's just on loan, Devereux.'

Kendra had never fainted in her life, but was near to it at that moment.

A man said, 'What cards did *you* have, Burford?' and made to look at them.

He was knocked to the floor with Burford roaring over him. 'Anyone who wants to see my cards pays for it.' He put his cards in the deck, shuffled them and scattered the pack over the man. He then strode out.

Devereux, who was gathering up the chips said to Kendra, 'Wait for me.'

The command in his voice infuriated her. She shook her head and hurried out. Mrs Dawson followed and caught her up.

'Don't be hard on your husband, Mrs Devereux,' she pleaded. 'He had confidence in winning.'

'Confidence? With five Kings—? Please excuse me, Mrs Dawson, my head is throbbing.' Kendra ran to the cabin.

She sank onto the sofa. She would have to leave. She must. It was an impossible situation. If it had not been so late she would have asked the captain if he had a single cabin. In the meantime—

When her husband came in Kendra was stretched out on the sofa, a blanket over her.

'What is this?' he demanded. 'Why are you on the sofa?'

'I would have thought an explanation unnecessary.' Kendra gripped the edge of the blanket.

198

'No matter what happened this evening you are still my wife.'

Kendra drew herself up. 'I'm glad you reminded me, sir, I've had little cause of late for thinking so. I've slept alone, your heart is with another woman and tonight you were willing to sell me to Bo Burford.'

'I had no intention of "selling" you, as you so wrongly put it. I knew I had winning cards.'

'How could you know? Five Kings is not an unbeatable hand.'

'But I knew Burford could not have been holding the five aces. It would be a million to one chance! In all the years I've played cards I haven't come up against such a hand or known anyone else who has. What's more, I know Burford, know his mannerisms. I knew he was not going to beat me.'

'It alters nothing as far as I am concerned, you *could* have lost, the million to one chance might have been tonight. You degraded me, I felt as though I were for auction. I can never forgive you for that, or forget it. Many people too will remember it. When we make our next stop I shall leave the boat.'

'Oh, no you won't! You are staying with me. I need you.'

Kendra lay down again and pulled the blanket over her. 'I'm afraid you will have to do without your good luck charm, sir.'

The blanket was flung from her, hands gripped her and she was lifted and carried over to the bed. 'That is where you belong, and where you will stay. Enough of this nonsense.'

Devereux began undressing. Kendra felt a stir of emotion and hated herself for it. Why should she submit to a man who was so uncaring of her welfare. For all he knew she could have been taken by Bo Burford, and would now be in *his* bed. She made to get up and was pushed back. When her husband turned to lower the lamp she slid from the bed. He caught her, wrapped her hair round his hand and drew her head back gently. His mouth covered hers, moving sensuously, hungrily.

Although Kendra knew she was no more than a substitute for Eleanor Lamartine she lay still. And when Pel removed her nightdress and pressed her body to the warmth and hardness of his own she gave a low moan and submitted, and she thought God help her.

CHAPTER NINE

There was a wildness in their lovemaking as though the tensions of the evening had to be released. This was at first. Later, when he took her again there was a control about Devereux, a teasing in withholding himself, so that it became a torment to her and she begged him to bring her to fulfilment. Their lovemaking lasted until dawn, when both fell into an exhausted sleep.

When Kendra awoke her husband was up and shaving. She lay watching him, admiring the muscular body. Even after the satiation of the night before she felt a stirring in her limbs. Last night, over the card game, she had despised him, been determined to leave him, yet here she was wanting to stay with him, wanting his arms around her. She made excuses for his behaviour of the night before. He was a professional gambler, knew what he was doing when he bid. He would never have sacrificed her to Bo Burford. Their lovemaking had proved it, his teasing, his tenderness afterwards.

He finished shaving then turning, saw she was awake.

'Good-morning, my love. Feeling lazy?'

She stretched herself, catlike and said softly, 'I could stay here all day.'

Devereux grinned. 'With me beside you, of course.'

'Of course.'

He splashed his face with cold water, dried it and said, 'And you my dear Kendra, were talking of leaving me last night.' His tone was jocular. 'Who else would satisfy you the way I do? Think what you would be missing. Oh, yes, my love, you would certainly be lost without me. Why, I had you begging for my love last night, remember?'

A feeling of disenchantment touched Kendra with a cold breath. Had this lovemaking all been part of a plan to keep her with him? Was he afraid of taking the risk of her leaving him and so change his luck? With superstition so strong in him he would see putting her up as collateral and winning as a miracle. He might even attempt to repeat it at some future time. Oh, no, she would definitely not stand for that. Kendra drew back the bedclothes and got up.

'My, such a sudden burst of energy,' her husband teased her. 'I thought you were waiting for me to slip into bed beside you.'

'I decided that eating is my most pressing need at the moment.'

'You disappoint me, Kendra, for allowing the mundane to take precedent over the poetry of lovemaking.'

'Poets are willing to starve in garrets, I shall never starve.'

She could see he was aware of a change in her and was puzzled to know the reason. He began to dress. 'You are not holding it against me about the cards last night, Kendra—are you?'

'As far as I am concerned the matter is closed.'

'Good.' His expression brightened. He began to talk about various card games, about the times he had made big wins on a bluff.

She interrupted to ask, 'Pel, the jewellery

that was stolen, who was the thief? You said you had an idea who it was.'

'I know where it is and I shall recover it when we get to St Louis.'

'If the thief is on board, and he must be, why do you have to wait to get to St Louis before reclaiming it?'

'You are asking too many questions, my darling. The story is long and complicated. I shall tell you about it one of these days. Now hurry up and get ready, I too feel famished.'

She was surprised he was eager to go into breakfast. The incident of the game would have spread over the boat like wildfire and she felt sure her husband would be ostracised by many. But to her further surprise he was greeted from all sides as though he had done something heroic.

'Congratulations, Devereux, heard about your win . . . Well done, sir, good to have taken Burford down a peg . . . Delighted to hear about your win, took courage to do what you did . . .'

The main topic at breakfast among the men was a speculation as to what cards Burford had held. And it was just a speculation, no professional gambler, with stakes so high, would allow anyone to catch a glimpse of his cards. Although one man did declare he had 'snuck' a look and the cards were 'five Queens'.

Devereux simply gave a benign smile all around, as though he knew exactly what cards

203

his opponent had been holding.

Bo Burford did not come into breakfast. When next Kendra saw him he was on deck. He was with two men and she was standing at the rail with Mrs Dawson, both waiting for their husbands. Burford acknowledged them briefly as he passed then, stopping, he came back and beckoned to Kendra.

She glanced at Mrs Dawson, hesitated a moment then went to him. He was smiling. He appeared to be friendly, but there was nothing friendly about his voice as he said, 'I'm warning you, Ma'am, your escape is only temporary, just as your husband's winnings are. I'll have you yet and when I do it'll be for keeps.'

Although Kendra's heart had begun a slow pounding she managed to force a smile. 'Why, Mr Burford, how kind of you to compliment my husband on his play. Most generous of you.'

A black scowl spread over his florid face. He chewed on his cigar and left. Mrs Dawson, who had heard Kendra's remark only, raised her eyebrows when she returned. 'Well,' she said, 'wonders will never cease. Who would have imagined Bo Burford paying a compliment.'

Kendra, who was more upset by Burford's vicious remarks than she would care to admit, replied, 'Who indeed?' then she added, 'Shall we go and find our husbands? I think they have talked politics long enough.'

When Mrs Dawson repeated Burford's 'compliment' to Devereux he laughed. 'Any compliment from Burford can be taken as a warning. He intends battle, but one I feel sure of winning. I'm on a lucky streak, I know it.'

Kendra said quietly, 'I think it unwise to tempt providence.'

Her husband knuckled her under the chin. 'You are too cautious, my love.' He was smiling into her eyes and she was drawn to him by his charm. She hoped if he played cards that evening, which no doubt he would, he would leave early to come to bed.

But her husband's routine of staying up all night and going to bed after their walk on deck was resumed. He was right about being on a winning streak though. Every morning he was jubilant, especially as Burford was the main loser. 'Soon,' he said, 'I shall have enough to buy a house and a plantation.'

Kendra looked up quickly. Although she was loathe to bring Eleanor Lamartine to his mind she could not resist reminding him that he had already won both and given them away.

'Oh, that—' he dismissed them with a wave of the hand. 'I disliked the house. I would never have wanted to live in it. I know exactly what I want and shall get it someday.'

The fact that her husband appeared to show no apparent interest in Eleanor gave Kendra hope she had slipped into the background and would stay there.

It gave her courage to take the initiative. She stood on tiptoe and clasped her hands about his neck. 'Pel, when are we going to have another night like—'

His mouth on hers prevented her from finishing the sentence. He teased, caressed, promising an ecstasy to come. But eventually he told her softly he needed all his energies to concentrate on the cards. Then he laid his cheek to hers. 'Wait until we reach St Louis, my darling, we shall dine out, have champagne— make love all night—'

When they docked at St Louis he told her he had to go ashore, he had business to attend to, but he promised to be back at eight o'clock for her.

With an afternoon to fill in Kendra spent most of the time on deck. There was plenty to see, and the usual noise of unloading, roustabouts singing. She was longing to go ashore, hoped she might be able to spend some time ashore the following day—with her husband.

Kendra was up on deck for the fourth time at six o'clock. In the darkness with the glow of torches and lights of the town the dockside took on a magic. In another two hours—she had already laid out the dress she would wear. The black velvet one which Pel liked. She was dreaming a little when she saw a familiar figure coming up the gangplank. Her heart missed a beat. Bo Burford! What did he want? He had left that morning.

He stopped on seeing her at the rail. 'Good-evening. I think I left my cigar case in the saloon.' He looked her up and down. 'Not waiting for your husband, are you?'

Kendra's head went up. 'I am expecting him.'

'You'll have a long wait.' His voice held a sneer. 'Where do you think he is?'

Hazarding a guess she said, 'Possibly playing cards.'

The laugh Burford gave was derisive. 'I take it you don't know about his lady friend. Or do you? He's with Eleanor Lamartine, saw them together. She arrived yesterday, on a faster boat.'

Kendra made a valiant effort to get a grip on herself and not let this man have the satisfaction of knowing he had upset her.

'Oh, Eleanor has arrived has she? She was boasting she would arrive before us. My husband will be bringing her aboard soon.'

Whether he was fooled or not Kendra could not tell. He brushed past her, and said he hoped his cigar case was still where he had left it. She waited until he was out of sight then she went to her cabin. Once there she sank on to a chair, and was unable to control a violent trembling.

Eleanor Lamartine—had Pel known she was coming to St Louis? Known there was a chance she would be there first? If so she was finished with him, this was the end of their marriage as far as she was concerned. She would not suffer further humiliation at her husband's hands. She would leave before Pel returned.

Decision brought a calmness. She would go ashore, wait there until Lloyd Francis arrived. He had offered her a job singing on the showboat. Although he had made it partly in jest she felt sure he was serious about it.

Then reason took over. The only money she had was the few sovereigns her father had given her. She had no idea when the showboat would arrive, they would make many one-night stands on the way. If she had to wait any length of time her money would run out and she would be at the mercy of heaven knew who—possibly someone like Bo Burford. She shivered.

Was there any money in the cabin, or did her husband carry it around with him? She began to search the wardrobe, look in his pockets. Empty. He had been carrying his small valise when he left. She searched the larger one. Empty. No—there was something in it.

Underneath a false bottom in the valise she found the jewellery, purported to be stolen. Kendra sat back on her heels, shocked at her husband's deception. He *must* have been the one to have taken it. He must have gambled it when he was losing, then recovered it later. She unrolled each piece. A brooch was missing, one set with a large emerald, surrounded by tiny pearls. She had come to be familiar with each piece. The brooch must have been sacrificed in the gambling. Pel had sworn never to gamble with it, sworn the jewellery was sacred to him. His mother's gift from the grave—for his bride.

Kendra tried to thrust aside one of her father's maxims that no man should be condemned without a trial. She was condemning her husband. The information about Eleanor Lamartine had come from an enemy of Pel. Eleanor might have come on a faster boat and she and Pel might have met, but it could have been accidental. He may have known nothing about her plan. She would know when Pel came for her at eight o'clock—if he came.

* * *

It was midnight when Devereux arrived. 'Oh, Kendra,' he wailed, 'can you ever forgive me. Poor darling, waiting for me all these hours. I met some friends, we had a game of cards, had drinks, I drank too much. I was shocked when I woke up and saw the time.'

Kendra sat staring straight ahead. 'Why do you bother to lie, Pel? You met Eleanor Lamartine. Your friend Burford informed me of the fact.'

'I did meet her but I had no idea she was in St Louis.'

'You lied about your mother's jewellery,' Kendra went on in implacable tones. 'I found it in your valise. One piece is missing. Did you give the brooch to Eleanor Lamartine, for her favours?'

'No, I didn't! I saw her for only a short time. I had no idea the brooch was missing, Burford must have kept it. I used the jewellery as surety. Yes, I know I told you I would recover it when I got to St Louis, I didn't want you to know I had used it for gambling. I never would again, I swear it.'

'Save your breath.' Kendra got up. She picked up a valise already packed.

'Where are you going?' Pel Devereux demanded.

'To a single cabin, and please do not make a fuss. If you do I shall walk off this boat and you will never see me again.'

'You are my wife, your place is here with me!'

'You have forfeited the right to keep me with you. Good-night, may your conscience keep you awake.'

Kendra left, closing the door quietly behind her. A crash from inside the room told her that her husband had picked up an ornament of some kind and thrown it against the wall. She walked with determined steps to a cabin a few doors away. As soon as she met the showboat she would board it, and hope for the best.

Kendra cried herself to sleep that night, but the next morning she made up her mind she would leave the boat when Pel had gone to breakfast. If he did by any chance call for her, then she would ignore his knock.

Her husband did not come for her and with the light of morning Kendra felt a reluctance to leave the security of the riverboat and plunge into the life of a strange city, a woman on her own was vulnerable to thieves and men wanting to pick someone up. Still . . . she would have to take that chance.

She put on a simple gown, so as not to attract too much attention. The bulk of her clothes would have to be left until a time when she had found somewhere to stay and could perhaps return when Pel would not be in the cabin. It would be impossible to carry with her more than her one valise. She could not afford to be driven around the city with the small amount of money she had. Her leaving passed unnoticed. There was so much activity going on she felt like a tiny cog in a vast organisation. It was easy to lose herself among bales of cotton, of tobacco, fur pelts, stacks of timber. Cattle in quayside pens were bellowing. Men were shouting orders and draymen cursed loudly at delays.

There seemed to Kendra to be miles of dockland. She passed taverns where, even at this time in the morning, men came rolling out singing bawdy songs. She skirted round these groups and averted her gaze from the painted women in doorways seeking customers. She went through narrow streets, hoping to find cheap but clean lodgings. She wanted to be as far away from the riverboat as possible, yet near enough to be able to see Lloyd Francis's showboat when it arrived.

After walking for what seemed ages and not finding any place that looked suitable, she came to a part where respectable looking women shopped in a market. She spoke to several, having eventually to put her question in French, as none had any English, but all shook their heads. There was no place they could recommend. Then an elderly woman came after her. She knew of a widow who might help, and gave Kendra directions. Which took her in a half-circle part of the way back to the docks.

Here she was offered a small back room, poorly furnished but spotlessly clean, and having the advantage of a window that overlooked a part of the river. The woman explained the fare she could offer would be simple. Kendra gave her a sovereign in advance and the widow's thin face, which still showed signs of a recent grief, brightened. She told Kendra if there was anything she needed she had only to ask.

Kendra spent the longest day she had ever known sitting at the window. At six o'clock, her body chilled, she got under the bedcovers, but the mattress was hard and the blankets thin. She thought with longing of the boiler deck on the boat with the lovely warmth of the glowing furnaces, the comfort of the cabin.

What was Pel doing? Preparing to have

dinner then go out somewhere to play cards? He might already have gone from the boat. It would be a good time to go and fetch her clothes, as nearly all the passengers would have left after breakfast. She got up and stood at the window.

The lanterns on ships and riverboats, and the small scows bobbing on the river, gave a deceptive air of magic to the scene. Candles and lamps in the rooms of the houses would give some light to the night but there could be stretches of complete blackness where she could get lost. She would have to ask directions.

Her landlady looked worried when she knew that Kendra planned to go out. It would be unsafe, sailors and riverboat men were always looking for an unaccompanied woman. Would Kendra accept the protection of her sixteen-year-old son? Although young he was capable. Kendra thought it advisable to accept.

Maurice was big for his age, broad-shouldered. He was polite but a youthful interest in the situation showed in his eyes.

Kendra was reluctant to explain her business, yet knew she would have to give a brief explanation of her reason for going to the riverboat. She said she had left her husband, they had had differences, and she wanted to collect her dresses. Maurice nodded his head as though understanding every aspect of marital upset. He said one of his uncles had an eye for

213

the ladies and that his father had drank and kept his mother short of money.

When they did come to stretches of blackness in the streets Maurice led her with confidence and Kendra thought of Mr Cartwright talking about piloting the boat in the blackness of the night, and saying one sensed something ahead and added one had to know the shape of the river to feel at ease.

Kendra felt at ease with Maurice 'piloting' her until they were nearing the dock area and she caught a whiff of cigar smoke. Although the saloon on the riverboat always held the smell of cigars she had come to associate them with Bo Burford, and felt a stab of fear.

She told herself she was being foolish, it was not likely that Bo Burford would be in this part of the city, but the feeling persisted. At last she could not resist looking back—and saw the red glow of a cigar. She stopped and the person smoking the cigar stopped. Kendra's heart began to race. She whispered to Maurice that she thought they were being followed and he said, an excitement at the intrigue of it in his voice, 'Your husband perhaps, Madame?'

'No, a man I hate. He has pestered me. I must get away.'

'At once, Madame, this way, I shall see you safe.'

Maurice had Kendra from one street to the other and along alleyways with such haste she had eventually to beg him to stop to catch her breath. After peering around a corner Maurice announced with triumph they had lost their follower, adding he would get her safely to the riverboat.

Which he did, but it was not to say Kendra felt completely at ease. Pel could be in the cabin. It was unlikely, yet life had taught her to be prepared for the unexpected.

But she was not prepared when she opened the cabin door to see Eleanor Lamartine standing in front of the mirror, eyeing her reflection. Anger gave Kendra voice.

'What are *you* doing here?' she demanded.

Eleanor turned slowly and the first thing Kendra noticed about her was the emerald brooch pinned to her deep blue satin gown.

'Waiting for Mr Devereux. What are you doing? I thought you had left him.'

The palms of Kendra's hands were sweating. Sweat trickled between her shoulder blades. The other woman looked cool and poised.

Eleanor Lamartine fingered the brooch. 'In my opinion a woman who leaves her husband is less than nothing.'

Kendra, although boiling, met the insolent stare unwavering.

'But do you have a right to an opinion, Miss Lamartine? After all, when a woman of your age has not yet *found* herself a husband—'

The shaft struck home, the shapely mouth tightened. 'It is not for the want of being asked in marriage. My suitors are too numerous to mention. It is simply that I happen to be selective.'

'In that case I would advise you not to wait too long. Your particular kind of beauty fades after a certain age.'

Kendra would not have believed herself capable of making such a cruel remark, yet found a great satisfaction when she saw Eleanor's hands clench. She went to the door and opened it. 'And now, Miss Lamartine, would you please go somewhere else to wait for my husband, I have things to do.'

'With pleasure, Mrs Devereux. I shall tell him you are here and aching to see him.' She laughed. 'That should amuse him. The last person he wants to see is you.' She walked up to Kendra, eyed her up and down, said, 'You poor specimen of a wife,' and swept out.

Kendra closed the door and leaned against it, eyes closed. How could Pel have taken up with such a woman? How could he have lied about the brooch? The hurt of his lying was suddenly overlaid by the thought that he could be here any minute. She went to the wardrobe and, after packing feverishly, she left without encountering anyone who mattered.

Maurice, who was waiting at the foot of the gang-plank, had taken one valise from her and was about to take the other when she froze. Standing a short distance away was the bulky figure of Bo Burford, with the inevitable cigar between his thick lips. She had tried to tell herself earlier she had been mistaken, that it could not have been him, but now she knew it had been him following her.

'Maurice,' she said urgently, 'the man who followed us is standing over there. How can we avoid him?'

'Follow me, Madame.' This time he wove a way between cartons and bales, and drays with horses snorting, past the cattle pens where the smell of urine was overpowering, and stopped behind a massive pile of timber. 'Wait here, Madame, keep hidden, I shall return soon.'

It seemed to be only seconds before he was back. 'Come, Madame, a friend has offered to drive us home in his wagon. Put this over your head.' It was a sack.

Kendra felt she ought to laugh at such an incongruous situation, but thought grimly that being perched on the seat of a wagon which stank of fish was an indication of her finances, and was not sure whether she was willing to accept such poverty, not after having experienced the luxuries.

The next morning, when she was sitting at her window, all sorts of thoughts tormented her. Was she, as Eleanor Lamartine had so scathingly remarked, 'a poor specimen of a wife'? How would other wives have behaved? Would they have felt duty bound to stay with their husbands, even though a mistress was involved? Many wives had to accept such a situation because they had no place to go, but if they could get away, as she had done—?

Kendra looked around her at the scrubbed bare boards, the small threadbare rug, the rickety washstand, and knew panic. She was living in poverty now, so what would happen when her money ran out—that is if the showboat did not arrive? She had only presumed it travelled between here and New Orleans. Maurice said he had seen showboats, but not often and had no idea if one of them had been the *Marie Louise*.

What if Bo Burford had had her followed, knew the conditions she was living in and was waiting until her money ran out? This was one reason why Kendra was afraid to venture out in daylight. She would only leave the house when she knew that the Marie Louise had arrived. Maurice said he would let her know if it docked.

By the evening Kendra was frantic with worry and indecision. Pel would be leaving on the riverboat. Was she to accept he had a mistress and ask him to have her back on those conditions, or take the risk of waiting for Lloyd Francis? It occurred to Kendra then there was more than one risk attached to the waiting. He might not be able to offer her a job singing on the showboat. He might even have lost his half-share in the boat. What was she to do? If the worst came to the worst she could earn her living by—No, Kendra covered her face. Not that. It was more abhorrent than the thought of

218

sinking her pride and asking her husband to take her back, and living with him knowing he was making love to Eleanor Lamartine. She straightened. She would wait, take her chance.

During the next two days Kendra helped Maurice's mother with some embroidery, which she did for a living, as well as washing up in a tavern during the early hours. Maurice did casual labour on the docks. He was always full of news and although it was not important to Kendra she looked forward to him coming to talk to her in the evening.

From where she sat at the window she could see only the bend in the river and the lovely forest land, but there was a constant moving of craft of all kinds. She was always hopefully listening for the music of the calliope, but all she heard were whistles, and blasts from smoke stacks.

Kendra was beginning to despair of ever seeing the *Marie Louise* when Maurice came bounding up the stairs one evening and announced that friends of his had seen the showboat. It was way up river and would not be coming to St Louis, but if Kendra wished, his friends would take her to it on their boat. They were leaving at five o'clock the next morning.

Kendra felt no excitement, only relief she was going to do something at last. If Lloyd Francis was not on the boat then she would have to take some other course. She said, 'Thank you, Maurice, I would be pleased to

219

accept the offer of your friends.'

The fact of leaving at such an early hour gave Kendra confidence that even if Bo Burford was still in St Louis he was not likely to be out searching for her at that time in the morning.

She said goodbye to Maurice's mother that night and gave her another sovereign, which the woman tried to refuse, saying she had been paid enough. Kendra insisted on her taking it, thanked her for her kindness, and was told if she wanted to return, the room would be ready for her. At least, Kendra thought, she would have an anchor if anything went wrong.

The morning was grey and chill with a mist that hung over the river and shrouded the masts and twin stacks of riverboats. They did not go right on to the dockside, but turned left where Maurice said his friends would be moored.

She had not thought of the kind of craft she would be travelling on and was surprised and much disconcerted to find it a large raft on which a husband, wife and their four young children lived. They were itinerant tinkers who sold and mended pots and pans, spending most of their lives on their raft plying the river's two thousand miles. They were quite a pleasant couple, reasonably clean, but Kendra was appalled that people could live on such a craft and sleep under what could only be described as canvas-covered tents. Maurice actually envied his friends their way of life. But then he was young, to him it would spell adventure. To Kendra it was discomfort, having to sit on two or three sacks, praying the journey would not take long.

They were on the river all day and moored at six o'clock because of deluging rain. 'In the morning we leave early,' the man said, 'then we see the showboat.' Kendra slept that night between the two youngest children, covered by damp blankets and with a feeling she was in the middle of a nightmare. If the people had not been Maurice's friends she would not have expected to reach the showboat.

They were all awake and up at five o'clock, with Kendra stiff and aching in every limb. The woman drew water up from the river to make coffee. Kendra had seen water from the river, it was so muddy she had heard one man describe it as 'food and drink'. The brewed coffee had a tempting smell, Kendra felt parched and sipped it. Although the water seemed not to affect the taste she had a job not to retch as she thought of all the river life that could be in it. She took two bites of the hard bread and left the rest.

The rain had stopped but the clouds were heavy. There was a depressing greyness everywhere. They passed lovely forest land but in between she could see the shanty towns, the negroes working.

'How much further have we to go?' Kendra

asked after they had been moving for what seemed to be about three hours.

'Soon—' The man pointed ahead. 'See—'

Above some low-lying trees around a bend in the river she could see coloured pennants. They hung motionless on the morning air. At last! Kendra sat up and began tidying her hair.

Then they rounded the bend and there was the *Marie Louise*, all of it beautifully painted now. It had a yellow wheelhouse, blue twin stacks, a white fretwork of balconies and decorations, and a colourful country scene painted on the nearest paddle wheel. Kendra then caught a glimpse of copper-coloured hair and her spirits lifted. It could only be Lloyd Francis. It had to be! She suddenly felt a warm glow as though she had come home.

But it was not the American . . . it was one of the players. 'Mr Francis left the boat five days ago,' he said. 'The new owner is aboard, would you care to see him—oh, here he is now.'

Kendra stood, frozen, staring at the man who was coming towards her. He stopped, eyed her from head to foot, his gaze lingering on her bosom. Then he took his cigar from his mouth, tapped off the ash and grinned.

'Good-morning, Mrs Devereux. I had a feeling we would be meeting again soon. Welcome aboard. Are you intending to stay?'

Kendra glanced over the side and saw the poverty, the dregs of coffee in the pan, the crusts she had left, she thought of the house in

222

St Louis, the hard bed, the thin blankets, the cold, and looked at the man before her. Her fear of him had gone.

She called to the people on the raft, 'Yes, everything is fine, thank you. Catch—' and she dropped her last sovereign onto the middle of a blanket. She then turned to the waiting man.

'Yes, Mr Burford, I am intending to stay.'

'Good, let us go and have a drink.'

CHAPTER TEN

Bo Burford took Kendra to a small cabin, which had been made into an office. He poured her a brandy but she shook her head and waved it away. He thrust it at her. 'Drink it, you look like death.'

She took a gulp and choked on it. It brought tears to her eyes, but she could feel the warmth of the spirit spreading over her body.

'What happened to Lloyd Francis, and what happened to my husband's half-share of the boat?'

'I won both halves in one game. The American's a fool. Reckless.' He guffawed. 'You should have seen his face when he realised he was cleaned out. I half expected him to produce a pistol and blow out his brains.'

'You seem to find that amusing,' Kendra said

coldly. 'I hope you are in that same position yourself some day.'

Burford tossed back the contents of his glass and poured himself another brandy. 'No, my dear Mrs Devereux, I have more sense. I shall always have a reserve. I would never, ever be as poor again as I was as a child.'

Kendra looked at him with interest and waited, but he did not enlarge on his life.

'You had better get tidied up,' he said, 'then I shall introduce you to the players. Oh, just a minute, Hannah will be opening up the box office, she'll need change. I'll come back for you.' He unlocked a safe, took out some bags and left.

When the door closed behind him reaction set in with Kendra. A wave of misery and despair swept over her. What was she doing here with a man she hated?

Kendra suddenly acknowledged the hopelessness of wishing. Pel had lied to her about the brooch, had treated her in a disparaging way by putting her up as collateral in the card game. The only time he would miss her was if he were on a losing streak. Perhaps he was already if he had lost his share in this boat. And poor Lloyd Francis. If only he had been here and she could have talked with him.

The sound of the calliope broke into her thoughts, startling her. Then she was sitting up, listening. The gaiety of the music had her first tapping her fingers, and then her toes. Her spirits lifted. At least she was better off here where there was some life instead of sitting chilled and miserable in her lodgings at St Louis.

Burford opened the door. 'Come along—'

When Kendra went out on deck she found herself reliving the scene that Lloyd Francis had described to her. People were coming across the levee in streams, struggling down the bank which had been churned to mud by the rain, then stepping onto a part strewn with cinders before going on to the boat, to book their seats for the evening performance. 'Come on,' Burford urged.

'Please, just a moment.'

There were many poor people, their cents clutched in their hands, as Lloyd had described, but there were also people who could be farm owners, storekeepers, clerks, and so on.

'Folks come from all over, from up and down the river,' Burford said, 'on horseback, in buggies, in wagons—'

'Why doesn't the boat go into St Louis?'

'The tax is too high. We can get as big an audience as we want stopping at the smaller places.' Burford put a hand firmly under her elbow and urged her forward.

To the left of double doors that led into the theatre was a small box office where a woman with auburn hair was dealing with the tickets. Burford gave her a nod, said he would see her later and pushed open the doors, holding them

225

for Kendra to go through.

She remembered coming through them with Lloyd Francis, going up the staircase that led to the balcony and upper boxes, remembered the smell of greasepaint. The theatre spread out below her with its tiered seats. She stopped as she saw a group of people on stage. 'They're rehearsing,' Burford said, 'this way.'

The players were standing in a tableau then a deep, resonant voice that came from a tall, attractive man said, 'Begone wench—' to a pretty fair-haired girl who cowered, hands raised in front of her face.

Burford chuckled. 'A lot of balderdash but the audience love it. Some of them have never seen a show before, they live it, cry over it, feel pain. I bet they die a thousand deaths when the heroine is threatened with a "fate worse than death".' He opened a door leading from the balcony. 'In here.'

The room was large and held a tester bed. Although the furnishings were adequate they lacked the luxury of the cabin on the riverboat.

Burford motioned her to a chair. 'Another drink?'

'No, thank you.' Kendra pressed her palms together. 'Mr Burford, when I agreed to stay on board the boat this morning I accepted the conditions I felt your invitation implied, but I want you to know I do not consider my stay to be a permanent one.'

His eyes narrowed. 'It will be permanent as

226

long as I want it to be. You'll have to stay, you haven't any money. You didn't come all the way on an itinerant raft to see the show. You threw away a sovereign, but I would like to bet it was your last. I know your finances, know where you were staying in St Louis. I knew that Lloyd Francis offered you a job singing—'

'He told you?'

'I hear these things.' Burford took a cigar from a carved oak box, clipped it and lit it. 'You can sing your heart out if you want to, but you'll not be paid. You'll get fed and clothed—'

Kendra said wryly, 'Fed and clothed—you put me in the category of a slave.'

'That's all women are to me.' Burford's mean little eyes went to Kendra's breasts. 'Don't get any big ideas that you own me, Ma'am, because I shall be keeping you.'

'And don't get any ideas, Mr Burford, that *you* own *me* because you are giving me food and shelter. I'm fulfilling an obligation, but when I am ready to leave not you or anyone will stop me.'

He blew out a smoke ring. 'It might be interesting breaking your spirit.'

'Don't try,' Kendra retorted. 'I might end up breaking yours.'

He roared with laughter and slapped his thigh. 'By God, Kendra Devereux, I like you, I like a woman with spirit.' Then his expression altered, became mean again. 'But I warn you, don't underestimate me. I told you some time

227

ago I would have you and I've got you.'

'You've got me on your boat, Mr Burford, but I came of my own free will, and am staying of my own free will, not because you forced me to. And when I'm ready to leave I shall go.'

'We shall see, Ma'am.' He stared at her. 'Yes, we shall see. I'll leave you to get tidied up.' He heaved his bulk out of the chair. 'I'll be back, so see you're here.' There was a menace in his voice.

Kendra was not prepared to accept having Bo Burford making love to her and what she would certainly not accept from him was brutality. If he attempted it she would stick a knife in him. For a moment Kendra was shocked at the direction of her thoughts, then dismissed them. She was on her own now, she would have to become hard, put on a protective armour if she were to survive.

Later Kendra met the players and the staff in the dining room under the stage. At first they were a little wary of her, then Burford mentioned she might eventually be doing a song in the concert after the show and after that she was accepted as one of them.

When Burford was not there Kendra mentioned Lloyd Francis and they all spoke with affection for him, said how sorry they were to lose him. They said nothing about Burford, cautious no doubt, not quite knowing Kendra's relationship with him.

She had a feeling during the afternoon that

everything happening was a build-up, not towards the evening show, but towards her relationship with Bo Burford when the show was over.

There was certainly plenty of things happening. Kendra helped to repair some of the costumes and was told about the bandsmen who played at the show, and how they were in the small town advertising the plays. When the bandsmen came back at four o'clock their bright red jackets made a splash of colour in the greyness of the day. They would play on the foredeck before the show, alternating with the calliope.

The stage was being set up and there was banging and hoarse shouts. Players went from one dressing room to the other, complaining about lack of space, the dressing rooms were tiny. Then when twilight came the odd job man arrived to light the auditorium lamps. He also lit the large kerosene seachlight on top of the pilot house, whose beam probed from the river bank to the levee. Kendra felt herself caught up in the noise, the music, but was glad she would not be singing tonight, she needed time to adjust to the excitement.

Soon a number of people began to gather, adults with bare-footed children, who could not afford to buy tickets but who would draw from the colour, the warmth of the lights from the windows of the showboats, the music, the intrigue of it all.

And when at half past six the torches stuck on pikes in the ground were lit they eyed the wavering orange and scarlet flames with wonder. The flames turned the commonplace into the mysterious, and gave a beauty to thin, starved faces.

Kendra longed for Pel to be with her, to share in the delight, to know as she had done, a primitiveness in the flaring torches. She wanted him to make love to her. Then she looked around her, feeling a shame at such lascivious thoughts.

Next to come were the ticket holders, scrambling down the muddy bank, the torches casting dancing shadows over them. Once aboard, members of the crew showed them to their places.

They were a quiet, orderly crowd, who whispered among themselves. When the more wealthy came into a box all eyes swivelled again. The bandsmen began to play, the lights were lowered, the curtain rose slowly, and there was complete and utter silence.

Kendra thought she would never forget that evening, the atmosphere, the faces; it was a make-believe world they watched, but they believed in it. They longed for the black-hearted villain to get retribution, and prayed for the innocent heroine to find happiness, and applauded mightily when right triumphed over evil.

When the plays ended the audience were

informed they could stay for the concert if they paid another fifteen cents. Many of the people did stay. All the players could sing and dance or play an instrument, and when Kendra watched their performance and heard the applause she knew she would find pleasure in singing to such an appreciative audience.

Later the theatre was emptied and the people wended their way, some back to shacks, with hopefully, some of the enchantment still clinging to them. The players and crew met on the stage to have supper and to discuss the plays and their audience.

What surprised Kendra was how the players, none of them young, had shed years acting their parts, especially the fair-haired woman who not only played the part of the *ingénue* but a ten-year-old girl. Kendra, caught up in the aura of the evening, decided she was really going to like this life.

Reality came for her when Burford came up to her and jerked a thumb towards his bedroom. 'Go on, you get undressed, I'll be with you in a few minutes.'

The loudness of his voice carried above the chatter of the rest of the people and voices trailed away. All eyes were on Kendra. The woman who cooked for them shook her head sadly. Kendra, colour flooding to her cheeks, turned and left, her hands clenched at her sides. The coarse oaf, she said to herself. He was certainly determined to put her in her place. Well, she would put *him* in his place!

She waited for him, still dressed, and attacked him right away.

'Don't you dare address me in front of anyone in the way you did a few minutes ago!'

'Get your clothes off,' he said, 'and get into bed.'

Anger flared in Kendra. 'I expect to be treated with respect.'

'Treat you with respect?' He eyed her up and down. 'Who do you think you are, a crowned princess of Europe? You're the daughter of a gambler and the wife of a gambler, so don't go giving yourself airs to me. As far as I'm concerned you're just a woman I want in my bed. Don't think you can't be replaced. The golden-haired Edna is panting to take your place.'

'Then you can stop her panting. I'm leaving.' Kendra picked up her suitcase. Burford snatched it from her and flung it across the cabin.

'You owe me for the food you've had today and no man or woman gets away without paying their debts to Bo Burford! Now get undressed and get into that bed before I take a whip to your back.'

The earlier fear of Burford returned. She was without means of defending herself and would be no match against his size and brute strength. Oh, God, why had she given in so easily this morning to stay with him? She was going to pay a big price in order to have a decent standard of shelter and food in her belly.

No, she thought, she was not going to give in to him. She said, 'You were talking about your earlier life and how bad it was. Well, I had a good childhood but when my father died I felt I wanted to die.'

He leered at her. 'But you didn't.'

'No, there were debts to be paid. I took a job, a menial job with hateful people. I was shouted at, pushed about by my boss. He got one of his servants into trouble and wanted to rape me.'

Burford was concentrating on what she was saying, his eyes narrowed.

'It had been arranged that I would be paid my wages every six months. At the end of the first six months he refused to pay me. He presumed it was impossible for me to leave because he thought I had no money. I did leave and came to America.'

'But you were on dry land,' he sneered. 'Here you are on water and I can assure you there is no way you will get off this boat.'

'That's no problem. I would simply jump over the side into the water and drown myself. Oh, yes, Mr Burford, I wouldn't hesitate. I think the Lord would take better care of me than you.'

She sensed his indecision. Then he said boldly, 'You wouldn't drown yourself, I know it.'

'No, you don't know it,' she said softly. 'I would rather be out of this world than be the chattel of a brute like you. I am willing to work, scrub floors, cook, sing and do any other job that's required, but I will *not* get into your bed.'

'A very determined bitch, aren't you,' he snapped. 'Get out of here.'

Kendra, unable to grasp that she was free picked up her luggage and walked slowly to the door, not sure where she should go.

'Go on,' he yelled, 'get out, but I'll have you in my bed before long and you'll be glad to be there!'

The lights were still on outside and she walked along the deck and met the auburn-haired Hannah who said, 'Why, hello, Miss Hollis, where are you making for?'

'I'm staying, but I don't know where to sleep.'

Hannah glanced towards Burford's quarters then said, 'Oh, oh, then I think you had better share my cabin for the time being. It's not very big but you don't have much luggage. We'll manage. This way.'

Her cabin was not far from Burford's and Kendra wished she could be below deck. But, beggars could not be choosers.

The cabin was larger than she had expected and there were two bunk beds. Hannah said, 'You can have top or bottom, I'm easy.'

Kendra smiled. 'I see that the lower one is

made up so I shall have the top one.'

Hannah opened a sizeable wardrobe and moved some clothes along. 'There's room for yours. I'll make a cup of tea.' She lit a small paraffin stove and put a kettle on. 'Everything at hand.'

'Where do you get your water from?'

'One of the men brings a bucket full of water every morning.' She pulled a curtain aside. 'There we are.'

There was a washstand with a mirror above and the pail of water was underneath. The lamp light was soothing.

Kendra was beginning to feel better. 'You certainly are fully equipped.'

'I love the boats, Kendra. May I call you Kendra?'

'Of course.'

'And you know that my name is Hannah. But there, enough of names. Let us have our cup of tea.'

She talked about the boat, how many owners it had had. She worked for Mr Burford but said she had very much liked it when Lloyd Francis had won it. 'He's a real gentleman,' she lowered her voice, 'and I hope he wins it back.'

'And so do I,' Kendra said stoutly, and then they were both laughing, which was something Kendra had not done for some time.

Over their cups of tea and biscuits Hannah talked of the players and what friendly people they were. 'Mind you,' she said, lowering her

235

voice, 'they're not fond of Mr Burford, but then, unfortunately, he isn't pleasant with anyone. I think I'm the only one who understands him. Or, should I say, he thinks I'm the only one who understands him.'

'And do you?'

Hannah hesitated a moment then nodded. 'Yes, yes, I do. I've known him for a long time. But let's talk about the show. You'll enjoy it, Kendra.'

Hannah repeated what Lloyd Francis had told her, about the people clutching their cents to pay for their seats and how many of the poorest people got their pleasure by standing on the banks of the river, listening to the calliope playing and simply enjoying seeing the people, and all the lovely lights.

'I often think of all the money lost in gambling,' Hannah said sadly, 'and what that money could do for these poor people, some of them having no more than a crust of bread for that day.'

'I know. Mr Francis was telling me how he had wanted to help these people but gambling was in his blood and he had lost three fortunes.'

'You know Mr Francis?'

'He's a friend of my husband.'

'Oh, I didn't know. Have you—left your husband? Sorry, it's none of my business.'

'It's a long story,' Kendra hesitated then said, 'Hannah, you know that I sing. If by any chance I was chosen to sing outside do you

236

think that Mr Burford would let me keep what I was paid? He told me it would be his money, but that seems all wrong.'

Hannah laid her hand over Kendra's. 'Oh, dear, this is all so difficult. You see he regards you as his property.'

'But I'm not his property. I expected to find Lloyd Francis here. Mr Burford wanted to sleep with me, but I refused.'

'And he accepted it?'

'He couldn't do anything else. I told him I would rather go over the side of the boat and drown. And, I meant it. The thing is, Hannah, I have no money. I'll never sleep with him just to have my keep. But I told him I was willing to scrub floors, to cook, to sing, to do anything else, but not to—'

'Sleep with him. I admire you. Look, Kendra, I don't know whether I should tell you this, but . . . no, perhaps later.'

'If it's anything you feel you can tell me about Mr Burford I would rather know about it now.'

'Well,' there was a short hesitation then Hannah went on, 'I knew Bo when we were young. We lived in a village and our families lived close to one another. He was big then, clumsy, and found it difficult to mix with other people our age. But Bo and I got on all right together. He told me one day that he had fallen in love with a girl, but he wouldn't tell me who she was. He was eighteen and I was sixteen

237

when he told me shyly that I was the girl he loved.'

Hannah sighed. 'I was a bit of a tomboy and I teased him. I had had boys teasing me, but was afraid of letting them go too far. It had been drummed into me by my mother so many times that I was not to let any boy kiss me, or ever be alone with one. On this particular day Bo and I were in the barn, just chatting. It was something we often did and I never thought of him as anything else but a big brother.'

Hannah got up and moved around the cabin, then sat down again. 'I tempted him, asked him if he knew what couples did when they married. He nodded and said he would show me. He touched my breast first then he tried to put his hand under my dress. I panicked, but he was roused and wouldn't let me go. I tried to fight him but I was helpless against his strength. When I shouted he pushed a handkerchief into my mouth. He then stripped me and . . . raped me.' Hannah's voice dropped to a whisper.

'What happened afterwards?' Kendra asked in an awed voice.

'His father, obviously hearing me trying to scream came into the barn.'

A look of pain came over Hannah's face. 'His father yanked him away from me and taking off his belt thrashed him so brutally that Bo all but died. When he recovered his father told him that if he ever laid a hand on a girl again he would kill him.'

The look of pain turned to one of bleakness.

'Because of my curiosity I was responsible for Bo doing what he did and I hadn't the guts to admit it to anyone. You are the first person I've told about this, Kendra, and I beg you to keep it to yourself.'

'I give you my word that I shall never repeat it to anyone.'

'I think that Bo longs to be thought of as a big man, having lots of women and always boasting about having any woman he wants.'

'How is it that you are still with him?'

'Oh, I didn't see him for many years. My family moved out of the village and I was not married until I was twenty-seven. He was a decent man, not very romantic but kind and caring of me. He died ten years later and it was not long after this that Bo came back into my life.'

'Had he sought you out?'

'No, I had to work, I needed money and I had a job on a showboat when he came on it to gamble. Old Mr Francis owned it then. A lovely man. I recognised Bo at once but he didn't recognise me. I was appalled at how he had changed, big man, loud voice, vulgar. He seemed to have amazing luck, always winning. It was weeks before he eyed me one evening and said, 'I know you from somewhere.'

'I admitted who I was and hurried away, feeling so ashamed. He sought me out later and I apologised for what I had done. He bore me no grudge, he said he should have had more sense. I kept seeing him when he came to gamble. He won the showboat and old Mr Francis died and his son took over. Then Lloyd won the showboat and I went from one showboat to another, looking after staff. Bo kept seeking me out, he always seemed pleased to see me and eventually he asked me if I would work for him, to look after his affairs and I agreed.'

'So how long have you worked for him?'

'Three years and I don't really know anything of his private life. What are your plans, Kendra?'

'I did think if I could get the chance to sing and someone was interested in me I might get the opportunity to get away.'

'I could speak to Mr Waterson for you. He deals with all the turns. He arranges rehearsals. He was saying today that he was a turn short. Someone had suddenly taken ill.'

'Would you, Hannah? I would be so grateful. I only hope it won't put you in Mr Burford's bad books.'

'No problem. It's part of my job. The trouble is getting money for you. Bo will have his sights on your contract.'

'We'll take it step by step.'

* * *

When she was in bed Kendra felt an

unbearable longing to have Pel's arms around her. Were his arms around Eleanor Lamartine, or was he sitting poker-faced in a card game? Eleanor might learn that cards took precedence in Pel's life. They did in any gambler's life.

There was so much crowding of thoughts in Kendra's brain she thought she would never be able to sleep, but she slept heavily and it was Hannah who roused her the next morning at half-past seven.

'Mr Burford dropped a note under my door, asking if I could go a little earlier for breakfast. He says he has some business to discuss. Breakfast starts at eight o'clock. I'll see if I can have a word with Mr Waterson. See you later.'

Kendra had felt a dryness in her throat when she first awakened, but by the time she had washed and dressed there was a definite rawness. Not a sore throat, she thought in despair, not when she hoped to sing that night.

She was at the door ready to leave when cold shivers began to chase up and down her spine. She went back for a shawl, but had hardly drawn it close around her when she felt as though her body were being consumed by fire. Oh, heavens, a chill, stemming no doubt from sitting shivering in her room at her lodgings, and culminating after travelling on the raft, lying on damp sacks, covered by damp blankets. What was she to do? A sick woman was the last thing Burford would want on the boat. Perhaps after a cup of something hot—she would have to pretend to be feeling all right.

There was nothing to help Kendra put on an act of brightness. When she came out of the room onto the balcony, the theatre, in the dimness, had a desolate, depressing air. She made her way down to the door that led under the stage. Before she reached it she could hear chatter and small bursts of laughter, smell coffee, and bacon cooking.

When she opened the door the volume of sound increased.

Most of the people were seated at a long table, at a smaller one sat Burford with the auburn-haired Hannah and two men. At the big, black stove the wife of the odd job man, who cooked for all of them, was handing a plate of food to Cal Caley, the tall, attractive man who played the part of the hero. This morning he looked to be fifty.

In spite of the concentration of talk Kendra was noticed and welcomed. Burford, seeing her, raised his hand, beckoning her. It was the pilot of the boat who drew out a chair for her. The other man acknowledged her with a brief smile and resumed what he had been saying to Burford.

Hannah said to Kendra, laughing, 'Just in time, another minute and all the food would have been gobbled up, we're a hungry lot. Did you—' She paused and added in concern, 'Are

242

you all right, Kendra? You're shivering.'

'Yes, I'm fine. I just felt a little chilly coming out in the morning air.'

'Good. I'll see Mr Waterson after breakfast. Excuse us for a few minutes will you?'

The other people at the table were interested in her and pleased that she might be singing that evening. 'We'll all give you a good clap,' one man said laughing.

A woman remarked smiling, 'You have a lovely speaking voice. I'm sure you'll pass Mr Waterson's test.'

Kendra began to feel a little better again. If only she could get Mr Waterson's approval and sing tonight she might get some money and leave the boat.

They had just finished breakfast when Hannah said, 'Ah, here is the gentleman we want.'

Mr Waterson was a tubby man, with a serious expression. Hannah introduced Kendra and asked if it was possible for her to have a rehearsal.

'Yes, of course. Are you free now, Miss Hollis?'

Kendra replied she was, and he called across the room. 'Maurice, the piano, please.'

A young man came hurrying over, sat down at the keyboard and ran up and down the scales. Mr Waterson turned to Kendra. 'Have you a favourite song, Miss Hollis?'

'No . . . I mean yes. Sorry, I like
243

"Greensleeves".'

'A good choice.'

Kendra had been taken aback, thinking he would have heard her in a quiet room. Then, common sense took over. With a bit of luck she could be singing in front of several hundred people this evening.

The pianist played the introduction then Mr Waterson gave her a nod, and Kendra sang the first verse in a low voice. When she glanced at Mr Waterson, however, she saw he was frowning. There had to be a change, so she raised her voice for the second verse, and this time he was smiling.

'Splendid, Miss Hollis. You pass with honours. You'll sing in the theatre this evening.'

Relief flooded over her. 'Oh, thank you, thank you very much.'

There was a great deal of clapping and a number of the other artists came and congratulated her.

One man said, 'With a voice like that, Miss Hollis, you'll get to the top.'

Mr Burford came up, a broad grin on his face. 'See you don't let me down tonight.'

Hannah took Kendra's arm and said in a low voice, 'Let's get back to my room. You're flushed.'

Kendra had not realised until now how hot she was.

Back in the cabin Hannah took two pills

from a box. 'They're for a fever. Here, take them then I'll mix you something for a gargle.'

She mixed a small quantity of salt and boric acid and put some water on to warm.

Kendra said, 'My throat isn't sore any more.'

'It could be. You'll gargle and keep on gargling and I'll give you some more tablets later. You must rest this afternoon. We must have you right for this evening. You really do have a beautiful voice. Oh, pray heaven there's someone in the theatre this evening who's looking for talent like yours.'

'I pray heaven I get some money.'

'Don't worry about that. Just keep well.'

CHAPTER ELEVEN

Kendra felt better for the rest and her pills and gargling, but the minute she walked on to the stage that evening she lost all her confidence. Heavens above, she was about to sing to an audience of eight hundred people. She would never do it.

The orchestra was playing the introduction and all she could see was a blur of faces.

When she did start to sing her voice was practically non-existent. Then suddenly she thought of all the poor people who had saved their cents for this occasion, and she was preventing them from enjoying her song.

She straightened her shoulders and sang 'Greensleeves', throwing her voice and feeling emotional.

There was a short silence when she had finished then a burst of applause and cries of 'Bravo!'

When they allowed her to leave the stage the people backstage crowded around.

Where had she learned to sing? Had she been in theatre before? What an asset she would be to the company.

Two middle-aged, well dressed men asked Kendra if she would be interested in singing in private houses in New Orleans.

Mr Burford came up and, pushing Kendra aside said, 'I am the young lady's agent. Would you please come to the privacy of my office, gentlemen?'

One of the men looked enquiringly at Kendra, but Mr Burford urged him on. 'This way, please.'

Kendra was furious and when she started to complain Hannah said, 'Let's get back to the cabin.'

On the way there Kendra vowed that she would not sing unless she was paid. 'Why should he have the money? I am the one working. I agreed that I would work, cook, sing and—' She paused. 'Sing? I said that, didn't I? Oh, he couldn't keep my pay.'

'Now calm down and we'll discuss it.'

In the cabin Hannah said, 'You haven't

signed anything to say you are apprenticed to Bo. I think the men would want you to be there. The men are not theatre people, they want you to sing in big houses. Sit down and I'll make some cocoa.'

Before the cocoa was made Burford was back and fuming. 'They wanted you there to sign and I told them I would contact them when we arrived in New Orleans. There are plenty of other people who will want you and who won't be bothered whether you sign or not.'

'But I do mind and I can tell you now that I want to be paid.'

'You belong to me and I tell you that you won't get a penny. You are my property.'

Property . . . that was how he saw her. It was then that Kendra decided she must get off this boat and the sooner the better. She turned her back to him. 'There's no more to be said.'

'No, there isn't, is there? When you leave here it will be with my permission. I'll see you in the morning.'

Kendra was astonished to realise that he had taken it that she had given in. Well, he would soon know differently. There were opportunities outside for her. She was prepared to leave the boat without any money.

When Burford had gone Hannah said, 'Don't worry, I'll help you to get away and I can direct you to a friend of mine where you can stay. I'll lend you some money. I'll also try and find out where these two men live.'

'Oh, Hannah, you're so good to me.' She burst into tears.

Hannah put her arms around her. 'You've had a raw deal, but don't forget that Bo had one too, when he was younger. I can't help but feel sorry for him.'

By the following morning Kendra had made her plans. After breakfast she would slip away to have a look in Burford's office and see if she could find the address of the two men. She didn't want Hannah to be too involved in getting her away. She had a living to earn.

Burford was very affable when she entered the dining room. 'Ah, good-morning, Kendra. Come and enjoy your breakfast. Everyone is talking about you.'

She found herself being congratulated from all sides, and managed to smile and thank everyone. Hannah smiled too, but said nothing. Always she and Burford would sit after breakfast with two other men, going over certain papers. When Kendra had finished her breakfast she was able to excuse herself quite easily. At the time Burford was having a heated discussion with one of the men, so Kendra was sure he hadn't even noticed she was leaving.

Her heart was beating wildly as she went into his office and began searching his desk. As everything seemed very orderly it was difficult to know where to start.

There was a filing cabinet and she had gone through the drawers without finding anything of interest. She pulled out one of the desk drawers and found a small leather bag with money in it. Dollars, dare she take some?

It was then she felt a draught. She had not heard any movement but when she looked towards the door she went rigid with shock as she saw Burford, an evil look on his face, a leather belt clutched in his hand.

He advanced slowly, menace in every step. 'So, what were you looking for, Miss Hollis? Money, was it, I wondered who had been robbing me.'

Kendra still had the bag in her hand, and shock had made her unable to speak. She shook her head, and as he moved closer she said, 'No, I haven't robbed you. I haven't touched any of your money.'

Another step forward. 'You know what happens to *Nigres* who steal, don't you? They get beaten.'

Kendra backed away. 'But I haven't stolen anything.'

'And I know you have.'

He raised the belt and she shouted, 'Don't you dare touch me, you—you impotent oaf.'

The florid colour in Burford's face receded for a moment then came flooding back. 'Why you—' He seized her, caught hold of her blouse and ripped it from her. The belt cut across her shoulders. Kendra screamed and getting out of his grasp she ran to the other side of the room, knocking over small tables and a chair on the way. Then, finding herself trapped in a corner she put up her hands to ward off further blows. He knocked her hands aside and the leather cut across her shoulders several times. She screamed and kept on screaming. As he raised his arm again she managed to duck under it and make for the door. But before she reached it he struck her again.

There was movement on the boat, footsteps running. A man's voice shouted, 'What's going on?' Then someone else hammered on the door calling, 'Burford, for God's sake.'

Kendra shouted, 'The door's open.'

Several men rushed in, grabbing Burford, overpowering him. Kendra sank to the floor, sobbing. It was Hannah who drew her to her feet, who soothed her. She draped a blanket around her. 'Come with me, Kendra.'

Hannah took her to her cabin, rubbed ointment into the weals on Kendra's back and shoulders. Kendra winced, tensing her body against the pain, but her sobs had subsided.

Someone handed in a cup of strong coffee then left. Hannah held it out to Kendra. 'Drink it up, it will make you feel better. When you've finished, it might help to talk, if you don't want to, it's all right.'

Kendra wrapped her hands around the cup, grateful for even that small area of warmth. 'I was looking for the address of the two men. Burford accused me of stealing from him. I wasn't.' She paused. 'I—I called him an . . .

250

impotent oaf. It was a dreadful thing to say to any man.'

Hannah nodded slowly. 'Especially to Bo, because it was not his fault.'

Seeing the pain in her eyes made Kendra realise that her own pain would ease in time, but with Hannah it would always be there.

'Well, he will soon find himself another woman. There will always be another woman. Now, Kendra, you must stay in bed for a day or two, then we must think what to do. I'll see you later.' She dropped a kiss on her brow.

Kendra lay on her stomach to ease the pain and when Hannah came in later she was able to say she felt a little better. She asked hesitantly after Burford and Hannah said, 'Very subdued. He had his lunch in the office. He refuses to speak to me. I did think if you were well enough tomorrow we could get you away from here. Two of the men will bring a carriage. I was thinking I might . . . well, go with you.'

'I would love to have you with me, Hannah. But do you really want to go? I think that Mr Burford depends on you.'

She sighed. 'I know. I'll make up my mind by tomorrow.'

The next morning Hannah said, 'A man will come with a carriage in half an hour. Do you think you can make it? I've packed your clothes. We'll go to a friend who will give you your breakfast and look after you. I'll decide what to do about leaving Bo later.'

251

To Kendra's relief she and Hannah were ashore and in a carriage without setting eyes on Bo Burford. The relief even made her forget her pain for a while, but the rubbing of her dress on the weals and the jolting of the carriage caused her such agony she had to bite on her lower lip to stop herself from crying out. And she was glad to be able to take off the weight of her cloak when she got to her lodgings. These lodgings at least were comfortable.

Hannah promised to come back that afternoon to let Kendra know how Bo Burford had taken the news of her leaving, but she was back at midday and greatly agitated.

'Oh, Kendra, something dreadful has happened. Bo, with a gang of ruffians, has been on your husband's boat and smashed it up. Your husband has been hurt, but I don't know how badly.'

Kendra struggled to her feet. Pel, here? Had he come to see her? Or, was Eleanor Lamartine with him?

She said, 'I must go to him. Where is the boat docked?'

'Lloyd Francis knows. He's here, waiting to know if you are well enough to go and see him.'

'Of course I am.'

Hannah went to get her cloak for her.

Kendra, for some reason, felt no surprise that Lloyd should be on the spot to help her. He took both her hands in his. 'Mrs Devereux,

252

I'm very sorry to be the bearer of such bad news, but felt sure you would want to know that your husband was hurt.'

They drove immediately to Pel's boat which was moored further down river, with Lloyd explaining to Kendra he had heard about the card game and about her leaving Pel. He did not say he knew she had gone with Bo Burford to the showboat, but of course he must have known for him to have sought her there.

'Were you on Pel's boat?' she asked.

'No, I was staying in New Orleans. I heard about the damage to the boat, and that Pel had been hurt.' He paused and laid a hand on hers. 'Try not to worry too much, Kendra, Pel is strong, and would hold his own with any man.'

'With one man, yes, or even two, but not against a crowd of ruffians.' She stared straight ahead. They had left the busy thoroughfare and were driving beside forest land. It was a peaceful scene. She usually felt a sense of peace with Lloyd Francis, but the lingering pain of her beating and the worry of Pel had her emotions in a turmoil. She would like to have known if Eleanor Lamartine had been on the boat, but would not ask.

When at last they glimpsed the boat a wave of anger swept over Kendra. Such wanton destruction! All the beautiful and intricate fretwork smashed, the blue and white striped awning ripped into shreds, the painting on a paddle wheel hacked at with an axe, deck chairs smashed up. The only people on board seemed to be workmen and crew. Mr Cartwright, seeing them get out of the carriage, was waiting for them at the top of the gangplank.

'Mrs Devereux—a sorry business, yes indeed.'

'My husband, how is he?'

'Well now,' the pilot rubbed his chin, looking embarrassed. 'You see it's like this, your husband needed a doctor and Miss Lamartine—well, she had him taken to her home.'

'A doctor? Mr Cartwright, how badly hurt is my husband?' Kendra's alarm was tinged with hurt that Eleanor Lamartine had taken charge of him.

'I don't rightly know, Ma'am.' The pilot's manner was distinctively evasive. 'Burford's men had clubs. There was a lot of them. Our men and men from the other boats came and fought them off. There were plenty of bruised heads. Burford didn't suffer none, he left.'

Any sympathy Kendra had felt earlier for Burford had gone. She said, 'I hope Bo Burford rots in hell, and may God forgive me for saying such a thing.'

'There's many as thinks the same, Mrs Devereux, and if any of this battered lot lay their hands on him, well, I wouldn't be answerable for the consequences. Come and see what the fiends have done below.'

Kendra was appalled at the destruction. The saloon was a shambles, beautifully polished tables hacked, chairs broken, pictures and curtains slashed. The cabins had come in for the same treatment, in the kitchen the broken crockery and crystal covered the floor.

Lloyd Francis said through clenched teeth, 'Hanging's too good for men who behave in this way.'

Kendra, her mind suddenly made up said, 'Lloyd, I want to see my husband. Would you take me to the Lamartine plantation?'

'Are you sure you want to go, Kendra?' His blue eyes were troubled. 'Eleanor will not welcome you, she may refuse to allow you to see him.'

Mr Cartwright said, 'If they'll not let you see your husband, Ma'am, you come back here. There's a hundred or more men spoiling for a fight, wanting their revenge. You will see him, I promise.'

'And I shall take you,' Lloyd said.

It was quite a long drive to the Lamartine plantation. During it Lloyd talked about his foolishness in losing his share in the showboat, and how grieved he had been. 'But there,' he said, 'I am the only one to blame. Since losing it my luck has been good, how long it will last remains in the lap of the gods.'

Kendra asked how her husband had fared at cards, and was told he had had a fantastic run of luck, unfortunate he had run into this trouble with Burford. Kendra experienced a pang of disappointment that she was not Pel's good luck charm after all.

They had left the forest and come to where the land had been shorn of timber and there was a continuing line of sugar plantations. On some were rows of wretched looking huts where the slaves lived. On others the huts were whitewashed, showing that these slaves had more caring masters. At least, this was the impression it gave.

Lloyd, as though aware of Kendra's thoughts, said, 'One of these days things will change. There's a great deal of unrest at the present time, and it could even lead to civil war.'

'Oh, surely not. Where would the slaves go? These are the only homes they have known.'

But Lloyd still looked grim, and talked further about the threat of war.

Pel had said he did not like the Lamartine house, but although it was not so elegant as some of the colonial type houses with their graceful columns, Kendra thought the Lamartine house impressive enough. Lloyd had pointed it out from a distance, but once they drew nearer it became hidden from view by a thick belt of trees.

There was a sweeping drive and as they rode along it Kendra felt a weakness in her limbs. She was still determined to see Pel, but was not looking forward to an encounter with Eleanor.

They were out of the carriage and a negro boy had come running to take the reins when Kendra turned as she heard the raised voice of a woman, a note of hysteria in her voice. And then she witnessed one of the reasons why slaves were rebelling.

Eleanor Lamartine was lashing the bare back of a negro youth with a many thonged short-handled whip. The boy, his hands tied to a post, uttered not a sound. Eleanor was doing the screaming.

'You did it on purpose! You'll pay for making a fool of me, you dirty, rotten bastard!'

Lloyd, without a word strode over and snatched the whip from her. Eleanor was so taken aback that for a moment she stood staring at him. Then she shouted, 'How dare you, how dare you interfere between me and my slaves. Get out of here!' Then, catching sight of Kendra she added, 'And take your woman with you! I don't know how either of you have the effrontery to come on to my property without permission.'

Kendra had difficulty in keeping her temper under control. 'I want to see my husband, Miss Lamartine, and whether I am on your property or not I am determined to see him. I shall not leave here until I do.'

Eleanor's lips tightened and her green eyes blazed. Even in the ugliness of rage there was a certain beauty about her.

'You will get off this land or I shall have you

thrown off. Did you really expect your husband to want to see you after you were responsible for his injuries, and the damage on his boat?'

'I was not responsible,' Kendra protested. 'How could I be?'

'You went off with Bo Burford, didn't you? If you had stayed with your husband, like any other sensible wife would have done, none of the trouble would have happened.'

'Sensible or not,' Kendra retorted, 'I am still Pel's wife and have more right to see him than you, who are only his mistress.'

Eleanor Lamartine slapped Kendra hard across the cheek, and would have struck her again had not Lloyd, who had been untying the slave, stayed her hand.

'I am not his mistress! I don't give my body to men, not as you did to Bo Burford, and don't tell me you didn't, because I know all the string of women he's had.'

'You know nothing about *me*, Miss Lamartine,' Kendra said, forcing herself to speak calmly, 'nor do you know anything really about Bo Burford. And I would say you know less about my husband if you think you can hold him. I will add one more thing. If you do not let me see him now, I shall see him sometime later. A hundred angry riverboat men are waiting to make sure I do.'

Eleanor's rage died. She stared at Kendra, trying to weigh up if this could be true, and how far she could go in getting rid of her unwanted

258

guests. At last she said, 'I shall speak to my father. And remember this, we own five hundred slaves, all ready to fight for us.'

Lloyd said, his eyebrows raised, 'Do you really believe that, Miss Lamartine, after your exhibition of a few moments ago? If war comes, and believe me it is imminent, you had better be prepared for having the same treatment meted out to you.'

'What nonsense.' Her expression was derisive but her words lacked conviction. She turned away. 'I will find my father.'

There was an arrogance in the way Eleanor walked towards the house, her head up, an elegance in the grey silk gown with its full skirts. Her hair was like polished ebony in the thin sunlight.

It seemed only seconds later that a servant came out and invited them inside. Mr Lamartine, a tall, thin-faced man, greeted them civilly, but with a coldness in his voice.

'Mrs Devereux, Mr Francis.' He gave both a brief bow then said to Kendra, 'I understand you wish to see your husband, Mrs Devereux. I can understand you wanting to see him, but I do object to you threatening my daughter with violence if you were not granted permission.'

Lloyd stepped forward. 'If I may be permitted to speak, Mr Lamartine. There was no threat of violence to your daughter, but I would point out that many angry men are determined that Mrs Devereux shall have the right to see her husband. Your daughter ordered us off your land.'

'Because you interfered when she disciplined one of our slaves. That is not your business, you had no right to interfere.'

'I interfered because I saw the incident that brought the punishment to the youth and I thought it unjustified and excessive. The youth, who was carrying a bowl of water slipped and a few drops splashed on to your daughter's gown.'

'That is not what my daughter told me, but as I did not witness the incident myself—' Lamartine raised his shoulders. 'The more important issue is Mr Devereux. It is essential he has rest and this is doctor's orders. He has had a very rough time.'

Lamartine's voice was less cold. Kendra took advantage of it.

'Yes, so I understand. If you think it would be unwise to see him today, would you allow me to see him tomorrow? I hate to intrude on your privacy, but the circumstances being what they are—'

'If you will wait one moment, I will see your husband myself, please take a seat.'

When he had gone into one of the downstairs rooms leading from the hall Lloyd and Kendra exchanged glances, both were smiling.

There was a murmur of voices for a few moments then Mr Lamartine came out and said that Mr Devereux would see them both. He added it would be unwise to tire the patient.

Pel lay on a day bed in front of a window, propped up by a mass of pillows. Kendra gasped when she saw him. His face was swollen out of all recognition and already showing signs of purple bruising. His right leg, in wooden splints, was resting on a cushion.

'Oh, Pel, oh my dear,' she said, forgetting she had forfeited the right to endearments. 'What have they done to you!'

Although his eyes were almost lost in the puffed mounds of flesh around them Kendra could detect a glint of anger in them.

'I have you to thank for my condition.' The words were thick.

'Pel, what are you saying? I had nothing to do with it. I knew nothing about it until Lloyd told me.'

'You left me to go off with Burford, didn't you? Well go back to him, you can tell him how I look and you can have a good laugh.'

'Pel, that is not fair.'

Lloyd said, 'You are doing Kendra an injustice, Devereux. She's not with Burford.'

'Oh, so she's living with you now, is she?'

Lloyd's hands clenched. Kendra laid a hand on his arm. 'It's no use, we had better go.' She turned to her husband. 'I hope, no matter what you think of me, that you will soon be well again.'

Lloyd commiserated with her as they walked

back to the carriage. 'I'm sorry, Kendra, it was terrible for you. You must have felt very hurt. It will not be easy for you to make allowances for your husband's behaviour, but if you think of the physical hurt he has suffered and, having his boat wrecked, it might help. I also think it a good thing that the Lamartines took him away from all the destruction.'

'Eleanor took him away,' Kendra replied stiffly. 'Pel became—friendly with her. I was perhaps foolish to leave him, but I felt so affronted, I had to get away. And now I know he has no wish to see me ever again, so I must start trying to make a new life for myself. I have the address of a man who offered me engagements to sing in private houses.'

Lloyd said he could be of help to her, as he had many friends in New Orleans.

* * *

A completely new life started for Kendra. She had had a touch of freedom when she left the showboat earlier, but it was nothing to knowing that she was now her own boss. Lloyd had found the two men who had called on the night she sang in the theatre and he had seen that the contracts were correct and she was well paid.

He had smiled and said, 'You are on your own now, Kendra. But if you ever need any advice you have only to ask.'

'I will and thanks for all you've done for me.'

262

She had a small apartment at first, wanting to save some money, not knowing how long her success would last.

Her appointments were at some beautiful houses and each time she sang she was asked by someone at that house if she would come and sing for them. Kendra never refused a request.

She had written a long letter to Hannah and had a short letter back saying she had left the showboat. She was delighted to know that Kendra was doing well and when she was settled she would write a longer letter to her. At the moment she was in lodgings. A long story, but she found it impossible to stay with Bo after what he had done to Pel's showboat. Hannah closed by sending her love and wishing her every success.

Although Kendra had Lloyd trying to find out where Hannah could be, he had no success and Hannah had not written again. Pel, she was told, had left the Lamartine mansion and no one knew where he had gone. She thought about him quite a lot but was determined she would not let him spoil her life.

She moved into a larger apartment and became selective about the houses she would visit to sing, choosing those where the slaves were cared for. Through a number of people she had learned a great deal about their lives; the terrible conditions under which they lived, scanty food, wretched huts and many of them being brutally whipped for small misdemeanours. And more often than not this was the treatment meted out by many of the richest plantation owners.

When the wife of one plantation owner asked Kendra why she would not come to sing in her house Kendra was honest with her and told her the reason.

The woman's face flushed, 'How dare you suggest that our slaves are badly treated. They have to be disciplined.'

'Other slaves are disciplined but not beaten.'

The woman argued with her but Kendra, having her information from a good source, remained adamant. She was then verbally abused and told she would never get into another house in New Orleans. However, she did, and it made no difference to any of her engagements.

Lloyd escorted her every time, but invariably ended up playing cards in another room. His luck was erratic, some good, some bad. Although Kendra knew he was in love with her he had never actually declared it, nor did she want him to. She was fond of Lloyd, found pleasure in his company, but as much as she longed to feel a man's arms around her it was Pel's arms she wanted to enfold her.

From time to time Lloyd gave her information about her husband. She knew Pel had recovered from his injuries, but was left with a bad limp, knew he had sold the riverboat and bought another, and named it *Caroline Ann* after his mother. Lloyd told Kendra that any rumour she might hear that Eleanor Lamartine had a share in the *Caroline Ann* was untrue, he had been there the day the deal was made and Eleanor had called Pel a fool for buying the boat.

To Kendra's tentative enquiry as to whether Eleanor was travelling on the river with Pel she was told no, Eleanor was living at home, but to further questioning Lloyd had to admit that Pel did visit her on occasions.

To Kendra's relief Bo Burford had disappeared from the scene. She had been afraid she might meet him and he would cause trouble. There were times when she heard the strident music of a calliope up river and would know a longing to see Hannah and the others, to perhaps sing once more on the showboat, but the *Mary Louise* never came to New Orleans.

Kendra did not lack for admirers. She did accept a number of invitations to dine, to go to the theatre and for drives, but always skilfully avoided any intimate relationships. When she eventually rented and furnished a house Lloyd was her only visitor.

Sometimes in the evening when she had no engagement and Lloyd was playing cards somewhere she felt an unbearable loneliness. Then she would bring out her 'dancing sailor', but although the antics of the toy would make her smile, she invariably ended up in tears as she remembered, with nostalgia, the day Pel had bought it for her. Did *he* ever think of that day?

* * *

Autumn and winter slipped by with Kendra feeling her life had little meaning. Perhaps in the spring something might happen. It was a time of new life, a time of hope. But with the spring came bad news.

Kendra was singing at the home of one of the wealthiest families in New Orleans, when her host, apologising, interrupted her in the middle of a song to announce gravely that the Confederates had fired on Fort Sumter. It meant war. They must get themselves organised.

There were cries of consternation from the women, murmurs of concern from the older men and excited talk from the younger ones who were all eager to be the first to offer their services.

Kendra began edging her way among the groups of people, hoping to find Lloyd, needing assurance that this war would be of short duration. She saw the men coming from the card room, saw Lloyd's copper coloured hair, then stopped, her breath catching in her throat as she noticed the taller, dark-haired man at his side—a man with a limp. She mouthed the word Pel, but no sound came.

Lloyd, seeing Kendra, came forward. 'You've heard the news.' He paused. 'Kendra, Pel is here, he would like to see you. Do you want to see him?'

She nodded. Lloyd motioned Pel forward then withdrew. Pel bowed and took Kendra's hand in his. 'It's been a long time, Kendra, may I offer my congratulations on your success.'

She found it difficult to assess his expression. There was a suppressed excitement about him, but this could be due to news of the war. Then he raised her hand to his lips, and when he looked up she saw desire in his dark eyes. Her pulses leapt in response. 'I've missed you, Kendra,' he said, his voice low.

She withdrew her hand, spoke lightly, 'But evidently not greatly. I was easy to find, an enquiry—many people know me.'

'Too many, I was jealous.' He was smiling as he said it, and she knew he had lost none of his charm.

'Surely you relinquished that right, sir. You told me when I saw you after the incident of the riverboat you had no wish to see me again.'

'I was a man in pain at the time, angry, my boat vandalised.'

'You were also at the home of a woman who had replaced me in your affections, or perhaps affections is the wrong word.'

'Indeed no, I have always had a fondness for you, Kendra. My feelings have not changed in

267

that respect.'

He sounded sincere but Kendra wished he would have told her he loved her, that Eleanor Lamartine meant nothing to him any more. When two men came up and asked her permission to speak with Devereux, she agreed and moved away.

The three men spoke earnestly. Kendra studied her husband. The only change in him she could see was a small scar on his left cheek. He was still so attractive, still had the arrogant tilt to his head, and just looking at him still had the power to bring a weakness to her limbs.

The two men left and Pel came over to her. 'Kendra, I have to leave, urgent business. May I see you again? Please say yes.' He spoke softly. 'I've never stopped thinking about you—never stopped wanting you.'

Kendra forced herself to ignore the throbbing of her body at his words. 'I'm sorry, Pel, I find that hard to believe. If you had wanted me so much you would have found me.

'It was pride that prevented me.'

He sounded so humble she had to smile. 'Pel, humility does not become you. You have no need to lie to me.'

He grinned. 'You never did mince words, my love. But then that is something I admire in you.' More seriously he added, 'I do need your help, Kendra. Can we meet tomorrow? There is so much I have to tell you.' He tapped his right leg. 'This wretched injury will prevent me from doing any "marching" to war, but there are other ways in which I can help, and you can aid me in this.'

'In what way could *I* help?'

'I would rather explain tomorrow. Some of my colleagues are waiting for me, we are to hold a meeting. Will you help, Kendra?'

'Why not ask Eleanor Lamartine?'

'It has to be someone I can depend on, someone capable.'

If there had been the slightest hint of flattery in his voice she would have refused, but as the statement was simply made, she gave him her address and it was arranged they would meet the following morning.

When she told Lloyd she was seeing Pel the next day, and added she hoped she was doing the right thing, he said gently, 'He is your husband, Kendra.'

It was thinking of Pel in terms of lover that gave Kendra a restless night. At times her body was on fire with longing and she felt she could hardly wait to have this sweet agony assuaged.

But all the longing was suppressed when Pel did arrive the following day, his eyes bloodshot because of having sat through an all-night meeting.

Without any preamble he began. 'Last night I asked your help, Kendra. Now I can explain why. The North will try and blockade the ports. We must prevent it, stop our people from being starved. We need somewhere to rendezvous;

269

and I have it. Recently I bought a house and plantation just outside New Orleans. I will need to be away from time to time and want to leave someone in charge.'

'And you want me to be the one in charge?' Kendra could not keep bitterness from her voice. 'Why not Eleanor Lamartine?'

'I told you, because it has to be someone we can depend on,' he said quietly. 'I feel you would be able to cope with any contingency. You have a strength that other women lack.' Pel smiled wryly. 'The women that I know, that is.'

'I would have to think about it,' she said.

He looked at her in mild astonishment. 'Why?'

'Oh, Pel, for heavens sake, I know it was I who left, but you stay away from me for months then come and ask me to take charge of a house and plantation for you. And make the excuse I would be helping to win a war that could peter out in weeks, or even less.'

'No, Kendra, this war will not peter out as you state. There has been too much unrest for too long. To say it will be over soon is wishful thinking. There will be a great many people killed before it is over.'

Kendra gave a shiver of apprehension. 'And you want me to be left alone in the house.'

'You will not be alone. The servants are trustworthy. The slaves have always been well treated. And I will not be away all the time.' He reached for her hands. 'I want you waiting for me, Kendra, when I come back. I need you, want you as much as you want me. Oh, Kendra, my love—' His voice dropped a tone. 'I want you now, I want to feel your skin, your lips on mine.'

He drew her fiercely to him and she clung to him, wordlessly. His lips, warm and soft, moved sensuously from her mouth to her cheek, her eyelids, to her throat, he undid the buttons of her bodice and slipped her dress from her shoulders, then sweeping her up in his arms he carried her, with a homing instinct, to the bedroom.

Oh, this beautiful madness, she thought, every pulse in her throbbing. It seemed only seconds before they were on the silken sheet of the bed, the excitement of flesh against flesh making it impossible this first time after so long, for any prolonged love-play. Pel took her quickly, and as his rhythm increased everything for Kendra was blotted out by her mounting ecstasy. When they reached fulfilment together she shouted, 'Oh, Pel, Pel,' and they lay motionless, wanting to savour to the last, each ebbing, pulsating moment.

When Pel eventually rolled away from her he gave a deep sigh of satisfaction. 'Kendra, you are wonderful, my darling.' He laid an arm across her stomach. 'Don't you dare go to sleep.' He sounded drowsy.

'Don't you!'

'I shall be awake all night and I promise you, my love, so shall you.' As he ended the sentence he was asleep.

Poor Pel. Kendra felt a wave of love for him sweep over her. She carefully removed his arm, turned on to her side and snuggled up against him, convinced he did love her without realising it. Why else would he want her with him in the new house? Not only, she was sure, because he thought her capable to deal with business. On this happy thought Kendra drifted into sleep.

It was daylight when she awoke. Pel had gone, leaving a note saying he would return that evening to make arrangements for her to move to the plantation.

Another phase of her life was about to begin. She hoped that this war would be of short duration and she could at last know a settled life now she was reunited with her husband, and perhaps even have children.

Children? Kendra drew herself up in the bed, feeling a small excitement. She could at this moment be pregnant. Last night was the first time Pel had not taken steps to prevent such a thing happening.

She lay back on the pillow. Pel's child, what a lovely sound it had. A son, most men liked a son for their first born.

Kendra threw back the bedcovers, humming as she slid out of bed.

CHAPTER TWELVE

They drove to the house the following day. Kendra was enchanted with it, a colonial type white painted mansion with graceful columns and a front door that looked wide enough to take a carriage.

She was enchanted with everything inside it, the satin beauty of polished floors, of craftsman-made furniture, beautiful rugs that came from far away Persia, fine oil paintings, crystal chandeliers, the exquisite silver. She was shown the gardens, the sweep of lawns, beds with a profusion of flowers already blooming, white waxen petals, a riot of honeysuckle, its perfume mingling with that of pink, deep red and pale yellow roses.

Pel showed her the slave quarters which housed a thousand people, their huts freshly whitewashed. She met smiling people, women who bobbed a curtsy to her, their beautiful white teeth flashing in their ebony faces. She saw respect in the eyes of the men, spoke to the overseer and liked him, a compassionate man. These were well cared for slaves.

There was a brick kitchen house with a huge fireplace, a sugar mill with machinery for crushing the cane. So much to see.

She turned to Pel, 'I love it all, I shall be happy here.'

'I knew you would like it.' He took his watch from his pocket. 'I must leave you for a while,

273

Kendra.'

'So soon, where are you going?'

'I have a meeting.' He touched her lightly on the tip of her nose. 'And do not start questioning me whenever I have to go out.' Although the gesture was teasing his tone was sharp.

'Go to the devil,' she said, and walked towards the staircase.

'Kendra! Come here!' She stood her ground, but her heart began to race. '*Come here*!'

She turned slowly, took a step and stopped. 'Yes?'

'Do not look at me in that arrogant way. You are my wife and I expect respect. I told you before you agreed to come here that I would be away from time to time. I am not going away at this moment, I am simply going to a meeting. Now, you either accept this position or leave right away. And if you do leave I shall wash my hands of you completely. I have suffered enough with your temper and accusations.'

'*You* have suffered enough. What about me?'

'I am not prepared to be involved in any argument. Do you stay or do you leave?'

Kendra would have liked to say 'I leave. I don't know how you dare call me arrogant', but she knew she wanted to be near him, wanted whatever affection he would give her.

'I shall stay,' she said.

'Kendra—come here.' This time he spoke softly. She clenched her hands. If only she had the courage to walk on and up the stairs, get her valise and walk out of his life for ever. She went to him.

'Yes—*sir.*'

He tilted her chin, kissed her on the lips, then said, 'Now you may go. I shall be back in time for dinner.'

He gave her a teasing smile over his shoulder as he left. Oh, he was so infuriating! Trying to blame *her* for having left him. If he had not used her so in that card game and then become involved with Eleanor Lamartine—Kendra let her body go slack, common sense telling her if she and Pel were to have any sort of life together she must forget Eleanor.

Kendra soon found that spending time alone with her husband was practically non-existent. If he was not away there would be meetings at the house with a number of men. Invariably when they left to go to New Orleans he would leave with them.

She had hoped to have a baby, but even this was denied her. One day Lloyd Francis rode out to see her. Kendra was so pleased to see him she all but threw herself into his arms.

'Lloyd! What a lovely surprise. Will you be staying? Pel is away, but you would be most welcome.'

He shook his head. 'No, this is just a quick visit, I'm on my way to Baton Rouge. I have friends to see there, then I'm coming back to New Orleans. I'm going to enlist, Kendra.'

'Oh, no.'

Kendra felt dismayed. News kept coming in, of skirmishes and men being killed. The talk she heard at the dinner table between Pel and his colleagues was of serious battles to come.

'Must you go, Lloyd?'

'Yes, I must. For the first time in my life I feel I shall be doing something worthwhile. I really have led a very empty life, Kendra, gambling and drifting.'

'*My* life has been more full for having known you, Lloyd,' Kendra spoke quietly. 'I'm grateful for all your kindness.'

'*My* kindness? I was just so pleased to be able to escort you.' His eyes, so blue, suddenly darkened. 'If things had been different, Kendra—' He got up. 'Forgive me for being so emotional. It's the leaving, not having a family to say goodbye to. I came to regard you as— family, as—as a sister.'

'Then, as a sister, may I embrace you and wish you well.' She stood on tiptoe and kissed him gently on the cheek. 'If you will let me know your address when you are settled, I shall write to you.'

'And for that you would have my undying gratitude. Give my regards to your husband, tell him I am sorry to have missed him. Take care of yourself, Kendra.' Lloyd paused, then added with a worried frown, 'I would wish that you were safely back in England.'

'I shall be safe here, the war will not reach

this area.'

'People are fighting for all slaves to be free, already there is unrest on the plantations.'

Kendra assured him she would be perfectly all right, their servants were loyal, grateful for a good master, Lloyd was not to worry. He held her hands tightly for a few moments, then with a quick, sad smile, took his leave.

She watched him from the window as he made his way to the stables to get his horse. He kept looking back and waving his hat. His copper coloured hair looked bright in the morning sunlight.

Kendra wondered when she would see him again. When he was out of sight she felt as though the sun had gone in.

That evening Pel came home on his own. He looked dusty and dishevelled, as though he had been riding all day. With only a perfunctory greeting to Kendra he went upstairs, shouting orders as he went for water for a bath. When he came down, an hour later, he went straight into his study, sat at his desk and began pouring over ledgers.

Kendra, who had followed him in, watched him for a few moments, then went upstairs and changed into a dress with a low-cut neckline, which she hoped might prove tempting to her errant husband. She took with her a piece of tapestry to work on when she went into the study and asked permission to sit there, promising not to make a sound.

Without looking up Pel said, 'If you as much as cough, out you go. I need to concentrate.'

The night was chilly and a log fire had been lit. Kendra settled beside it and although she had never been one to sew with any lengthy concentration, she forced herself to work steadily on the piece of tapestry. After a while, however, the quiet of the room, the soft glow of lamps and the deep red of wood embers had a soporific effect. She put down her work.

The slamming of a ledger startled her into wakefulness. 'Well, that is most satisfactory.' Pel threw down his quill then held out a hand to Kendra.

She came over to him and he pulled her onto his lap and laid his cheek against her warm skin. 'You wore this dress to tempt me,' he said.

'Of course. I thought you needed to be tempted after being celibate for so long.'

He glanced up at her, a teasing in his eyes. 'Who said I had been celibate?'

Kendra's heart skipped a beat. 'I naturally assumed it, you being a man of honour.' She laughed as she said it. 'But if, of course, I am wrong and you are so satisfied with whoring that you do not need me—' She got up, but he pulled her back almost savagely.

'I have not been whoring! You spoil me for other women, your face intrudes, torments me, I have never allowed any woman to wholly dominate my life and I will not allow *you* to do so.'

278

'But Pel, my only wish is to be a part of your life.'

'And that is all it will ever be.' He eased her off his lap, and gave her a slap on her rump. 'Now go upstairs and be ready for me when I come up.'

She wanted to say, 'like a slave', but left. And had to admit that the dominance of his words excited her.

With the first big money Kendra earned with her singing she had bought silk sheets. These she brought with her. Her young coloured maid had had the warming pan between them and Kendra, slipping into bed stretched, cat-like, enjoying the luxury of the silken warmth.

There was a time when her husband undressed that Kendra would look away. Now she watched him, unashamedly, enjoying the magnificence of his muscular body.

'You have no modesty,' he said, smiling at her through the mirror. 'You should look away, or lower your gaze.'

'Why? A cat can look at a king, so why not a wife?'

Oh, he loved that, he roared with laughter. 'A cat can look at a king! How true. A mouse can look at one, a flea!'

'A flea has more access to his body.'

'All right, *Flea*, you can have access to mine.' He strode across the room, flung back the bedclothes and got in beside her, sighing as their bodies touched. 'Pleasure me, woman,' he

279

commanded.

Kendra laughed softly. 'Fleas make you itch.'

'I'm itching already.'

She 'walked' her fingers lightly over his skin, going down his arm and up, then coming over his body, over his stomach, lower and lower. She was teasing him at his very masculine response when they were both suddenly startled by loud shouting outside. Pel drew himself up and eyed her questioningly. Kendra, fearful, said, 'Are they soldiers, are we being attacked?'

'I doubt it.' Pel got out of bed, put on his trousers and was reaching for his shirt when there was an urgent knocking on the bedroom door. 'What the devil—' he said.

'Master, come quickly, trouble—'

Pel flung open the door. 'In heavens name, man, what is going on?'

Kendra, hearing the words, 'Baton Rouge .. . Lamartines . . . and fire . . .' jumped out of bed and dragged on a robe.

'I shall come at once,' Pel said to the servant, then turned to Kendra. 'The Lamartine house has been set on fire, it's thought by a group of workers from the estate. As far as the messenger knows Eleanor and her father are all right. I must go.'

Kendra felt sick as she thought of the possibilities evolving from this trouble. Pel could be involved with Eleanor again and be a constant visitor to Baton Rouge.

As it turned out, it was worse than she anticipated. At daybreak Pel brought Mr Lamartine and his daughter to the house, and ordered guest rooms and food to be prepared.

Guests? Kendra wanted to run away. How could she possibly live in the same house with this woman?

Mr Lamartine, his face ashen, looked on the verge of collapse. He kept repeating, 'A life's work gone.'

His daughter was more voluble. Her jet black hair in disarray, her beautiful face distorted by anger, she paced up and down the room, swearing vengeance on the slaves responsible for the fire.

'Every single *nigra* will pay for what they have done,' she declared. 'I shall see to it personally. How dare they burn down our house, we who have shown them nothing but kindness. They have been protected, have good living quarters, are well fed and cared for medically. I shall round up an army, pursue them, and won't rest until every one is hanged or shot. Oh, yes, they shall pay for this.'

Pel, who had come into the room said briskly, 'I can understand how you feel, Eleanor, but you will do yourself no good by ranting and raving.'

'What do you expect me to do, sit down quietly and say, oh, goodness me, they have burned down our house, how mischievous of them? Am I to get no co-operation from you? Why are you not out now searching for the bastards?'

'Because I have a home here,' he replied, sharp voiced. 'I had to know that this house was not being burned to the ground. There was nothing to indicate whether this was one of many organised groups bent on destruction, or an isolated case. I suggest that you and your father have a meal then go to bed.'

'Bed? Do you honestly expect me to sleep when—'

'Eleanor! That is enough. You are in my home and I will not tolerate all this shouting. Is that understood? Now calm down.'

Eleanor stared at him, her eyes mutinous, then she tossed her head. 'I will *not* calm down, that is impossible, but I will go to my room. Will you ring for a servant, please.'

When Eleanor and her father had gone Pel spoke coldly to Kendra, upbraiding her for not having gone up with Eleanor to make sure she was comfortable.

Kendra had to force herself to speak calmly. 'Miss Lamartine would not have welcomed any interference from me, and I would have wished you had taken her and her father elsewhere. They must have friends in Baton Rouge. It is not pleasant for me having them here, not under the circumstances.'

'Not pleasant! Do you realise these people have lost their home?'

282

'I am not surprised, not after I saw the treatment Eleanor meted out to one of their slaves. She was brutal, lashed him—'

'And no doubt he deserved it. Do not spare sympathy for a man defying orders. No, Kendra, I will not listen to any more. You disappoint me, but get this straight, while Mr Lamartine and Eleanor are in this house I expect them to be treated with respect. I must go out and see if any of our neighbours have had trouble. Pray heaven they haven't.'

Respect? Kendra moved round the room, fuming. How could he expect her to have respect for a woman who had been his mistress? Perhaps still was. The situation was intolerable. Feeling unwilling to face the day Kendra went upstairs, intending to get back into bed for a while, but on the first landing she paused as she heard the upraised voice of Eleanor Lamartine coming from an open doorway.

'Papa, will you for God's sake stop complaining about what *you* have lost. I am the loser! You had already lost the house and plantation to Pel Devereux.'

Yes, Kendra thought, tight-lipped, and Pel was the fool to have made it possible for Eleanor to own it. She turned to go to her room when a door was slammed behind her, then came a second slamming as Eleanor went into the bedroom opposite. Kendra shook her head, wondering how she was going to cope with this wretched woman. But she would cope and would stand up to her, she would not be the one to leave, no matter how difficult the situation.

Kendra had breakfasted when Pel returned and told her there had been no trouble elsewhere. She would have liked to have said that perhaps he would now accept her explanation for the burning of the Lamartine house, but thought it wiser to keep a still tongue.

Pel went up to wash and shave and when he came down for breakfast she sat with him, drinking her third cup of coffee. They sat in silence for some time then Pel, spearing a piece of bacon on his fork said, 'All right, say what you have to say and be done with it.'

'I have nothing further to add to what I said earlier.'

'You surprise me.' Pel popped the bacon into his mouth, chewed it then drew his table napkin across his lips. 'I expected Eleanor, alone, to be a talking point with you for days.'

'She is your guest and I shall be polite to her while she is here. That is your wish and I shall abide by it.'

Pel studied her thoughtfully. 'I am not sure I like this compliant mood. It makes me feel uncomfortable. I ask myself what brew you are stirring, what trouble will evolve.'

Kendra eyed him over the rim of her cup. 'If anyone makes trouble it will not be me. I am determined on that. I will not give you or Eleanor Lamartine an excuse to get me to leave.'

'Kendra, that is an abominable accusation, and quite uncalled for.' He threw down his napkin. 'Do you really think I would be guided in my actions by what Eleanor said or did in relation to you? If I wanted you to leave I would tell you so, and may I remind you that you were the one to leave *me*.'

Kendra refrained from reminding him she had had good cause for doing so.

Pel had not left the dining room when Eleanor came in. She was dressed for riding and looked beautiful in a dark blue habit, a white curling feather in her hat. She smiled from one to the other with such charm Kendra could only stand and stare.

'Could I please borrow a horse from your stables? I must go to Baton Rouge to see if anything can be salvaged.' It was to Kendra she made the appeal. It was Pel who answered.

'Yes, of course, I shall come with you. Kendra, would you care to ride with us?'

Feeling surprised and pleased at this gesture she said, yes, she would, and in the next moment realised how thin the veneer of Eleanor's charm.

Although her chagrin was swiftly masked by a smile it was there. She said, 'Papa does not feel well. I thought it advisable for him to rest, at least for today. Could a message be sent to ask the doctor to call? I hate to leave him, but I must see to the house—'

'But if the doctor is to come—' Pel glanced at Kendra and she knew that for this once, at least, Eleanor had won a small victory.

'I shall stay,' she said.

Her sacrifice did at least bring a gentleness from her husband. He put an arm about her waist and kissed her. 'Thank you, Kendra, this is a kindness.'

Eleanor, no doubt hating to see this demonstration of affection, had turned away and was at the door when Pel said, 'We shall not be late back.'

It was midnight when Kendra, who had waited up, heard the ring of hooves on the cobblestones of the stable yard. She sat tense for a few moments then got up.

Eleanor came in first. Her emerald eyes held a brightness, but her expression was woeful. 'Oh, Kendra, what a terrible time we had. Such devastation, such heart-break sorting through the debris, everything blackened and that dreadful smell of charred wood. Look at me, what a mess, I feel filthy.'

Judging by Eleanor's immaculate condition Kendra felt sure she had not even laid a finger on a piece of blackened wood. Pel made the remark that fortunately only a part of the house had been destroyed, and immediately Eleanor gave a deep sigh.

'But how long will it take to rebuild? And

where do Papa and I live in the meantime?' She glanced at Kendra then her gaze came back to Pel. 'Dare we beg your hospitality? We have relatives in Baton Rouge, but Papa does not get on well with them.'

Kendra thought it was more likely that it was Eleanor who was not compatible with their relatives.

'You and your father can stay as long as it is necessary,' Pel said.

'Thank you.' Eleanor then stifled a yawn. 'Please excuse me, I feel utterly exhausted. I must get some rest.'

When she had gone Kendra said, 'She did not even enquire after her father,' and regretted having made the remark when Pel answered her shortly that Eleanor was most concerned about him, and had indeed been worrying about him all day.

Which brought Kendra to the conclusion that her husband must indeed be gullible as far as Eleanor was concerned, unable to see through her ruses. And so all Kendra could see ahead at that moment was a clash of wills between herself and this beautiful green-eyed woman.

* * *

But the clash of wills Kendra expected did not materialise, for the simple reason that Eleanor was hardly ever there. Neither was Pel.

Unhappily for Kendra, every time her husband planned to be away for a few days Eleanor would leave shortly after him presumably to go to Baton Rouge, and always returned an hour, or two or three, after he had.

Kendra suffered in silence for several weeks then one evening remonstrated with Pel about the coincidence. At her accusations, or at her inference of the situation, Pel became angry.

'When I go away I'm concerned only in business. What Eleanor does has nothing to do with me. I never see her, nor do I want to, I just don't have the time.'

'Oh, so if you did have the time you would be together.'

'God give me patience!' Pel said, rolling his eyes ceilingwards. 'In another few moments you will be accusing me of spending my time whoring!'

'Well, you certainly never come to *me* wanting *'wifely'* comfort.'

'Kendra—' Pel spread his hands and spoke quietly and carefully. 'I shall explain my position and I will not repeat this so listen to every word. When I leave here there are times when I have no sleep for forty-eight hours. There—is—a—war going on. Battles are being fought, men are being wounded, dying, hundreds are already dead. Guns are needed, equipment, boots, I and others try and supply them. When I come home I go to a room on my own because I need to sleep. Do you

288

understand this? I do not want any contact with a woman, not you, or Eleanor Lamartine or anyone else.'

'I'm sorry,' Kendra said, 'I had not realised.'

'Well you do now, so let it rest.'

'There is just one more thing I must say, it concerns Mr Lamartine. I have tried to talk to you about him before but you refused to listen. Yes, I know he is Eleanor's father and she should be responsible for him, but that is the trouble. She never goes near him. Now I am willing to care for him, but I will not be held responsible for Mr Lamartine if he should die.'

'Die?' Kendra at last had her husband's full attention.

'Yes, he has sunk into a lethargy and cannot be roused. I spoke to Eleanor about it but she dismisses it, says her father is shamming. The doctor told me he ought to be with people of his own. They do have relatives in Baton Rouge, Eleanor said so.'

'I shall speak with her about it.'

The following morning a carriage came for Mr Lamartine. Eleanor travelled with him. Before they left she said she would not be returning. She offered no thanks to Kendra for her care of her father, or the hospitality they had been shown.

Pel made apologies for her, said she was suffering from the loss of her home and was going to relatives with whom she had nothing in common. Kendra made no reply.

That evening Pel made love to her, but she felt no joy; she felt he was rewarding her for services rendered to the Lamartines.

CHAPTER THIRTEEN

The weeks went by with Pel coming and going. When he was home he was tense; poring over ledgers, riding over the estate with the overseer and going out to visit this person and that. There were men coming to the house for meetings, and to Kendra he was a stranger.

Once when she ventured to ask him what work he was actually involved in he snapped, 'Questions, questions, always questions from you, Kendra! The work I do is secret.'

Two women from neighbouring plantations called and Kendra was glad of their company. She was invited to their homes and met other women and from them learned snippets about the war. There had been no major battles, but their husbands felt it was building up for one.

In July she arrived at the home of her nearest neighbour to find an air of drama about the chattering group of women.

'Oh, Mrs Devereux, come and sit down,' said her hostess. 'Have you heard the news about the battle at Bull Run? A dreadful affair.'

With all the women trying to tell her at once it took Kendra some time to sort out that the date of the battle to be fought at Bull Run Creek, near Washington, had actually been announced, and people had gone to watch the spectacle, taking picnic baskets with them.

'Picnic baskets?' Kendra echoed. 'Was it a *real* battle?'

'Oh, it was real all right,' said one woman, adding with relish, 'Men lost legs and arms and some had their heads blown off. Hundreds were killed and many more than that were wounded. The people who had gone to watch were physically sick and ill at the slaughter.'

Until that moment the war had seemed remote enough to be unreal to Kendra. Now she thought of Lloyd Francis, who had told her in a short note that he was in Washington; she felt sick.

On successive visits Kendra learned more about the war. There was now no more talk about it being of short duration. There was concern when small groups of slaves left their plantations in the dead of night, as it was presumed they had left to go North to join the Union Army. And these escapes must have been well organised because none of the men were caught. Nor had Eleanor Lamartine been able to find the men who had fired their house. Kendra was also told of constant friction between Eleanor and the aunt and uncle she and her father were living with.

When Eleanor became the subject of discussion a gentle, dreamy-eyed spinster said,

'Miss Lamartine is very beautiful.'

'And wicked,' declared a buxom matron. 'She is sure to come to a bad end, always after the men.' Then she added to Kendra, 'And you had better be careful where your husband is concerned, Mrs Devereux. I saw the two of them together when I was visiting near Baton Rouge a few days ago.'

Kendra's heart began to beat so fast she felt almost suffocated, but she managed to say, 'Yes, he told me he would be calling. He had messages for Eleanor from friends.'

She had a feeling that some of the women looked at her a little pityingly, and found herself wondering what more they knew about her husband and Eleanor.

*   *   *

The following day when Pel came home, in spite of the fact that he looked drained she tackled him straight away about the gossip.

'If you must meet Eleanor could I ask that you do it a little more discreetly. I find it unpleasant being told that my husband is meeting his mistress instead of coming home.'

He stared at her, his expression cold. 'You are behaving like a child listening to a lot of gossiping women.'

'It might not occur to you that I am glad of the company of these "gossiping" women, as you call them! You come and go and treat me

292

as if I were a servant, or some stranger. I wish I had stayed in New Orleans. I did at least have pleasant company, people who talked to me, treated me with courtesy.'

'Men who wined and dined you! And for what favours?'

'Pel, you really are despicable. Do not judge me by yourself. You handed over a house and plantation to get Eleanor Lamartine's favours. I once said that neither she, nor you, would get me to leave here, but now that is certainly in my mind. I shall go back to New Orleans, I can earn a living with my singing.'

'You will do no such thing, you are my wife and you will stay in this house. If you leave I shall make it so unpleasant for you, you will want to run away and hide yourself in a nunnery.'

Kendra found the coldness underlying his anger quite frightening. 'You are worse than Bo Burford,' she said, 'more vicious.'

Pel thumped a hand on a table sending ornaments dancing. 'Do not class me with that—that—'

'Gentleman?' Kendra supplied. 'He *is*, in comparison with you.'

Pel came up to her and taking her by the shoulders, shook her.

'Don't you ever compare me with Bo Burford again, do you hear? When I think of what he did to my boat I have murder in my heart, and to think that you actually condone

293

such action.'

'I don't condone it, not at all, I was simply trying to say—'

'You saw the injuries he and his men inflicted on me,' Pel tapped his injured leg. 'I shall probably have this limp for the rest of my life and you—' He released her and threw up his hands. 'Oh, I have nothing more to say, I feel too disgusted.' He turned away, started to go to the door, then stopped to give Kendra a scathing look. 'I don't really know why I bothered to bring you back. Go to New Orleans, do what the devil you like. You are not worth any affection I had for you.' With that he went limping out.

Kendra felt a rising bubble of hysteria. She had started by admonishing him about Eleanor Lamartine and he had twisted the whole thing round so that she was the one admonished.

'All right,' she said aloud, 'I shall leave, *he* can go to the devil for all I care.'

But once Kendra was upstairs and had brought out a valise she thought better of it. If she left, Pel would bring Eleanor here. It was what Eleanor had been working for. No doubt she had been dropping poison in his ears when they met, probably told him a story about the hardship of living with relatives, turned on her coaxing act. Oh, yes, she had charm when she wanted. Well, she was going to be disappointed about living in this house. If Pel did bring her here then *she* would make Eleanor's life so unpleasant, she would be glad to leave.

But even as Kendra thought it, she knew if it came to a battle of wits between them she would be up against a very clever and cunning opponent.

*   *   *

Pel continued to be a mere visitor in the house until November, when the cane was to be harvested. He arrived in a surprisingly pleasant mood and declared that war or no war they were going to hold the harvest celebrations with the workers.

Although Kendra was naturally curious to know the reason for the change in her husband, she made no attempt to question him, as it was enough that he was happy. No expense was to be spared for the occasion, he declared. Friends were to be invited. The crop had been excellent and the workers were to be rewarded. There would be the usual barbecue, and the bonfire would be lit at midnight. There was also to be an extra innovation, but this was to be a surprise. Pel was grinning like a schoolboy as he made this last remark.

Kendra found herself caught up in the excitement of the workers, there was a lot of running to and fro, with children wide-eyed with expectancy. The dried cane had been piled into a huge mound, ready to be lit at midnight. The sugar was boiled for the children to take their half-pecan nuts later to dip into it. Large cuts of beef were being prepared for the barbecue. Hogsheads of wine were being checked in the warehouse, with an order from the overseer to make sure the door of the warehouse was locked.

Pel laughed. 'Can't have them getting drunk before the celebrations.'

'They deserve it, suh,' said the overseer, 'they work very hard.'

He was a big, amiable man, who had taught himself to read and write but although he was always most courteous to Kendra, he had never encouraged her to mingle among the women. He gave her the impression that her place was in the house and this was his domain.

'Well, my love,' Pel said, putting an arm about her waist, 'I think everything is under control here.'

She noticed as they walked away that his limp was not so pronounced. When she remarked on it he said yes, there was an improvement, but the leg still gave him pain and he was certainly unable to walk any distance. Kendra had a feeling he was excusing himself for not having joined the Confederate Army. He was the only man of that age in the area who had not done so.

She once overheard two women talking about him. The first one said, 'I know Mr Devereux has a leg injury but there are men a great deal older, with *ailments*, who have offered their services.' The second one replied that as far as she had heard Mr Devereux was doing valuable work for the army—and there the conversation ended.

Kendra said now, as they strolled back towards the house, 'Pel, you never mention gambling, do you still play cards?'

He smiled down at her. 'Let me say that my life is one long gamble these days, and if I come through it unscathed I shall consider myself very lucky.'

Kendra felt alarmed. 'This work you do is dangerous?'

He patted her hand. 'I take care of myself, great care. You are not to worry.'

There was such a happy atmosphere that evening when their friends arrived no one would have dreamed there was a war going on, that men were being killed. Pel said for that evening the word 'war' was taboo.

When they all went out for the bonfire to be lit Kendra found herself caught up in the atmosphere that was reminiscent of the people coming to the showboat for the evening's performance. It was the excitement, the air of anticipation of something wonderful about to happen.

Kendra and her husband and their friends stood in front of the bonfire waiting for it to be lighted and the black people were laughing and cheering. A torch was put to the pile of cane and a great shout went up as the flames crept up and up until the ground around held a warm glow. The blaze brought once more to Kendra a primitive feeling, as the flaring torches on the river bank had done. She drew in a quick breath. Pel, as though aware of her mood glanced at her then, putting an arm about her, drew her quickly against him. 'I want you,' he whispered, 'Now!'

She shook her head. 'Later, we must wait.'

The men had already rolled out the barrels of wine, the children had gone into the sugar house and the pieces of beef were cooking over the glowing coals, the spits turning. The appetising smell hung on the cool night air. When the fire had lost its first fierce blaze Pel brought out the surprise. A box of fireworks.

They cracked, they sparked, flew up into the air and burst into sprays of coloured stars. There were cries of awe, of wonderment. It had certainly been a night of revelry, and Kendra could not wait for it to culminate in her being alone with Pel.

They saw their guests away, waiting until the carriages had gone from view round a bend in the road, then made their way back to the house. There were sounds of revelry coming from the slave quarters. Small spurts of flames shot up every now and again from the dull red glow of the bonfire, as though having a final fling before dying.

Dying? A drifting light mist coming from the river hung in wraith-like spirals, adding to the already ghostly look of the trailing Spanish moss, hanging from the branches of the massive oak trees. Kendra shivered, feeling a sudden premonition.

'Cold, darling?' Pel took off his jacket, put it about her shoulders then said, a teasing in his voice, 'You will soon be warm, I promise.'

She moved closer to him. Then, determined she was not going to spoil the most important part of the evening, she gave him a provocative smile and ran ahead. He caught her up in the hall, swept her up in his arms and carried her upstairs, not stopping until he set her down in front of a blazing log fire in their bedroom.

'There, my love, I shall pour us each a glass of wine then I shall undress you.'

Normally, the thought of her husband undressing her would have been enough to send every nerve in her body throbbing, but Kendra felt nothing. She stared into the fire, catching the lovely fragrance of burning applewood as the top log ignited from the lower one.

There was the delicate tinkle of crystal then Pel came over with two glasses of wine and held one out to her. He touched her glass to his. 'To us, and a long night.' His eyes were dark with passion. Still Kendra felt nothing. She looked up at him.

'Pel, stay with me. Don't go away again.'

'I have to, but I am here now, so make the most of it.'

He put down his glass then began to undo the buttons at the back of her dress. There was no haste in the action. When the dress slid to the floor he lifted her away from it and sat her in a chair. 'Now have another drink of wine, Kendra.' She looked at him questioningly, but he simply smiled then drained his glass. He poured himself another. Then, after having drank half he ordered her to start undressing him. No—not an order, a request, gently given. Kendra laughed as she undid his cravat.

'How unusual for you not to be in a hurry.'

'I will be, my love, by the time we are both undressed.' He knuckled her chin. 'And so will you, I promise.' Had he guessed he had not yet aroused her? If so, did he expect her to respond to him with these delaying tactics?

After the next garment was discarded they stopped to have another drink, and Kendra said, amused, 'Was there ever such a leisurely seduction, I shall be yawning in a moment.'

'You will not be yawning when I start purring.'

'Oh, so you are a cat.'

He leaned towards her, speaking softly, 'A tiger.'

'How interesting,' she said lightly. 'Then shall you kill your prey in the end?'

'With love.'

Two simple words, but the implication, the warm sensuousness of Pel's tone, brought the first swift throb to Kendra.

The 'purring' was a murmur of endearments as a garment was raised. A fleeting touch of lips on flesh followed the garment's progress, up and up, soft lips over throat, on mouth, on eyelids—fingers through hair so lightly Kendra's scalp tingled. Then stop. Garment off. A drink put in her hand. Pel, smiling, oh, so tantalisingly.

Now she must do the same for him . . . 'No, not so quickly, my darling, take your time.' Her whole body was throbbing now, and with his last garment shed Kendra drew in a quick breath as hard warm flesh touched soft warm flesh.

'And now to my lair, to be devoured.' Pel whispered it, his grin wicked as he swept her up in his arms.

Oh, what joy, what bliss, what agony what ecstasy. May the 'devouring' never end. Satiated they fell asleep at dawn.

* * *

It was daylight when Kendra roused. Still sleepy she reached out a hand for her husband—and found an empty space. Even then she would have drifted into sleep again had her glance not caught a piece of paper propped up on the bedside table.

The note from Pel was brief. He apologised for not waking her to say goodbye. He would be home again in another few weeks. 'Take care of yourself,' he said. The note was unsigned.

She lay back on the pillow between anger and tears. Why could he not have told her he would be leaving? Common sense told Kendra she would not have enjoyed their lovemaking so much had she known he would be gone the next morning. But even then she grieved.

Later that morning there were ugly rumours of houses being burned in Missouri and of families dying in the blaze. Two days later married daughters of neighbouring planters arrived with their children, for safety.

And two days after this Eleanor Lamartine and her now frail father arrived to greet Kendra, with a mass of luggage, already deposited in the hall.

To Kendra's demand for an explanation Eleanor eyed her haughtily. 'Papa and I need a home, and before you attempt to turn us away may I say that I, at least, have every right to be here.'

'What right?'

'The right of a woman carrying the bastard child of your husband.'

Kendra had suffered shocks in the past but none as devastating as this. Pel's child! He had known about it, known Eleanor would come here. This was why he had tried to enslave her last night. Tiger indeed! He should be hunted and shot.

Although bristling with rage Kendra managed to force herself to some degree of calmness. 'I have only your word for your statement, Miss Lamartine, but as you have so obviously been turned away from your aunt's house you can stay here until my husband returns. Then we can verify whether your statement is true. He should be back in a few weeks.'

'A few weeks?' Eleanor gave a derisive laugh. 'Your husband, Mrs Devereux, will not be back for months, quite possibly not until his child is born.'

'Months—but he talked about a few weeks.'

'And you, you poor specimen of a wife believed him, as all women take for gospel everything Pel Devereux tells them. He's gone to England, to increase his already large fortune selling cotton at inflationary prices.'

'Cotton?' Kendra whispered.

'Oh—' another laugh from Eleanor, 'did you really think he was doing secret war work, dangerous work for the army? You are a bigger fool than I took you for.'

A plaintive voice came from behind Eleanor. 'Please, Mrs Devereux, may I sit down?'

The distraction of dealing with Mr Lamartine, getting him upstairs, helped Kendra over the appalling disclosures made by Eleanor. Later she would have to face up to her dilemma and try and work out how she would deal with it. At that moment she only knew she wished herself anywhere but in this house.

After four days of enduring Eleanor

303

Lamartine's arrogance, her bursts of temper and her giving orders to the servants as though she were mistress of the house, and Kendra's rage, which she had kept under control, erupted. A complaint had come from the kitchen that Eleanor had thrown a cup of coffee over the young girl who had taken her breakfast up to her. Kendra ran up the stairs and burst into the bedroom without knocking.

'This is the end,' she declared, 'tomorrow you leave.'

Eleanor, propped up by a mound of pillows, put down a finger of toast and looked at Kendra in an amused way.

'What in heavens name is going on? Why am I being asked to leave in such urgency?'

Kendra listed the reasons, stressing that she would not allow anyone to throw coffee over a servant.

Eleanor looked at Kendra in a pitying way. 'What a naïve person you are to be sure. I told the girl the coffee was cold and asked her to bring me some fresh. I held out the cup for her to taste the coffee and she spilt it over her apron. But no doubt you will prefer to believe the story of the girl.'

'Yes, Miss Lamartine, I do, because I've seen the way you treated one of your own servants. Well, you will not give orders to mine, nor do you have the right.'

Eleanor eased away from the pillows, her green eyes flashing. 'I have as much right to live here as you, seeing that your husband was responsible for my condition. And pray do not get the idea that I wanted this child. I hate it! I took numerous pills and wretched stinking potions to get rid of it.'

Get rid of it? Kendra stared at her appalled. How dreadful, and how unfair life was. Here she was longing for a child and this woman was trying to destroy the living embryo inside her. It was murder. Anger swamped Kendra.

'How dare you take such a decision on to your own shoulders. It was not yours alone to take. It is Pel's child too.'

Eleanor laughed harshly. 'And do you think he would care what I did about it? I should imagine he would be delighted if I got rid of it.'

'No, no, you are wrong! Pel longs for a son.'

A change came suddenly over Eleanor. She eyed Kendra in a speculative way. 'So, you want a child and I want it out of the way. Could you bring up another woman's child as your own, if the father of it happened to be *your* husband?'

'That would depend!' Kendra felt caution, not quite knowing what was in Eleanor's mind. 'I could accept a child and bring it up as my own, and love it, as long as the mother would never lay claim to it.'

'You would have my word on that. I would leave, go right out of your lives after I had recovered from the birth—on condition you allow me to stay here until then.'

'How do I know you would keep your

promise?'

'I told you I would give you my word.' Eleanor's voice held a coldness. 'I am a Lamartine, we have pride in our name.'

Kendra pointed out that her husband would need to be consulted but Eleanor dismissed this. 'He has no choice. He either installs me, *and* his child in a house of my choosing, or accepts you caring for it in this house.'

After some thought Kendra agreed but stated that she wanted to impose certain conditions.

'Such as?' Eleanor demanded.

'That I am treated with respect and that you ask what you need from the servants but do not demand.'

Eleanor flared. 'Why should I treat *you* with respect?' Her lips curled. 'Pel took you away from a life of drudgery, you were no more than a slave to some common people. A companion of sorts!'

Kendra walked up to the bed and spoke quietly.

'Miss Lamartine, let me make one or two things clear. I too am proud of my family name. Circumstances reduced me to working for the Bagleys. You have made disparaging remarks about me, taken me for a fool. Do not underestimate me. I have a strong will, and I have found over the past few months that I can be quite ruthless. If you plan to stay here then you will accept my conditions. If not I would

306

have no qualms in putting you out, whether you are carrying a child or not. Is that understood?'

Eleanor gripped the edge of the bedcover and her knuckles showed white. Then suddenly she released it.

'I cannot imagine you turning me out, but I am not willing to risk it. Very well, I agree to your conditions, but do not ever expect me to grovel to you.'

'I could not picture you grovelling to anyone, Miss Lamartine. Not under any circumstances.' With that Kendra turned and walked, straight-backed, from the room.

Although Kendra had the satisfaction of having scored a small victory over Eleanor she knew that life was not going to be easy living with her during the coming months. There was also Pel to be told.

To give Eleanor her due she did stop ordering the servants around but there were a hundred minor irritations that made Kendra long for the child to be born and to have them out of the house.

Eleanor, although suffering no discomfort, treated her pregnancy as an illness, and all Kendra's coaxing to take some exercise fell on deaf ears.

When she did get up she had servants running after her with her own special chair and cushions, she ordered delicacies then refused them when they were brought to the table, and asked for whisky to be poured. It had been useless trying to point out the injury she might do the child. According to Eleanor she was the one carrying the baby and she would eat and drink what she wanted and do what she wanted. Later she became careless of her appearance.

Kendra had stopped visiting friends, afraid of having snide remarks made about her giving a home to her husband's mistress. But her nearest neighbours had called and it was from them she heard all news of the war.

There were battles going on, both armies ill-equipped. Some soldiers were without uniforms, some without boots, many were sent to fight with only wooden staves. There was confusion, a great deal of corruption, casualties of killed and wounded were mounting.

When Kendra asked if it were possible for the Union Army to reach this area she was given an emphatic no. The two forts beyond New Orleans were well-gunned, and well-manned. A massive raft had been made and was secured with heavy chains and anchored across the river so if an enemy ship approached it would be sunk immediately. And, of course, New Orleans was teeming with soldiers. All was gaiety, wining, dining, dancing. No, they were perfectly safe here.

One day two young army captains, resplendent in grey uniforms, gold braid on collars and cuffs, came to call on Eleanor.

From being dull-eyed, listless, untidy, she

was transformed into a vibrant personality, beautifully groomed, her full skirt camouflaging her pregnancy. She asked all sorts of questions about New Orleans, played the coquette, angling for an invitation to go to the city. And got it, Kendra being included in the invitation. Kendra refused, saying that Miss Lamartine had been ill and was not yet fully recovered. Perhaps some other time. She was firm about it.

This, later, brought a storm of abuse from Eleanor, with Kendra pointing out that dancing and even the jolting suffered on the journey could bring on a miscarriage. At this Eleanor shouted, 'And a good thing that would be,' and stormed out.

The next morning she was missing. A note said she had gone to New Orleans and not Kendra or anyone else could bring her back until she was ready.

She was away four days and came back full of her enjoyment, talking non-stop to Kendra as though they were close friends. She described the beautiful dresses worn by the ladies at a charity dance to raise funds for the Cause, remarked how the materials had been bought in spite of the blockade, and added laughing, she would not be surprised if Pel had been responsible for smuggling some of it.

Kendra, who had been full of worry as to what the effect of all this dancing and gaiety could have on Eleanor, now sat up, alert. She had heard nothing from her husband since he had left. With thumping heart she said, 'Pel—did you see him?'

Eleanor said no, she had overheard a group of men discussing him. Pel was still shipping cotton to England, where the English were hoarding it to get higher prices. Some of the men had spoken of Pel affectionately as a clever rogue, getting the cotton through the blockade, and no doubt making a profit for himself. Others, less affectionately, dubbed him a cold-blooded gambler, while one man declared, with venom, he was spying for the North. Eleanor did say that all the others in the group refuted this, saying they would stake their life that if any spying was being done by Pel Devereux it would be for the Confederates. Then almost as an afterthought, Eleanor added that Pel held the rank of major.

Major? This settled Kendra's mind that her husband was not spying for the North. But she tormented herself wondering if Pel and Eleanor had been together in New Orleans. She worried all day then knew if she kept thinking in this vein she would make herself ill. She had plenty of other worries on her mind, Mr Lamartine for one. He demanded so much of her time. Eleanor refused to go near her father, saying she was more ill than he was. So Kendra was left to deal with the querulous old man.

It was a day of driving rain in the middle of

March when Eleanor went into labour. With the first pains she began shouting and Kendra, thinking it must surely be a quick birth, sent for the doctor. After examining Eleanor he snapped shut his bag, his manner impatient, announcing that the birth would not be for several hours. 'Such a fuss,' he declared as they came out of the room.

Kendra, making excuses for Eleanor said, 'It is her first child, I suppose it is rather frightening.'

The doctor, looking at her over the top of his spectacles announced it was not his patient's first child, and added he would be back in a couple of hours to have a look at her.

Kendra stared after him, stunned, unable to believe that Eleanor had had a previous child. Had it died, or had she given it away as she was so readily prepared to do with this unborn one?

Kendra had left a midwife from the plantation with Eleanor. When she went back into the bedroom the woman rolled her eyes as though to say there was going to be plenty of trouble with this young mother. Eleanor, between pains, glared at Kendra, denouncing the doctor as a fool and cursing all men who made women pregnant. She would take care that no man put his seed into her in future.

Kendra, thinking of the first child that had been born could not help but say, 'The choice was yours.'

Eleanor turned her head away. 'Oh, get out

of here, I'm sick of your platitudes, sick of your holier-than-thou attitude, sick of your face.'

Kendra stood for a moment looking at Eleanor, her black hair a cloud on the pillow, her beauty marred by her recent hysterical outbursts. She wanted to see Pel's child born, but at the moment she thought it advisable to leave. She was at the foot of the stairs when the shouting began again.

She went into the salon and stood at the window, thinking of the past trying months, of how she had coaxed and scolded Eleanor to get out of bed and take exercise.

During the two hours until the doctor came again Eleanor's shouting had changed to screams. Kendra suffered with her. She held Eleanor, soothed her, and Eleanor clung to her, begging her to stay.

After a six-hour labour she was delivered of a son, a puny child who looked as though he would not be long for this world. He was baptised Samuel, after Eleanor's eldest brother, as she said the baby resembled him. But after the birth Eleanor showed no interest in the baby, refusing even to feed him. Kendra, fiercely protective held the baby close. He *had* to live, he was Pel's son.

A wet nurse was brought in from the plantation, and within a week the baby had put on weight. Eleanor complained when little Samuel cried that she was losing sleep, and eventually she said to Kendra, 'Take your son out of here, I want nothing to do with him.'

Her son? Kendra, who already loved the baby, agreed eagerly.

Wanting the baby always close to her she put a crib in the small dressing room leading from her bedroom. With the door open she could hear him if he cried. The dressing room was also convenient in that the woman who nursed him could come in from the landing without disturbing Kendra.

Kendra found it difficult not to spoil Samuel. At first she walked the floor with him if he cried through the night, but after a while she began to know when he was in pain or just wanting to be picked up. If not in pain then he went back to his crib and she suffered his wailing.

She felt she could be the happiest woman alive if the war was over and if Pel, when he came home for good, would love the baby as she did. Then she would think, but what would happen if he took to the baby but wanted the maternal mother?

Although Eleanor had talked about leaving once she recovered from the birth, she had made no effort to do so and Kendra had decided to ask what her plans were when Eleanor, without a word, or a note, packed up and left. The coachman said she had asked to be taken to New Orleans. Kendra was furious that she had been left to care for Mr Lamartine, and later that day felt sick when she was told by a neighbour that Pel had been seen in New Orleans. So she concentrated on caring for the baby, as he was now the only warmth in her life.

*　*　*

Little Samuel continued to thrive. He was a solemn child but she loved to watch his changing expressions, one moment a frown pulling his brows together, as though debating some vital point, the next looking cross-eyed with a spasm of wind. Kendra laughing would say, 'Oh, Samuel, my darling, you are so funny, so lovely, and I adore you.'

One morning she had brought him downstairs and was watching him in his crib, his fists flailing as he tried to catch a sunbeam when the servant came in to announce a visitor. Visitors were rare nowadays and Kendra looked up expectantly. Then her heart seemed to skip several beats as she caught sight of a big figure in the hall from the open doorway.

Bo Burford! What was *he* doing here? What could he want? Her heart, which began a mad beating, would not be stilled. Her first instinct was to refuse him entry, but her next to face him. She asked to have him shown in.

For once Burford did not have a cigar between his lips. He came forward slowly, eyeing her up and down in an insolent way.

'So, Ma'am, we meet again.'

'I can only spare you a few minutes, Mr

Burford, so if you will please state the reason for your visit—'

'Still hoity-toity, eh?' He gave a deep belly laugh. 'You know, Kendra, I still like you, in spite of what you did.'

'In spite of what *I* did, why you—'

A movement from the crib caught Burford's eye. He gave Kendra a quick glance then went over to take a look. 'Well, well, well, what have we here? When did this happen? A boy, isn't it?'

'Does it matter?' Kendra spoke coldly. She went to the crib and stood at the head, in a protective way. The baby pursed his lips, blew some bubbles and kicked his legs.

Burford laughed softly and touched the baby's cheek. 'You're a lively little fellow, aren't you? Your mother won't tell me your name. I wonder what it is? Edward? No, you aren't an Edward.'

Burford began going through various names and Kendra could only stare in astonishment. There was a tenderness in Burford she would not have believed possible. She said, 'His name is Samuel.'

Burford nodded. 'Sam suits him. Doesn't take after you though, Kendra love. Nor his father. Reminds me of someone, but I can't think who.' He grinned suddenly. 'You haven't been misbehaving yourself, have you?'

'Mr Burford! You go too far. Will you please tell me why you came to see me, then I can—'

'Well, actually, it was not you I called to see. Disappointed? I've been away. I was passing through Baton Rouge intending to call on the Lamartines and heard about the fire. I was told they were staying with you, which I must say, surprised me, seeing that you and Eleanor are not exactly on the friendliest of terms.' His face had once more resumed an insolent expression.

Kendra, remembering seeing Burford and Eleanor talking together the night she left the showboat said, 'If it is Miss Lamartine you want she's gone to New Orleans.'

Burford pulled out his cigar case and extracted a cigar. 'As a matter of fact it is Eleanor I want to see. I'll take myself to the city and find her.' Burford took another look at little Samuel. 'Just see you take care of that lad of yours.' He walked to the door, lit the cigar, blew a smoke ring then, with a laugh, left.

Kendra stood, hands clenched, nails digging into her palms, incensed at Burford's attitude towards her. Eleanor was the one who had misbehaved but she, who had not only abandoned her child but her father, would no doubt be wining and dining and dancing, and quite possibly sleeping with Pel, the father of her child. Kendra sank on to the settee. Life was so unfair. Even Bo Burford who had been responsible for the injury to Pel's leg and smashed up his riverboat was quite uncaring. No grey uniform for him, he would simply drive to New Orleans and join in all the gaiety.

It was not that she wanted to be parted from little Samuel, he had become very much a part of her life, but if only Pel would come, if only for a day, or write a letter, anything so she knew how she stood with him.

A week later, Kendra who slept lightly since having the baby close to her, roused with a feeling of someone moving stealthily about the room. Fear stabbed at her. She had left the lamp on low, now she was in complete darkness. She lay rigid, listening. She became aware of a presence moving closer, then suddenly the bedcover was lifted and an icy hand touched her warm flesh. The scream that rose in her throat was stifled as lips covered hers, urgently demanding.

She began to fight, scratch, trying to kick out. There was a soft laugh.

'Kendra, my darling, is that the way to greet me?'

'Pel.' She pushed him away. 'How typical of you. I get no word from you for months then you expect me to be delirious with happiness and fall into your arms. Did you have to turn out the lamp? Do you realise I was petrified with fear, I—'

'Nag, nag, nag,' he teased her. 'I wanted to surprise you. Now, can I have a welcome home kiss?'

He was leaning over her when a wailing came from the dressing room. Pel sprang back. 'What the devil!'

He lit the lamp, paused then went into the room. Kendra followed him. He was staring into the crib. 'Good Lord, whose is this? Not yours—no, it couldn't be.'

It hurt Kendra that he thought her incapable of giving him a child. She spoke coldly.

'Samuel is the son of you and your mistress.'

Pel put the lamp on the bedside table and stood staring at her. 'What are you talking about?'

'I was meaning Eleanor Lamartine. She came back here, demanding shelter for herself and her father. She said she had the right to stay here, seeing that you were the father of her unborn child. Samuel was born here. Eleanor has gone to New Orleans. She wanted enjoyment. She didn't want the baby, nor her father. He is still here, and he is sick.'

Pel ran his fingers through his thick dark hair with an air of bewilderment. Kendra, watching him, thought how his uniform gave an added stature to his already impressive physique. Love for him was seeping through her angel. Pel moved away,

'This child is not my son, Kendra, I swear it.'

'You visited Eleanor, you were obsessed by her.'

'Yes, I visited her, but Eleanor was not generous with her favours.'

'Did you make love to her?'

Pel hesitated. 'Yes, once, but—'

'Once is enough, there is no more to be said.'

318

'There *is* more to be said, a great deal more! Eleanor could have had twenty or more lovers. She's always had men after her. Yes, I know I hankered after her, but—'

'And you got her. You say she was not generous with her favours, so perhaps she was only generous with *you*. Anyway, I don't believe you made love to her only once. You went there often enough, heaven knows!'

'She took advantage of you, Kendra, knowing I was away. She would never have accused me of being the father had I been here.'

'But you were not here,' Kendra said bitterly. 'You went off, leaving the responsibility of house and plantation to me. I had to give decisions on a number of things. The only word of you I had was indirectly, from Lloyd Francis, you did not even think me worthy enough of putting pen to paper. You've made a pawn of me from the first time we met. I was even saddled with your mistress, put up with her tantrums, her arrogance, her accusations, looked after her sick father, and her bastard child.'

Kendra's hand flew to her mouth. 'Oh, no, how could I call dear Samuel a bastard, he's become so dear to me, even though he is Eleanor's son. I want him, Pel, and you will have to accept him too.'

'No, never! That child is not mine, he shall be returned to Eleanor, I shall find her.' He recoiled from the cot. 'I will not be made to look a fool, I would hate him, knowing that his own father will be somewhere laughing that I had taken over the responsibility.'

He left the room and Kendra followed him.

CHAPTER FOURTEEN

'Pel, listen. I will not let Samuel suffer if I can help it.' She spoke in impassioned tones. 'You have denied being his father, but *could* you be?'

He stood with his back to her and was silent.

'I want the truth. This is too important an issue for any prevarication. Samuel is the victim of lies and deceit. The truth, *please.*'

There was aggression in every line of his body. Then his shoulders suddenly went slack. He turned and faced her.

'I don't know, Kendra, I just don't know. I would have said it was impossible that I had fathered this child, but—I would hate to deny my own son. We must talk again in the morning, then I must see Eleanor. At the moment I am looking forward to sleeping in a decent bed.'

Pel was starting to undress and Kendra, watching him, thought how easily a man could dispense with an urgent problem. A decent bed and a woman to make love to were obviously all that was on his mind at this moment. She said,

'And if you see Eleanor and she convinces you that Samuel is your son, what then?'

'I shall naturally bring him up as my own.'

'And will you accept me as his adoptive mother?'

'You did say you wanted the child.' There was a touch of irritation in her husband's voice. 'If you have changed your mind now is the time to say so, not when he is older, and perhaps grown fond of you.'

'I want him! I only want your assurance that you will not bring Eleanor back here. I will not become part of a *ménage à trois*. It was intolerable enough having her here without you in the house.'

'Will you please leave the matter until another time.' Pel spoke in controlled tones. 'All I want to do at this moment is sleep.'

He slid under the covers. Kendra got into bed and flung herself away from him on to her side. 'And so do I. Pleasant dreams!'

She lay rigid and was aware of the tension in Pel. No doubt in a short while his body would relax and he would be asleep. It had happened in the past when they had quarrelled. She was always the one to stay wide awake. She thought of the endless weeks she had waited to hear from him, thought of the nights she had longed for him to be close, to have him make love to her, nights when her body had throbbed, and now she felt a misery sweep over her.

He moved his leg. It touched hers, but it was

only momentarily, he drew it away quickly as though he did not want her to get the impression he was making advances.

At that moment the baby started to cry and Kendra, pushing back the bedclothes, made to get up. Pel said in grumbling tones, 'If you get up every time he gives a whimper you are going to store up a pile of trouble for yourself.'

'Samuel was a sickly child when he was born,' she retorted. 'He's needed a great deal of care, but he has not been spoilt. And anyway, I am the one to get out of bed.'

'And disturb my sleep.'

'You were not asleep and you know it.'

'No, I wasn't. How could I sleep? I came home longing for you, and what welcome do I get? Have you any idea what I am suffering? I've been celibate for months.'

'Do you really expect me to believe that?'

'You can please yourself whether you do or not, it's the truth. Oh, Kendra—' his tone lowered, 'I want you, need you.' He reached out to her but she lay rigid. 'Kendra—' he pushed her hair back, made gentle nibbling bites on her ear lobe. Her body began to respond, but remembering that Pel was in New Orleans when Eleanor went there before the baby was born made Kendra reject him.

He pulled her over to him and his fingers did a butterfly dance up and down her spine. She arched her back. Pel's lips moved from her throat to her breasts. 'I shall take you,' he said

322

softly, 'so you would be better to respond than fight me.'

She wanted to fight him but his caressing fingers were bringing a sweet, agonising fever to her blood. Every nerve in her pulsated.

'I hate you,' she whispered, rubbing her cold foot against his warm leg. Pel drew in a quick breath.

'You can go on hating me forever, my darling, if this is your method of loving. More please.'

She moved her knee up over his hard, lean thigh and when she knew it excited him she leaned across him, her parted lips covering his.

Her nightdress had moved up to her waist. Pel now divested her of it. She rolled away from him, laughing softly, wanting to go on teasing him. He lifted her bodily, so they were lying flesh to flesh. He urged her to make love to him, and when she attempted he demanded to know who had been teaching her, who had taught her the ploys of lovemaking.

She drew a finger from his brow to his nose to his mouth. 'You did, sir, have you forgotten so soon? I was a virgin, remember?'

'Have you been with any man while I've been away?'

'No, I haven't, you should know that without asking! Don't judge me by yourself. You've spoilt everything.' Kendra flung herself away from him. 'You can go whoring with Eleanor Lamartine, or any other woman, and you—'

He leaned over her, his mouth on hers, stopping any further protest. When she was quiescent he leaned up on his elbow smiling at her. His eyes were so dark with passion she wondered how he was managing to restrain himself from taking her. He twined a strand of her hair round his finger.

'I do not go whoring, and I shall punish you for suggesting such a thing.' His voice was soft. He began kissing her eyelids, her cheeks, just pecks, he moved to her throat, then sitting up he pulled her up and wrapping her hair around his hand he tugged her head back in the gentle way that was so sensuous to her she gave a little moan.

Then, as though all passion was unleased, he explored every part of her body, was brutal with his kisses, and roused her to such a frenzy she was begging him to take her.

Abruptly, he put her from him, said good-night and turned over on to his side. Kendra was so astonished she lay still for several moments before anger made her turn to him and thump his chest. 'Why you—!'

He laughed. 'I told you I would punish you.'

'But you're punishing yourself!'

'I can survive until tomorrow. Then I shall find Eleanor.'

Kendra knelt up in the bed and pummelled his body with clenched fists. 'You lied to me, lied! You said you had only made love to her once. You've been seeing her in New Orleans, she *is* a whore—whore, whore, whore! And you are worse, there's no name bad enough to call you. Did you know she had had another child? No, I'm sure you wouldn't know, I wasn't going to tell you, but I want you to know the kind of woman she is. Go to her, give her twenty children, I don't care.'

Kendra dropped on to her back, exhausted by her burst of temper.

Pel lay motionless, and silent. When the seconds ticked by and he still said nothing Kendra put her hands over her face. Oh, God, she felt awful, felt as though she had betrayed a trust, even though the person was a woman she hated. It had been unforgivable of her to resort to petty jealousy to try and destroy Eleanor in her husband's eyes. He loved her. She said, in a low voice, 'Pel, I'm sorry.'

More seconds ticked by before he answered. 'What proof have you?'

Not wanting to involve the doctor she told him none, it was just hearsay, adding, 'It was wrong of me to malign Eleanor. I was jealous.'

Pel turned over on to his left side and Kendra to her right. They lay back to back, quite close, but with a gulf between them that to Kendra was filled with animosity from Pel and regret from her. Was she to let it widen or try and bridge it?

'Pel, please forgive me.' She thought her plea was going to be ignored, then Pel slipped his hand under her neck and brought her head to rest on his shoulder.

'I goaded you.' His fingertips moved gently over her cheek. 'And I had no right, considering all you've gone through.' He cupped her chin. 'It was you I missed when I was away.'

His kiss was gentle, it was a gentle wooing, beautiful to Kendra, and although their lovemaking rose to a crescendo and the ecstasy had her moaning with pleasure, there still remained a tenderness in the act. She felt this to be the real consummation of their marriage. And this part of the night still remained with her, even though there was a greater passion between them before morning.

Pel was getting dressed when Kendra roused. 'Surely it's still early,' she said.

'Yes, I know,' his tone was matter-of-fact. 'I must go to New Orleans.'

Kendra's heart plummeted. 'To—see Eleanor?'

'Of course. I have to know the truth before I can accept the child.'

Half an hour later he had gone, with no promise of when he would be back. Kendra wept with despair.

For a week Kendra watched constantly for Pel's return, sometimes walking down the long drive then standing, waiting, looking up the road. It was not only that she wanted to know if he had seen Eleanor but to have him here to deal with the unrest among the workers. Joseph, the overseer, had told her about it. It had been slowly spreading among most of the plantation workers since so many slaves had been freed in the North, but now it looked like erupting on a large scale.

Joseph threw up his hands with a gesture of despair. What would happen to the land if all the people left? No, not all, he added, he and his family and others would stay. They had a good boss, good houses, good food.

It was at the beginning of April on a day of deluging rain when Kendra heard urgent hoof-beats on the drive. She went to the window, then seeing it was the young grandson of her nearest neighbour she ran out into the hall, and was on the porch when Stevie reined. His hair was plastered to his head, the horse steaming. He did not dismount.

'The Yankees have taken New Orleans,' he called. 'It's burning!'

Oh God—Kendra ran out to him, disregarding the raindrops bouncing off the forecourt. She pressed her hands to her chest. 'What happened exactly, Stevie?'

He was already wheeling the horse around, preparing to leave. 'Grandmama is following, she will tell you, I must let the others know.' He went galloping off down the drive.

Joseph, who had been standing near, came over with long loping strides, a strange grey pallor touching the ebony face. They both stood watching the young rider receding into the distance. The rain ran in rivulets down

Kendra's face.

Hardly had Stevie gone from view before a second rider appeared. It was Mary Hall, the boy's grandmother. Kendra turned to Joseph. 'Do your best, Joseph, to keep your people together.'

He nodded, but there was a hopelessness in his eyes. Mary Hall dismounted and threw the reins to the boy who came running.

'Stevie told you the news, Kendra?'

'Yes, come on in, I'll get you a hot drink.'

Mary said she would come in for a few minutes but no drink, she must arrange a meeting among the women. They went into the hall and stood there, pools of water spreading on the tiled floor.

'How bad is it?' Kendra asked.

Mary told all she knew. The Union ships had come up the river and the Confederate defences had proved useless. The enemy guns were heavier. The people of New Orleans had started the burning to keep goods from enemy hands. Wharves, warehouses containing bales of cotton, sugar had been burned, wine and molasses ran down gutters. Mobs hurled abuses at the Yankees. Many prisoners had been taken. Kendra went cold. Had Pel gone to England, or—?

Mary said, 'I must go, Kendra. There are other women, like you, who are alone. Plans must be made.'

Would plans be any good? In other captured

territories houses had been burned, women and girls raped.

Kendra said, 'Pel has a gun, Mary. My father taught me how to use one.'

'Pray God you will never need to use it. Reinforcements could arrive, the city could be recaptured.' There was the same hopelessness in Mary Hall's eyes as she said it as there had been in Joseph's. She left with the promise to keep in touch.

Kendra stood at the window, her soaked dress clinging to her.

Was ever a scene so desolate? In the driving rain, the Spanish moss that trailed from the oaks normally looked ghostly on dull days, now it looked positively sinister.

It was difficult to believe that yesterday people had been dancing in St Louis and St Charles. Yesterday the bedraggled garden had been ablaze with colour.

If only she could be sure Pel was in England it would ease her mind. But even if he were in New Orleans and had not been taken prisoner he would be more concerned with the safety of Eleanor Lamartine than with his wife's welfare.

Kendra squared her shoulders. So, seeing she had a sick man and a baby to care for she must stop standing here feeling sorry for herself. She must make her own plans. Food stores must be hidden, she must enlist Joseph's help, talk to the servants.

That night Kendra was lying wide awake

when she became aware of a sound that she identified as wagon wheels. She leapt out of bed, expecting one of the servants to come hammering on her door to tell her the Yankees had come. Several of the men were standing guard. Instead there was a gentle tap and a whisper, 'Ma'am, is yo awake? De boss am here, him.'

'Pel?' Kendra could not believe it. She dragged on a wrap and raced downstairs.

He stood in the hall, giving orders to servants, his uniform enhancing his powerful physique; and yet Kendra felt no tremor go through her.

Pel, seeing her, raised a hand in greeting. 'I've brought you some stores, Kendra, thought you would need them.' His voice was as matter-of-fact as though he had left her minutes before.

'For heaven's sake, Pel, you ought not to have come here, you could be caught, taken prisoner, shot.'

'Not me.' In the soft glow of the lamp his smile showed ego. 'It would take a wily one to catch a Devereux.'

'Stop boasting! And anyway, we do have stores, you are risking your life for nothing.'

'I am risking my life, my dear Kendra, because you need two lots of stores. If the Yankees came and found none they would tear the place apart searching. One lot you hide, the other you let them take. And let them have

330

your jewellery, don't attempt to hide it. Your life is more important than gee-gaws. Give them your wedding ring if you have to.'

Kendra twisted it on her finger. 'No, never that!'

'Give it, Kendra. Don't try heroics.'

'And do I allow them to rape me?' she asked tartly. 'Or should I fight for my honour?'

'That is up to you, Kendra my love. It depends on how much you value your life.' Although Pel spoke lightly there was a fierceness in his eyes and Kendra noticed that his hands were clenched. 'Every Yankee is not a rapist,' he added, 'But in any case Joseph and the men will look after you. If they have warning of the soldiers coming they will hide you.'

'I can take Samuel with me, but what about Mr Lamartine? Will they hide him too? He's a very sick man.'

'He will be taken back to his relatives, he is not your responsibility.'

'Have you seen Eleanor?'

Pel's face took on a closed look. 'I have no time to talk about Eleanor. I have to leave right away. The men will see to the stores. Joseph is out there, we have quite a number of the men loyal to us, others will leave, you must be prepared for conditions to get tough.'

'Pel—can't you stay? We could hide *you*.'

'Tempting, but I have work to do, I have a lot of money to make.'

'Oh, stop talking about making money at a time like this.'

'Kendra, the army needs money to fight, yes, I do make some for myself, but whatever else I am I *do* have a loyalty to the South.'

A man called softly from the doorway and Pel nodded and said yes, he was coming. He gripped Kendra by the shoulders. 'Take care of yourself.' He kissed her briefly and swung away.

When the door closed behind him she sank to her knees and covered her face with her hands. Would she ever see him again? Heaven knew what dangers he would be in.

It was not until later that she realised how cleverly Pel had evaded any talk of Eleanor, or any talk of whether the baby was his son. Perhaps poor little Samuel would never know who his father was. Kendra went back to bed with the thought that at least some plans had been made. Mr Lamartine would no longer be her responsibility. If the enemy came, Joseph and the men, who would be on the alert, would get her away with the baby to hide.

* * *

The Yankees came without warning the next morning, so stealthily Kendra heard nothing until six or more of them burst into the house, guns at the ready. She felt no heroics, her body, in her own silent words, was a 'lump of

332

quivering jelly'.

The men were certainly no ragtag and bobtail; their uniforms were neat, and they were seemingly well disciplined. They stood expressionless until their captain came in, then they snapped to attention.

The captain, a middle-aged man with a not too severe manner came towards Kendra, a paper in his hand. 'Mrs Devereux?'

'Yes.'

'You and everyone in the house are under arrest but you will not be harmed, not so long as you comply with our demands.'

He listed them. They must hand over their horses, livestock, grain, valuables and food stores. The captain then asked how many people were in the house. Kendra named the servants, then said, otherwise only an elderly sick man, a young baby and herself. She was told to ring for the servants but no one came in answer to the summons.

Kendra felt surprised, she would have thought the house servants loyal, but the captain simply shrugged, as though the running away of servants was expected.

The soldiers were then ordered to search the house, with Kendra leading two men to the rooms upstairs. She took them first to the main bedroom and, remembering Pel's advice, brought out what jewellery there was, which included Pel's cravat pins. She had laid them on a table when the sandy-haired corporal, the younger of the two men, came over and touched her breast. She knocked his hand away and eyed him steadily, feeling coldly calm. He gave a leering grin, showing missing teeth.

'I want a woman and I fancy you, I'll be back tonight.'

'Are you prepared for death, Corporal?'

'What?' His grin faded. He looked from her to his companion, who guffawed, then back to Kendra. 'I'll have you,' he said, 'and tonight, so be prepared!'

'Oh, yes,' she said, 'I shall be prepared, *well* prepared. Now pick up that jewellery and leave before I call your captain.'

The corporal called some obscenities as they were leaving, but the other soldier had gone quiet. Kendra had hoped to retain her wedding ring, but the captain asked for it when they were ready to leave, apologising that it was an order, they needed the gold.

They had stripped everything of value in the house, ornaments, paintings, and had taken silk bedcovers. Even poor little Samuel had been searched for any jewellery that might have been hidden in his clothing. There was only one thing that Kendra had managed to hide, the toy sailor. It was not that it had any monetary value but one of the men might have taken it for a child and Kendra wanted it, the dancing sailor was precious to her, a reminder of the early days with Pel when she had been so happy with him in London. She got the sailor out from his hiding place and set it dancing.

It could always make her smile and she smiled now, but tears were not far away. She replaced the toy in one of the pockets of the dress she had made to hold Pel's jewellery. She had been tempted to hide some of the jewellery the men had taken, but guessed that brocaded settees and chairs would have been ripped in a search for it.

Half an hour later the house servants returned. They had left by the back way when the soldiers came in at the front. They had helped Joseph to hide some of the livestock in the swamps. They had hidden just enough so as not to arouse suspicion.

The food store had been taken to an old barn, well away from the house, and hidden from view by a thick belt of trees and foliage. Joseph took Kendra to see it. He and the men had worked on the barn, creating a false partition. Kendra had not detected it until it was pointed out to her. At home a cellar would have been created but here so much was swamp land. Even the dead had to be buried in mausoleums. Kendra thought the barn would be a good hideaway, should it ever be needed.

A good three-quarters of the slaves had fled, but those who had stayed worked all hours to cope with the land. What Kendra hated the most was the isolation. Although she was allowed to go into the grounds she could not go further, sentries were posted. The captain had said it was as much for her own good, with groups of vagabonds attempting to loot houses, but Kendra longed for intelligent conversation. Mr Lamartine was still in the house, no doubt arrangements for taking him to relatives had fallen through, but his mind wandered and when he was sensible he kept asking constantly for Eleanor. Once after he had had a nightmare Kendra pretended to be his daughter to soothe him. Then bitterness soured her tongue that Eleanor was possibly now consorting with officers in New Orleans, wining and dancing. According to Joseph, who got snippets of news from somewhere, the city was getting back to normal, the people were accepting the new regime.

One evening when the air was still and the night black with a threatening storm Kendra, knowing she would be unable to sleep, stayed up late and sat on the porch. Everywhere was so eerily still the soft thud of moths throwing themselves at the damp glass seemed magnified a thousand times.

She had undone the neck of her dress and was fanning herself when she sat motionless, alert. There was movement to the left of her. The next moment a voice whispered, 'Ma'am, it is Joseph. I have message for you. Come to the end of the house. Be calm, someone may be watching.'

Kendra, her heart thumping alarmingly, forced herself to rise slowly and to stroll in the direction of Joseph. There she stopped and leaned against the wall, and wielded the fan.

'Yes, Joseph?'

'Master in barn, he want you to come. I take you.'

'No, Joseph, I shall go alone, I know the way. It will be safer. I shall wear something dark.'

Kendra strolled back to her seat, forced herself to sit there for a while, then, with a sigh she snapped the fan shut, and went indoors, doing it leisurely.

Five minutes later, wearing a black cloak and hood she crept out the back way and made her way among the trees, stepping back startled when a moth or trailing moss would touch her cheek.

Every now and again Kendra paused to look back but there was no movement, no sound, it was as though the night was holding its breath. Her footsteps quickened as she reached the barn. There was foliage growing all around it and branches had been laid against the door. Kendra pulled them away, tapped three times on the wood, then whispered, 'Pel—'

The door opened, she was drawn inside and the next moment strong arms wrapped around her. 'Oh, Kendra, darling, how I've longed to see you, are you all right?'

'Yes, yes, and you?'

Pel's mouth covered hers, hungrily. She clung to him. He laughed softly, a little shakily. 'A clandestine appointment with my own wife!'

The complete blackness, the earthy smell, was suffocating for a while then Kendra felt a faint stream of air on her cheek.

'Pel, where have you been? What have you been doing, why are you here?'

'You ask that?' The urgency was back in his voice. 'I *had* to see you. I shall be away for some time, I have to go to other countries, organise cargoes, make trade, for the army.'

'And make big money for yourself?'

'Are you going to quarrel with me?'

'No, Pel no, when is this war going to end, I want you home.' Kendra paused, 'That is, if you want to be with me, or is it still Eleanor?'

'Forget Eleanor.'

'I can't, do you want her, is Samuel yours? I *must* know.'

'Eleanor says he is, I accept him as my son. Now, will you let me make love to you? And if you mention Eleanor's name again I shall put you outside.'

'I promise not to say another word,' Kendra whispered. 'Just love me.'

They made love as if it were for the last time, wild, undisciplined, the ecstasy of fulfilment making them both cry out. But even when they were spent there was no peace between them.

'I've been hungry for you, Kendra my darling,' Pel said in a second burst of passion. 'I had to see you, I would have killed anyone who tried to stop me.'

'Pel, do you *love* me?' Kendra asked

urgently, having to know before he left. 'Or is it still—'

He put his lips to hers, preventing her from saying the hated name. 'I am here, is not that enough?'

'Yes,' she said, her arms tightening around him.

*   *   *

The first crash of thunder came when Pel said he must leave. 'Oh no, not yet,' she pleaded. 'Ten minutes more, five.'

'Impossible, I must leave before the sky lightens, and so must you.' She began to cry and he wiped her tears away. 'No weeping, my darling, I want to take away happy memories, not sorrowful ones.' Then he cupped her face between his palms and said softly, 'Kendra, I must be in love with you, or I would not long to see you so much.'

Oh, the bliss, he had said it at last. Did he mean it, or was it just the idea of parting in war—she dare not ask.

Pel kissed her, gently this time. 'We must leave, you go first, and wait for me in the shelter of the trees. I shall see you to the house.'

'No, I can find my way. You get away from here as quickly as possible. Yes, you must, please, you cannot risk being caught now.'

Pel gave in. A quick patter of raindrops on

the roof was followed by a heavy rattle of thunder. 'You must go, Kendra.' They clung together for several seconds then he put her away from him. 'Now—' He opened the door and looked out. 'Go quickly.'

A flash of lightning showed an anguish in his eyes.

When Kendra looked back the door was closed, the foliage back in place and Pel out of sight. She felt as bereft as though a loved one had died.

Large raindrops spattered her face, thunder rumbled. Sheet lightning made spectres of branches, of trailing moss, and the following blackness unknown caverns to enter. She had come with such eager steps to meet Pel now she knew fear, she stumbled over exposed roots. Suppose someone had watched her leave the house, and was now waiting for her return.

A crash of thunder overhead made Kendra pause and hold her breath. It seemed to shake the ground. The rain was heavier now. She tried to hurry and stumbled more.

Not much further. Ahead she could catch a faint glimpse of lights from the house. She relaxed.

Which made the shock all the greater when, in a succession of flashes a man loomed before her, a soldier with a gap-toothed leer. Kendra, recoiling, automatically put out a hand to keep him away. He caught it, drew her to him and the next moment she was on the ground with him astride her. 'Told you I'd have you,' he gloated. Kendra screamed once. The next scream ended in a moan, the blow he gave her bringing the taste of blood to her mouth.

He was not a big man but he had a wiry strength. All Kendra's kicking and punching at his body with clenched fists had no effect. His slobbering mouth was on hers, making her want to retch. With a feeling of despair she thought of her boast to kill him. She had not even a piece of wood to defend herself.

It was rage in the end, rage at his attempt to violate her after Pel's lovemaking that gave her strength to push his face away from hers. Then she drew her nails down his face, digging deep.

The blow to her head brought a dazzle of lights in front of her eyes—then came blackness.

The rain deluging down revived her. Her clothes were up to her waist, her thighs bare. Oh, God, oh God in heaven. Kendra tried to draw herself up, but the blackness clamped down on her again.

When Kendra roused the next time she lay in a drowsy state, feeling that something terrible had happened, but could not recall what it was. Then suddenly the events of the night came flooding back. Her lids flew open. The trees, the soldier—but she was in her own bed, sunlight spilled onto the bedcover. She must have dreamt it, a nightmare.

A turn of her head told Kendra it had been

a nightmare of reality. A hundred hammers began beating in her brain. Oh, Pel, Pel—he had told her he loved her—but that foul man. A sob escaped her. She closed her eyes against the horror, the degradation of the rape.

'M's Devereux, Ma'am, you awake?' The gentle voice belonged to Martha, Joseph's wife. A hand touched hers.

Kendra gripped it. 'Last night, the soldier—'

'He dead, the men bury him.'

'Bury? But the danger, if he were found?'

Martha assured her he would not be found. The men had taken him right away from here. Joseph had seen to that. It was he who had found her. He had been watching for her but she had come back from the barn by a different way. When he found Kendra, Martha's expression held compassion and understanding—he had come for her to help, no one else knew exactly what had happened, none of the men had seen Kendra. For this, at least, Kendra was grateful.

She had no qualms about the soldier dying, he deserved to die, but it tormented her that her body had been violated. She became so agitated that Martha went to mix her a potion to calm her down, Martha explained she had mixed her one the night before to make her sleep. She and Joseph thought it unwise to bring the doctor. The fewer people who knew about the incident the better.

342

Kendra's real agony began two weeks later when for three successive mornings she was sick on rising. Whose baby, Pel's or the soldier's?

At first she had all sorts of wild notions to try and get rid of it, there were concoctions the plantation women took. But she couldn't. For one thing the child could be Pel's, and for another there was Samuel. Eleanor had tried to get rid of him before he was born, and look how adorable he had turned out to be. A wave of love for the baby swept over Kendra. An unwanted child who had wrapped himself around her heart.

But what of this child she was carrying? It was different with Samuel, he was part of Pel, but although *she* was a part of this baby the father could be a foul-mouthed rapist. Could she love it?

Kendra felt the answer had to be yes. No child should suffer because of parentage. Pel would be the biggest problem. Joseph and Martha could testify to the rape but would he accept another man's child?

A thought crept into Kendra's mind that Pel need never know. Samuel did not resemble either Eleanor or Pel. If this child happened to have sandy coloured hair this was easily explained. Her mother's two sisters had this colouring. It occurred to Kendra then that *she* might never know who the father was.

The worry of this, plus the fact that her

343

sickness lasted often until midday, had her drawn-faced and listless. It seemed, the one brightness was in a victory for the Confederates, albeit it could be a temporary one.

The whole of the Mississippi, apart from three miles in the middle, had been in Union hands, but the Confederates fought back and now controlled several hundred miles. New Orleans was still occupied by the Yankees, but they did withdraw sentries from the plantations to send the soldiers North to fight. It meant that Kendra had friends calling once more. From them she learned that both sides were suffering heavy losses, casualties running into thousands. Food was becoming short, and men were marching bare-footed. Medicines were in desperately short supply, meaning that soldiers were having limbs amputated without being given anything to deaden the pain. Surgeons were working as long as forty-eight hour stretches without sleep. And yet New Orleans danced on.

It was late August when Kendra, who had left the house to go visiting, paused as she saw a figure appear in the drive. The man, bearded and stooped, walked slowly and was too frail-looking to cause her any alarm. Men, some of them deserters, called to beg for shelter and food. Kendra always handed this type of person over to Joseph for him to deal with the situation. No matter if the man was Union or

Confederate, if he was desperately in need of food she would not deny him.

She was about to call to one of the men to fetch Joseph when something about the figure coming up the drive was vaguely familiar. The man's hair was long, matted, his clothes tattered, and rags were wrapped around his feet.

He was coming nearer. He raised a hand in a feeble greeting and she saw that the left-hand sleeve of his jacket was empty. Then she recognised him, and her heart began a slow painful thudding. She walked a few steps towards him, then ran, arms outstretched, too choked with emotion to call his name.

CHAPTER FIFTEEN

Lloyd Francis too was unable to speak. They just held one another then he put Kendra gently away from him. 'I had no right to hold you, I'm filthy, verminous.'

Kendra shook her head, tears brimming. 'Oh Lloyd, Lloyd, what have they done to you?' He swayed and she called frantically to the men standing near. He collapsed before they reached him.

They stripped him of his rags, washed him, cut his beard and hair, put him in a nightshirt between linen sheets and fed him with gruel. He began to recover and his blue eyes that were still so blue, held a gentle smile when he talked to Kendra.

But she knew, even before the doctor came that Lloyd Francis had not long to live, and was heart-broken.

His lungs were affected. He spoke of the time he had lost his arm and made a jest of it. 'Do you know why I was so upset about it, Kendra, I thought I would never be able to play cards again.'

'Oh, Lloyd—'

In spite of having lost his arm he had tried to rejoin his regiment, but it had been practically wiped out and the few men who were left, scattered. Lloyd said he had just kept on walking, begging food on the way, adding quietly, 'I had only one aim, Kendra, I had to see you before I die. Yes, I know I am dying, and please don't grieve, Kendra, I've had a good life, a full one.'

She took his hands in hers. 'I shall get you well and strong. You shall stay here, Pel would want you to. Even though you were opponents in card games he had a liking for you. He trusted you. He may soon be home.'

'Cards,' he said softly. 'They've played such a part in my life. Do you know, there were times when I lost the showboat that I felt pleased. Crazy, isn't it? I used to think, well I shall have the excitement of trying to win it back.' He was

346

silent for a few moments then said, 'Tell me about your life, Kendra.'

She spoke of Samuel, speaking as though she were the mother. She told him about the coming baby, and seeing a wistfulness in Lloyd's eyes, she wept inwardly knowing he had wanted a home of his own and children.

Kendra brought Samuel in to see Lloyd, the doctor said there was no risk of infection as long as he did not kiss the child.

Lloyd laughed at the solemn-faced Samuel, who eyed him unblinkingly. 'He'll make a good poker player,' Lloyd teased, 'but I can't say that he resembles either you or your husband at the moment.'

'One card player in the family is enough!' Kendra changed the subject.

Lloyd grew weaker day by day. His skin took on a transparent look. Sometimes through the night Kendra would get up and sit beside the woman who was nursing him. Then came the day when he slipped into a coma. It was a day of storm. Kendra never left the bedside. Rain lashed against the windows. At two o'clock in the morning the storm died away. Lloyd opened his eyes and smiled at Kendra. It was such a lovely smile. She said, 'Oh, he's going to get well.'

But his eyes remained open. Kendra closed them. 'God rest his soul. He's at peace.'

The night was so calm then it was as if the whole world was at peace.

Lloyd was buried in the grounds, as he had wished. A simple ceremony, and Kendra shed no tears, she had shed them all. A week after the funeral Bo Burford came again. The servant had hardly time to announce him when Burford came striding in, pushing the man aside. Without any greeting to Kendra he said, 'I want him, I want my son.'

Kendra, taken by surprise, actually glanced behind her, as though expecting someone to be there. 'Your son,' she said, 'I had no idea you had a son and he is certainly not in this house.'

'Oh, yes he is. I saw him last time I was here, although I didn't realise then I was his papa. It's Sam. *Sam,*' he repeated, shouting the name as though Kendra was deaf.

She stared at him. 'I have no idea what you are talking about Mr Burford. Samuel is Pel's child.'

'Oh, no he isn't, he's mine. Mine and Eleanor's.'

'But that is ridiculous. Eleanor told me herself that Pel was the father.'

'Ah, yes, she said that because she wanted to get her own back on you, and she had to have somewhere decent to stay where she could be looked after and have the baby.'

Anger made Kendra rigid. 'And now she's trying to blackmail *you.* You are a bigger fool than I took you for, Mr Burford.'

348

'It's not blackmail. It's truth. You see, Kendra my love, your husband wasn't near Eleanor when she conceived. I had been living with her for a month.'

The anger drained from Kendra, leaving her with a feeling of terror. She felt sure Burford was lying, but at the same time he was so convincing she had this dread he was going to take Samuel from her, that if it came to a court of law he could easily prove his fatherhood. She put on a front of bravado.

'This, of course, is quite ridiculous. *You* and Eleanor? Who is going to believe you?'

'I have proof he's mine, but I'll show you that later. I didn't like the look on your face when you said in that disparaging way, "*You* and Eleanor?" Yes, me and Eleanor. Perhaps I had better sit down and explain one or two things to you.'

Burford seated himself and lit a cigar. He did not ask permission to sit, or to smoke. He crossed one leg over the other and leaned back, all earlier urgency to get Samuel, gone.

'You see, Ma'am, Eleanor Lamartine and I are two of a kind, both misfits in this world. Most people, like you, would jeer at the thought of the beautiful Eleanor and me having an alliance. But that is because they know nothing about us. I have a grudge against women, for a reason. Eleanor has a grudge against men for a reason only *she* knows. She wants men to run after her, to beg her favours,

349

and she encourages them—but Eleanor gives nothing.'

'You are wrong, there, Mr Burford. My husband was most unwilling to admit paternity of Samuel, but eventually he agreed that such a thing *was* possible. And my husband would not lie.'

Burford leered at her. 'Do you think he's going to admit he couldn't lay her after all the times he's chased after her? Of course not, a man has his pride.'

Kendra, stung by his attitude, retorted, 'Are not you doing a bit of boasting yourself about living with Eleanor for a month. What did she get from you?'

He half-rose from his seat, his cheeks suffused with blood, then he sank back again.

'Eleanor is the kind of person who loves only one man and that man is me.'

'Eleanor loves only herself,' Kendra retorted. 'She doesn't know the meaning of giving.'

'And you don't know Eleanor.' Burford spoke quietly. 'I'm not in love with her. But I'm the only one she can give to.' He waved his cigar. 'Don't ask me why, I can't explain it. But that's not important to me, my son is, and I want him.' Burford got up. 'Oh, yes, you want proof.' He drew a small package from his pocket, talking as he unwrapped it. 'Do you remember my remarking that Sam reminded me of someone, but I couldn't think who it was? Well, this is the person.' Burford held out a miniature to Kendra. 'This was my father as a baby. Now you tell me that Sam is not my son.'

The miniature was beautifully done and the baby portrayed so like Samuel they could have been identical twins. But even then Kendra was not going to give up without a fight, not even if she had to lie.

'Yes, Samuel does resemble your father, but then Pel says the baby takes after *his* side of the family.'

'But he couldn't be your husband's child. I've explained, he wasn't in New Orleans when Eleanor conceived. He was miles away, in England!'

Burford wagged a podgy forefinger at her. 'I shall have my son, whether it's now, or next week *or* the next, so you'd far better hand him over now than that I get someone to kidnap him. They might not be very gentle with him.'

'But Eleanor doesn't want him,' Kendra wailed.

'I know she doesn't, and I'm not taking him to her. Hannah's going to look after him.'

Kendra was still. 'Hannah? On the showboat—?'

'I've bought a house, we're going to get married. He'll be well looked after, you needn't worry about that. Now go and get him. I have a woman waiting in the carriage, a wet nurse. Go on! *Get him*! I've been patient long enough.'

Although Kendra felt better knowing

Hannah would be looking after Samuel she could not bear to part with him. 'Leave him for a while longer,' she pleaded, 'a few weeks.' Tears welled.

'Oh, for God's sake! Stop snivelling. The boy will live like a king.' Burford eyed Kendra up and down. 'And anyway, judging by the looks of you, you'll have your hands full looking after another Samuel soon.'

Kendra turned away before he could see the despair, the misery in her eyes. A child, who could have a rapist for a father. She went upstairs.

Samuel was sleeping and Kendra stood looking at him. How could she possibly bear to part with him? And why should she? With a fiercely protective gesture she lifted him from his crib and held him to her. She would sneak out, take him to the hut in the woods, and from there she would make plans. The fire suddenly went out of her. What plans? Where could she take him to be safe from Burford? He had said he would get someone to take him if she did not hand him over. And were not her motives purely selfish ones? She had to do what was best for Samuel. He would have loving parents. Pel might never really take to the baby.

She was dry-eyed when she came downstairs but the wrench of handing Samuel over tore so much at her emotions she was unable to speak.

Burford handled Samuel as though he had been handling babies all his life. 'Now you

352

behave yourself, old son, do you hear?' The gentleness, the love and pride in his voice were balm to Kendra, and the fact that Hannah would love Samuel as much as Burford, a consolation.

'Well, we're going.'

Kendra turned her back, unwilling to watch them leave. She said in a low voice, 'Tell Hannah I'm glad you are getting married. I hope—you will all be very happy.'

Burford came up to her. 'You needn't worry, Kendra, he'll be well looked after.' He spoke gruffly, 'It is for the best.'

For days Kendra moved aimlessly about the house, torn in an agony of regret and loss. She had done wrong to have let Samuel go. How did she know Burford was telling the truth, that he did intend to marry Hannah? He could have gone to Eleanor.

It was only by convincing Joseph and Martha and friends who called, that Kendra was able to convince herself she had done the right thing— for Samuel.

Even then she was far from happy. The baby she was carrying was a constant source of misery to her. She was sure it was not Pel's child. There had been no movement. Perhaps it was dead inside her.

No, no, she must never think in that way. The tiny little creature had a right to live. There could be movement at any time.

Three days later she felt the baby move and

it suddenly became a person in its own right, needing love and care—no matter who the father was.

* * *

With all sickness gone Kendra began to feel better, to take part in the household, the plantation, but then came more worry. The cane was nearly ready to be cut and there was talk that the crop would be confiscated by the Union Army, as the cotton had been with other plantation owners. Kendra knew if this happened they would be in a bad way, they needed money to live, to plant more crops, to feed the workers. Food stores were disastrously low.

Mary Hall, with a four-woman delegation, went to New Orleans to plead their case, and came back full of despair. They had to relinquish their yield of sugar cane and no payment would be made. When the women threatened they would burn the crops they were told their houses would be burned.

'So there it is,' Mary said with a deep sigh. 'It looks as if we are on the road to starvation. It makes one wonder how it will all end. According to the news the soldiers on both sides are in a bad way, marching and fighting on a diet that wouldn't keep a cat alive.'

Then she added, her face twisted with bitterness, 'Only those in New Orleans feed well, especially the corrupt ones.'

'Mary—did you by any chance hear anything of my husband?'

'No, nothing, but I did hear that Eleanor Lamartine has a dozen or more officers at her feet. I also heard she is losing a little of her beauty with all her high living. Eleanor, I fear, will come to a bad end. She deserves to, after the way she treated you, Kendra, leaving her father with you to look after. How is he, by the way?'

'I think poor Mr Lamartine is hanging on to see Eleanor. If I could get a hold of her,' she added grimly, 'I swear I would drag her here by the hair of her head. But, she seems to have temporarily vanished. I only hope I'll hear about her soon. Her treatment of her father is disgusting. *She* is not fit to go on living.'

When the time came for the cane to be cut there were no celebrations, no beef barbecue. The children did, however, enjoy themselves just running around, playing games and singing little songs, some of their parents making an effort to put their despair from their faces and trying to join in.

Many of the slaves had left and a lot of them had gone to join the noisy camps below New Orleans, with their riotous living.

Oil had become short and a blight had hit the myrtle berries so Kendra was able to make only a few candles, which she used sparingly to do repairs to clothing by the light of the log fire.

Bread became their staple diet. All the animals, apart from the cows, which they had kept hidden in the swamps the day the soldiers raided the houses, had been killed and eaten. Kendra had one cow alive, determined if she was unable to feed her baby herself, the baby would have a chance to live. The milk had helped to keep two children alive, born to mothers who were 'dry'.

But then, two weeks before Kendra's baby was due, the cow fell sick and died and she wept for the hopelessness of it all.

There were times when she thought of denying Mr Lamartine food to have the little extra for herself, in the hope she might have some milk for her baby, but she couldn't do it. She marvelled that the old man, who was no more than skin and bone, had managed to exist. Perhaps God, sometime, would perform a miracle. As it was now, lack of food had Kendra so listless in the mornings it was a job to get out of bed.

One day Joseph came to her and said that he and some of the men were going to New Orleans to try and get some food, to beg or steal it. When Kendra pointed out they could forfeit their lives if they were caught, Joseph raised his shoulders. They would die if they had no food so . . .

They left in the blackness of the night by river, on a home-made raft, and returned three nights later with stores of flour, coffee, ham and beef. The jubilation of their safe return had to be kept subdued because of the secrecy and Kendra was sure she would never forget the mingled aroma of coffee and the smell of beef roasting, the fat spitting into the fire. She ate the beef, with a chunk of bread, her eyes closed in an ecstasy of enjoyment, savouring each mouthful, chewing each piece carefully.

She was grateful later for the strength the food gave her because when she went into labour it was a long one. To make the situation worse the day was humid and after five hours of pain, her body and the sheets drenched in perspiration, Kendra wondered why she was bothering to fight, to perhaps bring a rapist's child into the world. Then she remembered her thoughts that no child should be made to suffer because of its parentage, and she gritted her teeth and endured the pain.

At the end of twenty-four hours she was so weak she could only whisper, 'It's no use, I have no strength left.'

The doctor, exhausted himself, begged her to make a final effort. 'You cannot now deny your husband his child.'

Kendra was in a semiconscious state when he announced, 'You have a son, Mrs Devereux, a fine fellow!'

A son? But which man was the father? Kendra kept her eyes tightly closed, not wanting to see sandy coloured hair.

Then Martha said, 'Yo' take a look, M's Devereux, Ma'am, he image of his daddy, him.'

The squalling cries of the baby filled the room. Kendra slowly opened her eyes, then a joyousness filled her whole being. Oh, blessed Mother of God, she was looking at a replica of Pel, thick dark hair, long legs kicking, hands fighting the air, a look of outrage on his screwed up face at all the indignities he had suffered.

She held the child to her, tears running down her cheeks and laughed weakly as the cries became hiccups when her son's seeking mouth touched her cheek.

Just born and demanding food. The darling, so vigorous, so strong. She would name him Daniel.

Kendra's one regret was her husband not being here. How proud Pel would be to know he had a son—a legitimate son. She would not allow herself to think that Daniel might never know his father. She must live on hope, it was the only way to survive.

Kendra soon found it needed more than hope to be able to survive. She had plenty of milk at first and Daniel thrived on it. He was a demanding child; demanding food, demanding attention. When he got it he was sunny, lovable. Just like your father, Kendra would say. There were times when the baby would fall asleep, his head against her shoulder, his tiny hand warm on her throat when she would be near to tears. If only the war would end and Pel would come home. Kendra was sure if he did come home and saw Daniel he would no longer be interested in Eleanor.

But the war went on and as the store of food diminished so did Kendra's milk become less, and there was no wet nurse on the plantation to call on. She became desperate, and had thoughts of trying to get to New Orleans, where she could sing and earn money to buy food. But there was no means of conveyance. It was one thing having men go on a raft and risk being caught but it was something she could not do. Joseph did want to try again to get another store of food but Martha said no, it was stretching providence too far that he could escape a second time. She wanted her man, the children their father. Something would turn up.

But nothing turned up and the situation became desperate. Fruit was picked before it was barely ripe and raided sometimes by vagrants before the slaves had a chance to pick it. It was the same with greens. Kendra's saviour was Mary Hall, who although her own family were near starvation, managed to bring something with her when she called: an egg, a piece of bacon, some soda to make bread.

Mary also brought the war news. There were victories, defeats, chaos, more and more men were marching in rags, feet bare, even captains in some cases were bare-footed. There were so many wounded there were not enough bandages to go round. The men who were prisoners in the forts below New Orleans were too weak to move, they had sores, were verminous. But then the men taken by the Confederate Army were in no better state; the futility of it all.

Things became so bad that Joseph began to make definite plans for going to New Orleans. But before the plans were completed he said he had had a dream in which he had seen a food store behind the partition in the hut, and on investigating had actually found it there.

'My husband,' Kendra said eagerly, 'only he could have brought it, did you see him?'

Joseph said no, and although Kendra did not believe the story of the dream she could not move Joseph to say any different. Had Pel been in danger? There had been soldiers patrolling the woods for the past few days. It seemed so terrible to Kendra that her husband had been so near and she had not seen him.

She was beginning to think that someone else had brought the food when she found a note from Pel in a packet of coffee. It said simply, 'I am safe, take care of yourself and S.'

S—Samuel.

Many times Kendra had wondered what Pel would say when he came home and found Samuel gone, but she had deliberately thrust the problem to the back of her mind, not wanting to face up to it.

Now, with Pel specifically mentioning the

baby she began to realise the enormity of what she had done. He had left, accepting he was the father of Eleanor's child, would have thought about his son, wondered how he was behaving, and if he was a strong child.

She had accepted Burford's proof of paternity. Pel, however, not only hating the man but knowing how she felt about Eleanor would say she had been glad to get rid of the baby. Oh, God, was there to be no end to her worries!

It was worry that was wearing most of the women down, not knowing anything about their husbands, their sons. Paper was so scarce even those who had been in the habit of writing no longer did so.

When Kendra wanted to give Mary Hall a portion of coffee she had to find a jar to put it in. Mary popped the jar into her reticule and smiled her grateful thanks. No one asked questions. The food was carefully doled out to make it last. There was no having a feast this time.

During that year, whenever they had reached a starvation level, their food store was replenished. And always there was a slip of paper with the same message, not a word more nor a word less.

Although Kendra was grateful for the food she was utterly frustrated at not being able to see her husband. When the store was low she would hang about the woods, hoping to catch a glimpse of him, yet knowing he would not come in day time, and coming through the night to the hut was out of the question since her last experience.

Kendra had not contemplated the fact of the food stores coming to an end, but one day they did and she was frantic, not because of starving, although this was bad enough, but the thought that Pel had been captured—or was dead.

Martha said, 'Yo' not to worry, Ma'am. The master take care of himself, him. And the Lord will provide the food, he always has.'

And Martha was proved right, but the food came in a most unexpected way.

On a wet, blustery day a carriage, followed by a small wagon, came up the drive. A vehicle of any kind was such an unusual sight everyone stopped what they were doing to watch. Kendra, snatching a shawl flung it round her shoulders and went out onto the porch.

Joseph came up and Kendra said, 'Who can it be? It will not be my husband.' Joseph shrugged.

The carriage drew up and an army captain got out. He approached Kendra. 'Mrs Devereux?'

She acknowledged it and he introduced himself, then said, 'I have a Miss Lamartine in the carriage. She is ill, I was asked to bring her home.'

Home? Anger flared in Kendra. How dare Eleanor call this house her home. She was about to tell the captain he could take his passenger back from whence she had come when she caught sight of Eleanor trying to step down. She looked appalling.

Kendra and the captain went forward to help her and by the time she was out of the carriage Martha had arrived. Eleanor was too weak even to speak. Kendra asked Joseph to send someone for the doctor, asked the captain to come inside and wait, then she and Martha helped Eleanor upstairs.

A few sips of brandy brought a faint touch of colour to Eleanor's cheeks but against the pillows her face held a sickly pallor. The doctor, who had been on the plantation, arrived within minutes. After examining Eleanor he said she was recovering from a fever and rest would soon have her well again. Before he was out of the room Eleanor was asleep. Kendra left Martha with her and went downstairs to talk to the captain.

To her questioning he was cautious. Miss Lamartine was not known to him personally, she was a friend of his commanding officer, and it was he who had asked him to bring Miss Lamartine to the Devereux plantation. The lady had been very ill.

Kendra could imagine the CO wanting to be rid of Eleanor, a sick woman would not be part of his scheme. The wagon contained Eleanor's luggage and food, with the captain explaining that knowing the shortage of food everywhere

. . . He left the sentence unfinished. And so he might, there was obviously no shortage in New Orleans. Still, it was something to be grateful for, even though Kendra felt it did not make up for having Eleanor thrust on her once again.

Unhappily food was not the only thing that came with Eleanor. She had carried the germ of her illness, an illness that swept through the slave quarters and laid low all but two of the house servants. Kendra prayed fervently that she and Daniel would escape the scourge. For scourge it was. The doctor, run off his feet said no, it was not cholera, nor typhoid or yellow fever, it was one of those mysterious illnesses that occur in wars, never to be diagnosed or appear again. He added he thought it might come through the putrefaction of bodies left unburied, which had Kendra suffering from waves of nausea. She was already coping, with the help of Martha, with the vomiting and bed-dirtying patients, feeding them gruel, giving them copious drinks of water, wiping fevered brows with cold wet cloths, and being so exhausted at times she was sure if she caught the fever she would have no strength left to fight it.

The doctor used what medicines he had which he thought might help, and when they were finished he suggested Martha mix some of her concoctions. Martha did, using herbs and unmentionable ingredients, which stank the house in the brewing. Martha said it would take

364

two days before any results would be seen.

In that time half the patients showed signs of improvement and those who succumbed were mostly elderly people.

But even those who survived the fever did not recover right away. They still needed nursing. Daniel, to Kendra's relief, escaped the illness, but was as demanding as ever for attention, which she was unable to give. As well as all the other tasks to cope with there was Mr Lamartine, who was at his most querulous, complaining he was being neglected.

There was also Eleanor lying in bed, even though she had fully recovered, and refusing to even take a walk to her father's bedroom and talk to him.

Kendra had almost reached the limit of her endurance one night when Daniel's bad-tempered screaming and Mr Lamartine's high, thin wailing penetrated the sleep she so badly needed. The next day her nerves were so taut she felt they would snap.

Even then she kept on going, sometimes finding she was walking about with her teeth tightly clenched.

Twice Eleanor had got up when army officers called to see her. Then she was lively, full of talk and flirtatious. The day after each visit she went back to bed. After the second occasion Kendra went into the bedroom that evening and found her propped up with pillows reading a novel and eating sweetmeats. Kendra snatched both from her and flung them across the room and told her if she did not get up and attend to her father she would drag her out of bed.

Eleanor just eyed her in an insolent way and said, 'What are you going to tell Pel about giving our son away to Bo Burford?'

Kendra, taken by surprise, stared at her and her heart began to pound.

'*You* know why, because Mr Burford fathered him.'

Eleanor laughed. 'Is that what he told you. Bo would say anything. He wanted a son, but what woman would give him one? Oh, your face, Kendra—'

Kendra, trembling so much she felt her legs would not hold her, turned and went out. She had to think, work things out. She knew it would come easy for Eleanor to lie to put her in the wrong, but at the same time there was a fear in her that it might be true. It did seem ludicrous that Eleanor would live with a man like Bo Burford. And yet he had the miniature, there was the likeness. He had also said that he and Eleanor were the misfits of the world.

Kendra's mind went from one thing to another with such rapidity she felt she would go mad. How could she ever stand up against a woman like Eleanor who had so much cunning? But she must, or she would lose Pel. Perhaps she had already lost him. He could have been visiting Eleanor in New Orleans, and had perhaps stopped sending the food when he knew what she had done about Samuel.

It was sheer exhaustion that made Kendra drop off to sleep, and it was Mr Lamartine's whining voice that penetrated it. At first she felt she was pushing her way through curtains of mist, but once they cleared she became coldly calm. She straightened her dress, went along to Eleanor's room and walked in without knocking. Eleanor, who was still reading, looked up, a sneer on her face.

'If you have come back to beg me not to tell Pel what you've done you can save your breath.'

'No, I came back to deal with you. You are getting out of this bed and going to attend to your father and you are doing it now.' Kendra flung back the bedclothes. Eleanor tried to snatch them back.

'Get out of here.'

'No, you get out.' Kendra grabbed hold of Eleanor's arm and began pulling her towards the edge of the bed. Eleanor struck out and caught Kendra a blow on the side of the head. Kendra grabbed the long black hair, wrapped it round her hand as Pel had done with hers, but there was nothing gentle about the way she tugged it. She kept on tugging and Eleanor screamed and kept on screaming. She shouted curses and was half-way out of the bed when a voice spoke sternly:

'In God's name Kendra, what do you think you are doing?'

367

Kendra released the coil of hair and stood rigid, unable to believe what she heard. It was her mind, it had snapped. It could not be Pel, not in this room.

Then Eleanor, swinging her legs over the bed, dropped to the floor, thrust Kendra aside and ran across the room. 'Oh, Pel, Pel, thank God you came when you did. She would have killed me, she's mad, mad!'

Kendra turned slowly, saw Eleanor fling her arms round her husband, saw Pel's arms close around her. But it was not the woman he was holding whom he was looking at, it was her, and there was a coldness in his gaze that filled Kendra with despair.

Eleanor went gabbling on. 'Do you know what she did, she gave our baby away to Bo Burford. *Our* son. She hated him because he was ours, hated me. And shall I tell you something else? You wife has a bastard son, and God knows who is the father. She's lain on her back for every Union officer who came along.'

Kendra walked over to Eleanor, pulled her away from Pel and began slapping her across the face with all the force she could muster, first the right cheek, then the left, and went on hitting until Pel grabbed her hand.

'Kendra, for the love of heaven, what has got into you. Do you want to kill her?'

'Yes. She's not fit to be alive. Your mistress is a liar, the worst kind.' Kendra was surprised

368

there was no anger in her voice.

'I'm not a liar,' Eleanor shouted. 'Ask her about our baby, ask her if she gave him to Bo Burford.'

'Yes, I did,' Kendra said.

Pel's cold gaze was still on her. 'Why?'

'Because *he* is Samuel's rightful father, not you.'

'Do you expect anyone to believe that?' Eleanor screamed. She turned to Pel. 'Do *you*? Can you imagine me allowing Bo Burford to make love to me, he makes me feel sick just to look at him. I hate him, always have. Samuel is *our* child. You must believe me, Pel. Say you believe me!'

He looked down at her, hesitated a moment then said, 'Yes, I do.'

Kendra turned and walked from the room.

CHAPTER SIXTEEN

So that was it, their marriage was over. She felt all frozen up inside her. Pel had not even given her a chance to explain about Daniel. Well, he would not get his son, she would take him away from here.

But when Kendra went into the ante-room where Daniel slept and lit the stub of a candle to look at him, she knew as she saw his dear face in the flickering flame of the light that whatever plans she made must be thought over carefully. She must not let Daniel suffer for any rash move on her part. There was shelter here, logs for warmth and some food at least for the moment. If Eleanor left, and she surely must after tonight, she would no doubt take the rest of the stores with her.

But then, where could Eleanor go without transport? She too could be a prisoner until one of her lovers came to visit.

Her lovers? Was Pel still with her? Were they at this moment making love? Kendra went into the main bedroom, the thought tormenting her and the heat of anger at the injustice of it melted the ice in her. Why should she allow Eleanor Lamartine to get away with her vicious lies. Let Pel see Daniel, see the child was his own son! Kendra started to cross the room when the door was flung open and in the sudden spurt of flames from the log fire she saw Pel outlined, aggression in every line of his taut body.

He came towards her. 'Seeing that you have given your favours to the damned Yankees, I think I might, as your husband, claim *some* rights!'

He grabbed at the neck of her dress and ripped the bodice open and Kendra, who had dreamed of being made love to by her husband gently, or with wild passion, was incensed because he had ruined the careful repairs she had made on the dress.

'You fiend!' she screamed at him, and tried to fight him off. 'You have no rights, get back to your wretched mistress! Get her out of here before I kill her!'

Pel's mouth covered hers and although Kendra felt the familiar throbbing she still tried to fight him. 'I won't let you touch me, I want nothing more to do with you. I hate you, hate you.'

'I don't care if you do hate me,' he said. 'After tonight you'll never see me again. But I'll make you suffer for what you've done, giving my son away.'

'He's not your son, he's not, Bo Burford is the father, he has proof.'

There was a slight hesitation then Pel picked her up and threw her on the bed. 'Lies, all lies.' His body covered hers. He began to bite her ear lobes, sharp bites, and Kendra grabbed him by the ears and forced his head away from her.

'Find Burford, ask him for the proof. How could you believe Eleanor Lamartine! She had all the best luxuries in New Orleans, was kept by an officer and came back here ill, and brought her fever with her. I nursed the sick, looked after her father—she's never once been near him. Oh, *you* make me sick. Leave me alone, I don't want to be even touched by such as you!'

'What do you mean by such as *me*?'

'A fool, a weakling, who is taken in by a beautiful face, unable to see the evil behind it.'

371

'A weakling, am I! I'll show you!'

His anger, his urgency to punish her for her words made his lovemaking brutal. Kendra, determined not to respond, went on fighting him.

Pel, who had got up right away afterwards, said in a gruff voice, as though ashamed of his behaviour, 'Oh, come on, there's no need for all that fuss.' Then he added, his tone more sharp, 'I'm sure you suffered more than that from the Yankees you took to your bed.'

Kendra, who was more hurt than angry, got off the bed and began tidying herself, saying in a low voice, 'You will not get the opportunity of humiliating me the next time you come, I shall not be here.'

'What about the way *you* humiliated me?'

Kendra made no reply. She walked to the door and opened it, then stopped as she heard someone calling. Realising it was Eleanor's father she wanted to ignore him but she knew she would have to go. It was not his fault that he got into such a state. She went to his room.

He was sitting up in bed and when she went in he held out his arms and there was a mystic look on his face. 'Oh, Eleanor,' he whispered, 'I knew you would come.'

Kendra felt deeply touched. She went to him and putting her arms around him she rocked him gently to and fro, hoping he would think she was Eleanor. 'Yes, Papa, I'm here.'

'I knew you would come some time. I've

372

tried not to be a nuisance but I was so lonely. I needed you.'

Tears sprang to Kendra's eyes. 'I know. I'll stay with you. Life can be so difficult at times. Do you want to lie down?'

'No, Eleanor, hold me, please.'

'Yes, I shall.' She again rocked him gently, thinking at the same time how he seemed to be all bones.

'I think I'm going to die,' he said.

Kendra felt a terrible coldness. 'No, of course you're not.'

'I want to be buried here,' he went on. 'In the garden. Will you promise to bury me here, near the rose arbour?'

'Yes, I promise, but you are going to get better. The war will soon be over and—'

His body went suddenly limp. 'Papa ... Papa—'

Oh, no, she thought, feeling distraught. She laid him back on the pillow and smoothed back the thin grey hair, glad now that she had never neglected him.

A voice behind her said, 'Is he—?'

It was Pel. Kendra put her finger to the pulse in his wrist then nodded. Pel touched her on the shoulder and she got up and drew away from him. 'I'm sorry for the way I behaved,' he said. 'I never guessed.'

Tears ran slowly down her cheeks. 'Just leave us,' she whispered.

'I want to help.'

'You're too late. Please go.'

He went out and she leaned over the old man and crossing his arms over his chest murmured a prayer. Then she pulled the sheet over his face and went downstairs. She would have to see the vicar and arrange the burial.

Pel was in the sitting room. He said, 'I'll send James for the undertaker. I think we'll have to have Mr Lamartine buried this afternoon in case anything crops up. I'll see to it.'

'Where is Eleanor? She will have to be told.'

'She knows. She said she's not interested.' There was a bitterness in Pel's voice, but Kendra felt no pity for him.

The undertaker arrived later with a coffin and the vicar followed soon afterwards. He offered condolences and asked where Eleanor was.

Pel said, 'She's in her room. She doesn't want to come to the funeral.'

'Death is a sad thing,' the vicar said. 'But so many people have died. One has to face up to it.'

Nether Pel nor Kendra answered this. Martha and another woman washed Mr Lamartine and dressed him and the men lifted him into the coffin.

Kendra said in a low voice, 'I feel they're rushing to get him buried.'

'Far better that than he was left behind unburied, as people have been when the enemy have stormed towns.'

Kendra looked at him in alarm. 'Are you expecting it to happen?'

'Pray it doesn't happen but one must be prepared.' Kendra felt a cold shiver go up and down her spine.

The grave was dug near the rose arbour and a number of the coloured people came with small posies of flowers, but Eleanor did not come near.

The vicar said the prayers and everyone waited until the grave was filled in. Then the posies were laid on the dark earth, giving solace to Kendra.

Pel walked by her side back to the house and he said, 'I despise her. She wouldn't even make the effort to come to her father's funeral.'

Kendra wanted to say, and I despise you for the way you treated me, but the words stuck in her throat.

Back at the house they parted.

It was dark outside when Kendra sat over a log fire in the sitting room feeling glad she had Daniel. He was the only person she had in the world to care for. She would not do anything about Eleanor but prayed that Pel would order her out of the house. If not she would certainly not go on living here. How could she live in the same house with such a woman.

There was a knock on the door and Pel looked in. 'I shall be leaving soon.'

'Aren't you going to take a look at your son before you leave?'

'He's not my son.' He did not even glance at the crib where Daniel was sleeping.

'Now I really do hate you. And someday you will hate yourself for having listened to Eleanor's lies.'

'I must go,' he said stiffly. 'I have to—'

Pel broke off suddenly and stood in a listening attitude. Then came the sound of pounding footsteps along the landing. There was a hammering on the door. 'Master, master, dey Yankees, dey coming!' Pel strode across the room and flung open the door. A young boy stood there shaking. Joseph came running up.

'You must get away, sir, that woman betrayed you. Take M's Devereux with you, a lot of soldiers, a lot of guns, she'll be safer from here. I go with you to boat.'

Kendra was already throwing on a cloak. She grabbed a blanket, ran for Daniel and wrapped him in it, praying he would not start crying. She was afraid Pel would refuse to take her but he said, 'Come on, hurry up.'

There was the sound of rifle fire as they went out by the back way. Kendra thought at first they were making in the direction of the hut, but then they changed direction, although still keeping to the woods.

Pel took Daniel from Kendra and caught hold of her by the elbow when once she stumbled. She asked if the boat was near and was told not far away. It seemed to Kendra to be a great distance but the consolation was the further they went the fainter the rifle fire. Joseph talked as they hurried in the direction of the river. He told of how he had been watching for Pel to leave the house, then had seen Eleanor Lamartine come out, and because there was something furtive about her movements, he followed her. She met a soldier and Joseph, from behind the trunk of a tree, heard the name Devereux mentioned. Eleanor had been pointing towards a window of the house. The soldier disappeared and Eleanor set off down the drive, walking quickly. Joseph, feeling sure something was about to happen, alerted his people and the servants in the house and they sent the boy to alert Pel and Kendra. Then Joseph, seeing soldiers creeping towards the house, followed to stress the urgency.

Kendra was just about out of breath when her eyes, becoming accustomed to the blackness, thought she saw the outline of a boat. It was a sturdy boat with two men at the oars.

Once Joseph had seen them into the boat he left, saying he must get back to his people who were hiding in the swamps. He wished them Godspeed.

The two men rowing pulled away from the bank, their oars dipping with barely a sound.

'Are you all right, Kendra, not cold?' Pel's tone was solicitous.

'No, quite warm, thank you.' She looked at Daniel in her arms. Amazingly he had not uttered a sound and still slept cocooned in the thick blanket. Pel's glance went twice to the baby but then he became more interested in the boat's progress, as they left the inlet, keeping close to the bank.

On a dark night there was nowhere quite so black as the blackness of the river. Kendra remembered Mr Cartwright on the riverboat saying a pilot must know the 'shape' of the river, and that it was a different shape going to coming back. Kendra, in spite of all the unhappiness she had known on the riverboat thought with nostalgia of the comfort of the furnaces on the boiler deck, the glow on the water from the flaring torches in their baskets, the beauty of the saloon when all the chandeliers were lit.

Here there was no sign of life, no light anywhere, not even the glimmer in a window of a guttering candle. Where there were trees the blackness seemed to swamp them, bare branches touched the water. They travelled in comparative silence to the dip of oars. Kendra, realising the need for secrecy whispered to Pel, 'Where are we going?'

'I shall take you to Mrs Hall. You will be safe with Mary and her sisters.' Kendra wanted to ask Pel where *he* was going but knew she would never get to know.

Although Mary expressed concern with the trouble at the Devereux plantation and gave Kendra a warm welcome, the worry at having an extra mouth to feed was there in her eyes. Then Pel assured her that food would be delivered from time to time. She left husband and wife together to say goodbye.

Kendra wanted to say so much but felt the first move must come from Pel. He was obviously thinking the same thing because they both stood silent, looking everywhere but at one another. Then he said, 'Well, I must be going.'

'Without hearing my side of the story, without taking a look at your son, your *real* son? Oh, Pel, have you no faith in me? Do you think I would be living in your house if I had been consorting with Yankee soldiers? The only soldier who had my body was the one who raped me in the woods, the night I left you in the hut.'

A look of shock came over Pel's face. 'Raped you?'

'Yes, he knocked me unconscious. Joseph and his men found me. They killed the soldier and buried him up river. When I knew I was pregnant I lived in dread that the baby would be his, but the minute I saw Daniel there was no doubting who his father was. Will you take a look at him?'

Kendra undid the blanket. Daniel, one fist against his mouth, screwed up his face in a bad-tempered scowl at being disturbed, before emitting a loud wail. Pel laughed softly.

'Oh, he's a Devereux all right. Daniel did

you say you had named him? That is the name of my great-grandfather! An irascible old gentleman by all accounts.' Pel took the baby from her and although handling him clumsily there was a tenderness in his voice as he said, 'Hello, Daniel Devereux, this is your papa. And you just stop that howling. At once, do you hear?'

Daniel, dry-eyed, closed his mouth, punched Pel on the chin then grinned. And Pel held his son against his shoulder and there was the glint of tears in his eyes. 'He's a fighter,' he said softly, 'he will survive.' He looked at Kendra. 'About Samuel—?'

Kendra told him about Burford, about the miniature photograph and how he said he had lived with Eleanor for a month.

'Burford spoke about he and Eleanor being misfits in life,' she said. 'I thought he was impotent, but there was no doubting that Samuel was his child, just as you seeing Daniel know he is your son.'

Kendra waited for her husband to talk about Eleanor and when he said nothing and she pressed him about her a look of pain came into his eyes.

'I know Eleanor has many faults but I never thought she would betray me. I had finished with her a long time ago but when I came into the bedroom and heard her screams and the way you were treating her I felt sorry for her.' Pel raised his shoulders. 'I have to be honest with you, Kendra. I had been fed so many lies about you, and all stemming from her, I can see that now. When I left Eleanor to come to you—I had told her it was you I loved—'

Kendra's eyebrows went up. 'You said that? Yet you took me as though you hated me.'

'It was love, jealousy, hate, all mixed up together. I wanted to punish you because I thought other men had had you. I never loved Eleanor, I know that now, it was an obsession, but the wound resulting from her betrayal goes deep. It was a terrible thing she did. You know what they say, there is no fury like a woman scorned. This war is bound to end soon and, when I come back . . .'

End soon? Kendra reflected they had said that when the war had been going on for six months, but she refrained from saying so.

'Pel, promise me one thing, you will keep in touch, let me know you are safe?'

He promised, then handing Daniel over to her he kissed her gently, kissed the baby and left. At the door he raised his hand in salute and was gone.

*　　*　　*

Kendra stayed with Mary Hall for six weeks then went back to the plantation, wanting to be home to welcome Pel when the war was over. There was more and more talk of it ending, but it dragged on month after deadly month. All

381

but Joseph and Martha and their family and four other families had left. Kendra could not blame them. The food that came mysteriously to the shed became less and less and with longer spaces in between. The notes enclosed said, 'Love to you both.' And that was all.

Two weeks later Joseph came to tell her that Eleanor Lamartine had been shot. She had been spying for both sides. A year ago Kendra thought she might have felt exultant that her rival was no more, but all she could feel was sadness that Eleanor had lived such a tormented life.

The people knew the war was at last coming to an end when soldiers, scarecrows for the most part, came trudging back to their homes, some of them to die; the Confederates had lost.

Every day Kendra would wait at the bottom of the drive looking up and down the road, watching for Pel, with Daniel playing at her feet. As he grew his tantrums became less. He was tall for his age, and in spite of having very little to eat seemed to grow stronger day by day. 'Mama,' he would say, clinging to her legs and looking up into her face with his lovely smile, 'is today the day Papa is coming home?' And always Kendra would reply, 'Perhaps tomorrow.'

When Pel did come home Kendra was at the top of the drive and Pel was half-way up. Her heart began to beat in suffocating thuds. He was walking so slowly and there was an air of dejection about his drooping shoulders.

She started to walk towards him and he looked up and saw her. And his slow smile took the awful grimness from his face. He paused, then came hurrying, his hands outstretched.

They went into each other's arms. 'Oh, Kendra, just to be home.'

All the misery of the war was in his tone.

'You're safe,' she said, 'which is all that matters.'

'Mama, Papa!' Kendra turned at the shrill cries.

Daniel, leaving Martha, came toddling towards them. He fell, picked himself up and came on, laughing.

Pel swept him up and held him tight.

They walked towards the house. Reaching it they stopped and Pel said, 'We shall plant again in the spring. The plantation will live once more.'

'And from this moment,' Kendra whispered, '*our* lives will begin again.'

They went into the house.

We hope you have enjoyed this Large Print
book. Other Chivers Press or Thorndike
Press Large Print books are available at your
library or directly from the publishers.
For more information about current and
forthcoming titles, please call or write, without
obligation, to:

Chivers Press Limited
Windsor Bridge Road
Bath BA2 3AX
England
Tel. (01225) 335336

OR

Thorndike Press
P.O. Box 159
Thorndike, Maine 04986
USA
Tel. (800) 223-2336

All our Large Print titles are designed for easy
reading, and all our books are made to last.